This wonderful new book by Delbanco filled me with wonderment all over again about his family's survival, its joys and successes and all the rest—although the note of "lacrimae rerum" is much in evidence, especially toward the end. In combination with his natural writerly eloquence: "the long looping syntax of things"—a paragraph I read several times with admiration—it is more than enough.

— Charles Baxter, author of
There's Something I Want You To Do

"What a gorgeous novel. From the opening pages, I was captivated by Frederick and his world. I love how the novel moves backwards and forwards in time, how it navigates the long lines of history and the complicated story of Frederick and his splendidly unpredictable brother, Peter. As always, Delbanco makes it look easy with his lovely lucid prose which conjures characters and situations onto the page with such seeming ease and such conviction."

— Margot Livesey, author of *The Flight of Gemma Hardy*

It Is Enough

Nicholas Delbanco

IT IS ENOUGH

DALKEY ARCHIVE PRESS
McLean, IL / Dublin

Library of Congress Cataloging Number: 2018026150

Names: Delbanco, Nicholas, author.
Title: It is enough / Nicholas Delbanco.
Description: First Dalkey Archive edition. | McLean, IL : Dalkey
Archive Press, 2018.
Identifiers: LCCN 2018026150 | ISBN 9781628972856 (pbk. : alk.
paper)
Classification: LCC PS3554.E442 I8 2018 | DDC 813/.54--dc23
LC record available at https://lccn.loc.gov/2018026150

www.dalkeyarchive.com
McLean, IL / Dublin

Also by Nicholas Delbanco

Fiction

The Years
Sherbrookes
The Count of Concord
Spring and Fall
The Vagabonds
What Remains
Old Scores
In the Name of Mercy
The Writers' Trade, & Other Stories
About My Table, & Other Stories
Stillness
Sherbrookes
Possession
Small Rain
Fathering
In the Middle Distance
News
Consider Sappho Burning
Grasse 3/23/66
The Martlet's Tale

Nonfiction

Curiouser and Curiouser, Essays
The Art of Youth: Crane, Carrington, Gershwin, & the
    Nature of First Acts
Lastingness: The Art of Old Age
Anywhere Out of the World: Travel, Writing, Death
The Countess of Stanlein Restored: A History of the
    Countess of Stanlein ex-Paganini Stradivarius Violoncello
    of 1707
The Lost Suitcase: Reflections on the Literary Life
Running in Place: Scenes from the South of France
The Beaux Arts Trio: A Portrait
Group Portrait: Conrad, Crane, Ford, James, & Wells

Books Edited

Dear Wizard: The Letters of Nicholas Delbanco & Jon
    Manchip White
Literature: Craft & Form (with A. Cheuse)
The Hopwood Lectures: Sixth Series
The Hopwood Awards: 75 Years of Prized Writing
The Sincerest Form: Writing Fiction by Imitation
The Writing Life: The Hopwood Lectures, Fifth Series
Talking Horse: Bernard Malamud on Life and Work
    (with A. Cheuse)
Speaking of Writing: Selected Hopwood Lectures
Writers and Their Craft: Short Stories and Essays on the
    Narrative (with L. Goldstein)
Stillness and Shadows (two novels by John Gardner)

Acknowledgments

"The Window" was published in Michigan Quarterly Review, Winter 2015, "Cuba" in Moment Magazine, Spring 2017.

Elena, again

On my way a moment I pause,
Here for you! And here for America!
Still the present I raise aloft, still the future of the
    States I harbinge glad and sublime,
And for the past I pronounce what the air holds of
    the red aborigines.

Walt Whitman, Leaves of Grass

It Is Enough

Prologue

A FAMILY ALBUM: leather-bound, thin, its pages yellow with age. There are images on every page—black and white to start with, then Kodacolor. The reds have dimmed to orange, the blues to pale blue-gray. Most of the photos are dated, and some of them name names. These identifying markers have been written in pencil or pen. *Onkel Harry, Tante Lotte. Biarritz, 1921.* The images are glued—sometimes two, sometimes three, rarely four—to the black album sheets.

There are pictures of children and dogs. There is landscape and seascape, a series of weddings; there are houses, furniture, and tombs. A hand hovers above the binding, its fingernails jagged and needing to be filed. The back of the hand is spotted with age, its liver spots light brown. The index finger curls. On the desk a glass of water, on the lamp a shade.

The Window
2011

FREDERICK HOCHMANN IS seventy-two. A widower, with two grown sons on the West Coast, he still calls Connecticut home. New Canaan is the town where he and Sarah lived, and though the house can make him sad it also can console him: *this* is where they sat together by the fire, drinking their nightly martini; *this* is where the children played Ping-Pong and baseball and basketball and chess. He knows the colonial structure is too large for a single man, in need of the kind of attention he no longer wants to pay. In time gone by he'd stand on a ladder, cleaning the gutters or nailing back shutters himself. For the larger projects—plumbing, trimming the high protective hedge, replacing the broken slate shingles or storm windows that needed re-glazing—Sarah had known whom to call.

But maintenance seems unimportant or beside the point. The point is to continue with a minimum of fuss.

This, Frederick is good at. Retired, he reads the *Wall Street Journal* and the *New York Times*. For the first part of the week, and sometimes through to Saturday, he does the crossword puzzle; three or four times monthly, he takes the train to New York. He goes to museums or concerts at the Grace Rainey Rogers Auditorium—a chamber-music series he and Sarah used to patronize. Since she no longer plays the piano he no longer has to keep tuned, he put aside his violin. For similar reasons he stopped playing tennis, although he likes to watch the sport on television; the tournament at Wimbledon or the U.S. Open can

4

claim his attention for days. He admires the players' raw power but dislikes the way they shriek.

And he still listens to music, the piano trios and string quartets of Franz Joseph Haydn in particular. When asked what it is about Haydn—as opposed, say, to Mozart or Schubert—that he finds attractive, he has a ready answer: *self-control, restraint.* These are qualities his parents praised and tried to instill in their sons. Sarah too had valued self-control, and only at the very end of her long losing battle with cancer did she turn to Frederick and raise her ravaged face and cry, "Why me, why *me?*"

He has an elder brother in a nursing home outside of Guilford, and two or three times yearly he drives to visit Peter. These visits are not a success. They talk about the things they have in common—their childhood, their parents, the weather—and Frederick stays for lunch with what he thinks of as his brother's fellow inmates, then drives home. In the 1960s, Peter belonged to a commune, and the drugs he took seemed somehow to have leached away all sense of professional purpose; the jobs he held were dead-end jobs, the women he lived with were feckless. While Frederick climbed up the corporate ladder—his career was in commercial real estate, and early on he had the idea for a model of self-storage and a warehousing system that would gain national traction—his elder brother drifted from address to address and liked to quote Timothy Leary: "Turn on, tune in, drop out."

This he has done with a vengeance. Nearing eighty, Peter sits all day in a rocking chair, holding a spy story in his lap, or someone's cast-off magazine, and staring at the wall. He still believes in Marx, he says, and that the revolution was betrayed by inside agents, a cadre of FBI operatives he calls "capitalism's moles." His gaze is blank, unfocused; what hair he has is white. Their parents, he tells Frederick, were the unwitting pawns and apparatchiks of what Eisenhower labeled the military-industrial establishment, and any self-respecting Jew should study the Talmud instead. In the Talmud and the Kabbalah you can find the answer to life's questions, since the question *is* the answer if you know how to pose it. What seemed complex will look simple if you poke the ground for moles.

A certain skein of logic runs through Peter's nonsense, and his brother finds this hard to deal with: when should he argue and why disagree? So he sits an hour by Peter's side, talking about how cold or hot or wet it is, and then returns to New Canaan and watches a movie on television or treats himself to dinner at the restaurant he likes. They know him there; they bring him his martini without asking—straight up, with pimento olives on a toothpick—and about the nightly specials the waitress tells the truth.

His sons are raising families and urge him to fly west for Thanksgiving or their children's birthdays. The older son, John, practices real estate law in San Francisco; Daniel, the younger, teaches history at Berkeley. In the years since Sarah's death, Frederick has stayed with them—apportioning the length of his visits—on six separate occasions. His daughters-in-law are respectful, and Daniel's wife Eileen in particular will sometimes put her hand on his, and leave it there, as if she understands and shares his need for contact. For such a slender woman, her breasts are surprisingly large. Arriving and departing, she embraces him, and the embrace has human warmth.

Yet he cannot shake a sense of loss: how glad Sarah would have been to watch her grandchildren growing, how happy it would make her to spoil those wild-haired boys. This increases the pain of her absence, and returning from his visits he feels almost a kind of relief. The furniture is furniture she purchased, the curtains are curtains she hung. She has been dead for five years. From May to October he works in the garden, a little, and reads books on the Civil War, or biographies of statesmen, and from time to time has dinner with a widow or old friends. At such gatherings he drinks red wine, but does not open a bottle at home; he cannot finish a bottle alone, and it does seem wasteful to let the wine go sour and then pour it out.

He understands, of course, that this is what old age entails: a shutting down, a closing in, a lessening of the desire to try something new. He understands also that he is depressed. In the watches of the night, or in the early mornings—standing by the kettle and measuring the coffee grounds for his French drip coffee pot, warming a bran muffin on which to spread marmalade—he remembers how his parents, refugees from Hitler's Germany, had had their own set of habits: lox and bagels, fresh-squeezed orange juice, two boiled eggs every Sunday morning, and how they spoke German together when they did not want the boys to join the conversation. Therefore Frederick learned German.

His father's ancestors were bankers—moneylenders in the sixteenth century—his mother's in the import-export business. They had been prosperous people. His father's father owned a private bank, and they had "wanted for nothing," in the phrase his father used. In the way of such things, the families frequented similar circles and, once, took the same walking tour in the Tyrol. It is almost as though, when his parents married, the nuptials of Johann Hochmann and Gisela Lefchinsky had been prearranged.

There were distinctions, however. His mother's people were "artistic," with a penchant for collecting the paintings of Nolde and Klimt and, early on, African masks. They had come to Hamburg from Vienna. The Hochmann family, by contrast, was conventionally strait-laced and had lived in Germany for three hundred years. In his childhood Frederick heard stories about chauffeurs and upstairs maids, and the time when his father at six years old grew so impatient with a gourmandizing uncle who helped himself to too much whipped cream he cried, "*Das ist genug, Onkel Max.*"

"That's enough, uncle Max," became a slogan—a way of saying that the slice of chocolate cake or pudding should be distributed around the table so that everybody present would get a sufficient portion when that person's turn arrived. Brother Peter did not feel this way, and did not act as though the whipped or clotted cream would come to his plate in the fullness of time, if he waited patiently. Frederick tried to be patient; there was always enough to go around.

The Third Reich destroyed that, of course. When their families were dispossessed—the houses and bank accounts plundered, the exit duties levied—his parents fled to America via a sojourn in Cuba. They settled in Westchester County. In their community of refugees, men smoked cigars and wore blocked hats, women owned crocodile-skin handbags and sensible shoes. Because of the import-export business, there were connections in New York, and his father found employment with a cousin of his mother's, taking a train to the city. His parents rarely spoke about the years of exile or the way their fortunes changed.

"We were luckier than most," his father said. "My father arrived with his parents. And only a few of the family died."

"Why is that lucky," Peter demanded. "What sort of score were you keeping?"

"Don't be impertinent," said their mother, and Peter went up to his room.

The Oleskers invite him to dinner; they have something they want to discuss. "Is next Saturday good?" Judy asks on the phone, and Frederick accepts. Sam and Judy are a couple he had known with Sarah; they played mixed doubles as a foursome in the years when everyone played tennis, and dropped by in the final months with casseroles and wine. Sam too had been in real estate, and they live in a Breuer house not two miles from the Hochmanns; there'd been easy camaraderie between the couples. Sarah and Judy confided in each other for what could seem like hours in the kitchen, or when they went out walking.

"What do you tell each other?" Frederick asked.

She smiled at him. "Women talk. Girl talk. You know."

He did not know. He never knew what Sarah found to talk about, or why she and Judy would huddle together in corners, drinking coffee, gossiping with an intimate intensity he found somehow disquieting. There were secrets she should not disclose. There was the public world, the private world, and the two were adjacent but not interchangeable; there were things he told his wife in bed, and things they did together, he would never discuss with a third person, no matter how sympathetic that third person seemed. *Das ist genug, Onkel Max.*

Sarah, however, had few boundaries. When she had a second martini, she could be the life of the party, and her antics made him nervous; she would twirl around the living room, or raise a corner of her skirt as if performing flamenco. She would twitch her hips at him and say, "Oh come on, Freddy, don't be such a prude."

On Saturday evening the rain is cold, and he regrets the need to drive to the Oleskers; he could have stayed at home. The roads are wet, the branches bare; springtime has not yet arrived. The car's right headlight slants off at an angle, making a solid-seeming cone of light, and he reminds himself to have the lamps aligned. This is the sort of maintenance—an oil change, a tire rotation—he still attends to regularly, and his Volvo runs like a clock. His wife's Mercedes station wagon remains in the garage; he has not had the heart to put it up for sale.

Inside the Olesker house—with its stripped modernist arrangement, its fire burning brightly, its Calder mobile in the dining space—things do feel familiar. Harry and Clarissa Wilson have been invited also, and a divorcee with her cheeks pulled tight by plastic surgery and an elaborate necklace Judy praises: her name is Jane Markou. She has a sister down the street, but her sister and brother-in-law are renting a condo in Sarasota this winter; she's been house-sitting in New Canaan for three months. Un-plain Jane sits next to Frederick at dinner—sorrel soup, a leg of lamb—and tells him she works as a PR representative for luxury hotels and resorts, as well as for the State of Utah, and if he ever wants to go to Utah or to any of the various hotels and resorts she works with he should let her know. She then proceeds to list the places in Malaysia, Indonesia, Africa she represents, and he has heard of none of them and feels so keen a longing for Sarah that he excuses himself and goes to the bathroom and, peering at his white face in the mirror, says aloud: *How could you leave, why am I here alone?*

The Oleskers are going to Europe. They have a trip planned for May. They are flying to Vienna and traveling by train to

Budapest and Prague and Dresden and perhaps Theresienstadt and ending the trip in Berlin.

"Why don't you join us?" asks Judy over crème brûlée, and he cannot tell if she is serious, but Sam says, "That's what we want to discuss, it's what Sarah wanted."

"Excuse me?"

"To keep an eye on you," says Sam. "She made Judy promise."

He turns to his hostess. She nods.

"I don't follow . . ."

"Oh, only that she asked me—you know, right before the end of things—to, as Sam puts it so elegantly, 'keep an eye on you.' Take care of you. She meant, I mean, to try to make certain you weren't so alone, to keep you in the loop of life."

"'The loop of life,'" says Harry Wilson, who sits across the table. "Hey, that's a good one." He circles his neck with his hands and makes a strangling motion. "You mean, the *noose*."

"Don't be ridiculous," Clarissa Wilson interrupts. "It's the red wine talking," she tells Frederick. "Pay him no attention. *I* don't."

"Truer words were never spoken," Harry says. He drops his hands.

"Are you serious?" asks Frederick.

"Oh, I do know it was years ago, and we haven't asked before, but this seems like the perfect trip and I've been wanting all along to honor my solemn—the word *is* solemn—promise." Judy smiles. "Last year we took a cruise to the Greek islands: Cyprus, Rhodes, and Crete. And we promised each other the next trip we took would be something we'd ask you to join."

"Think about it," Sam repeats, and Jane Markou—whose PR accounts do not appear to include resorts in Eastern Europe—asks everyone at table if the rain will turn to snow, if spring is routinely so late in New Canaan, and where to find seedlings and plants.

The conversation shifts, continues, lags. He leaves at eleven o'clock. He should have brought an umbrella, he thinks; the wind-blown rain is hard.

"I will," he says.

"Will what?" asks Sam.

"I'll think about it," Frederick says, surprising himself, and Judy says, "Oh, perfect. It's what Sarah wants."

They travel in some style. They stay in expensive hotels and eat at restaurants the concierge recommends and then reserves for them; they hire drivers to show them through cities or guides for walking tours. The Oleskers are, he comes to see, practiced travelers; they have gone on such trips often, and follow established routines. At nine o'clock each morning they eat large hotel breakfasts of eggs and sausage and cappuccino and croissants and by eleven are in a museum—admiring the Rembrandts and the Brueghels and Monets.

On alternate mornings they ramble down boulevards or visit open-air markets or, in Budapest, the Museum of Terror, and walk through synagogues and cemeteries; in Prague, they tour the house where Kafka lived and the ancient castle on the hill. Afterwards, they improvise lunch—a light lunch, Judy insists. In Vienna they view the stables of the Lipizzaner horses and walk side streets off the Ringstrasse with its buskers and musicians. They visit the Opera house. In each of the cities they listen to concerts, having earlier decided which program is of interest and which they will forgo. Frederick photographs his friends at the base of statues of Goethe, Beethoven, and Mozart; they photograph him standing on bridges or on the deck of a boat on the Danube while they take an evening cruise.

He and Sam Olesker get along. He finds himself respecting the man's breadth of knowledge—how much Sam knows, for instance, about the Holy Roman Empire and the music of Webern and Schoenberg and the lifetime ERA of Warren Spahn. Early on, Olesker acquired a fortune in White Plains, understanding that the city center was seriously undervalued as a commercial locale. It was ripe for development, and throughout the 1980s he had been a major player in the construction boom

and downtown renaissance; now, he says, he sits on the sidelines
and no longer has the get-up-and-go to be an entrepreneur; you
need to believe in the future, he says, and like these tourists
here—Sam waves his arm at the *Kunsthalle* entrance where they
wait on line for admission—he mostly believes in the past. His
own people came from Odessa, so this part of Europe is virgin
territory, and it interests him as a builder to see what's been
restored and what destroyed. When they get to Berlin, he says,
he wants to see Frederick's place.

"There's nothing there," says Frederick. "My mother's apartment was bombed."

"Well, what about your father's house?"

"We can look for it, maybe. I have the address."

"Good. So then you can go home again."

"Except it isn't home. It's just where my father was born."

"Close enough," says Sam.

Judy tells him, when they are alone, or while her husband
studies the wine list, that Sarah was the *most* empathetic listen-
er, the one who could process whatever you said and come up
with something wise, incisive, some way of solving a problem
that hadn't occurred to you before, or anyone. It's why she really wanted—he must have wondered, hadn't he?—to take this
journey together, to feel as if she, Sarah, was traveling also and
there at their side; oh, not *exactly*, not in physical terms, but in
all the ways that count. Judy wants to be clear, to make certain
he understands how much she shares his—what should she call
it?—bereavement, the sense that nothing would or could ever
be the same again. But nonetheless he, Frederick, should know
how much his wife had hoped he would continue on without
her and begin again.

"I don't."

"Don't what?"

"Want to begin again. And sometimes not even continue."

"Don't say that," she protests.

The trip is uneventful. He knows even in the viewing that the museums and the palaces and synagogues and cemeteries will conjoin in memory—that the Ephrussis in Vienna and the Lobkowicz clan in Prague will be hard to keep apart. Conductors on the trains they take are fat or thin and short or tall, but all of them do business with a minimum of fuss, and all of the trains run on time. He remembers a room full of portraits by Rubens, but not in which city they hang. He remembers a painting by Brueghel of a wintry scene, with peasants, but by the end of the first week cannot remember where it was displayed, or what was the price of admission. Even concerts lose their focus; did they play Dvorak chamber music in Budapest or Prague, and which Brahms piano concerto did they hear that first night in Vienna, in the splendid hall?

Hotel breakfast buffets—muesli and fruit and scrambled eggs with bacon, or alternatively yogurt and smoked salmon and eggs benedict—grow indistinguishable, as do the evening meals. The ancient gravestones and Holocaust Memorials succeed each other implacably; the monuments and cobbled streets and central squares grow too numerous to name. He knows, for example, that Dresden was bombed—that the firestorm the Allies dropped on Dresden wrought the equal of the damage inflicted on Hiroshima. Yet visiting the city he feels neither triumph nor shame; it has been reconstructed and is its own imitation. The Jewish Museums do move him, but in the way good theater can; the commemorative spaces and display cases full of artifacts and photographs loom like a stage set, unreal.

He tries to keep up with his reading. He studies maps and local histories and the pamphlets they acquire. But where Sam seems to know and retain the distinction between Frederick I and Frederick II, he cannot remember his own namesakes' histories, and which of them was nicknamed "the Great" or was celibate or had a string of mistresses and was a great warrior; there is mad King Ludwig and Ludwig of Bavaria and he is not certain if they are one and the same. In bed at night he tries to remember the names of the concierge and chambermaid, and though their names are written on their uniforms he forgets them every morning and must keep his greeting impersonal; he would like to say, "Good morning, Hans," or "Good afternoon, Elsa," but does not trust himself to be sure of their names and it would be unmannerly to peer at their shirtfronts, then speak.

Unbidden, a memory comes. When he first acquired the rudiments of German he said he had learned a whole German sentence and wanted to show off his accent; he had been seven years old. The elders ignored him. His mother sat at the long table's head, his father at the foot, or perhaps it was the other way around or the oval dining-room table had, technically, two heads; in any case he and Peter sat between them, together with his second cousin Judith—his mother's cousin's daughter—who was visiting from London, and his father's parents, who came each Sunday for dinner, his grandfather Benno with a gold watch on a watch chain, and his grandmother Ilse white-haired, with pearls. There was also a business partner of his father's with whom, he now suspects, his mother had been having an affair.

There had been wine, he remembers, and lobster bisque, which he did not like and a roast beef his father carved and, for dessert, a Sachertorte. In a momentary lull in the adults' conversation Frederick repeated his claim that he knew a whole sentence and, when given permission to speak, enunciated clearly: "*Mutti hat die dicke Beine.*" He still does not know if "Mommy has fat legs" should properly contain the article *die* or not, but he remembers the ensuing silence that fell across the table and the way his mother's cheeks suffused with color, then went pale. Now, sixty-five years later, he believes what he was doing was challenging his mother for her flirtation with her husband's partner—the way they touched each other's hands across the chessboard, the way she poured him cognac or passed the silver salver of whipped cream for his cake. In college, when studying German, Frederick acquired the sentence, "*Wenn man eine Operation durchgemacht hat, dann braucht man ein bisschen Erholung.*" But the sentiment, "When someone has had an operation, they need some time to recover," had less effect, and although in his junior year he took a course in German literature—reading Goethe and Schiller and Rilke and Mann—he never acquired fluency in the language or felt at ease with its guttural speech. What he remembers is loud silence at the dinner table and the way his father cleared his throat.

Cousin Judith said something about Trafalgar Square and the statue of Admiral Nelson, the difficulties with the tube and the Northern Line to Hampstead so often running late. No one replied. His grandmother, he can remember, spoke about the problem of getting decent *Schinken* in Larchmont and how the man behind Broderson's counter would lean on the scale with his thumb. His grandfather corrected her; the men at Broderson's are honest, he insisted, and their *Lox und Schinken* is good as any you find in Berlin, and when at length his mother spoke it was to ask if someone wished a second helping of dessert.

In Berlin they arrive at the *Hauptbahnhof* and take a taxi through town. The Hotel Adlon Kempinski is a stately place just beyond the Brandenburg Gate and the border of what used to be East Germany; the taxi driver tells them it is very good, very luxe. There is a Bristol Kempinski also—older, smaller—but this is the chain's showpiece, with several doormen waiting and bellhops retrieving the luggage. Businessmen and young blond women in short skirts and a group of what he can hear by their accent are Irish tourists cluster in the lobby; the girl at the reception desk offers Frederick and the Oleskers a "welcome" glass of prosecco or, if they prefer it, champagne. Two bottles protrude from ice buckets on a table by her desk. The President of Ecuador is, they learn, paying a state visit, and dark-haired men with briefcases confer at the rear of the large entrance hall.

The multilingual bustle and the elaborate furnishings put Frederick at ease; all it is, he thinks, is money, all it takes is an American Express card, and the room is his. In his room he hangs up his jackets and unpacks his suitcase carefully—his laundry had been done in Prague—and, fingering the fabric of the curtains, remembers how he first traveled to Europe with Sarah on their honeymoon. This sort of hotel is not what they

then could afford or where they had wanted to stay. They had
gone to Italy, avoiding the land where his ancestors lived and
from which they were expelled. *"Kennst du das Land wo die
Zitronen blühn?"* he can remember reciting—one of the po-
ems by Goethe he'd learned—and, repeating the poet's question, asked, "Do you know the country where lemon trees are
blooming?" In a hill town in Tuscany, while they sat on a patio
and shared a plate of antipasto, he can remember Sarah saying
she was almost glad for Hitler—not glad, of course, for his ex-
istence or the horror of the Holocaust—but grateful that he
came to power, since otherwise the Hochmanns would have
remained in Berlin and the two of them would not have met
as students and she would not be happy. Although she herself
in any case would have attended Pembroke, he would not have
gone to Brown; they would never have dated or married. So
they would not now be staying in their *pensione* or have seen the
frescoes in Arezzo or be sitting at this table in the sun.

"I suppose that's true," said Frederick. "I would have been a
German."

"And not my husband," Sarah said. She put her right hand
on his knee and played, or so she told him, the opening bars of
"Für Elise."

"I can't hear but I can *feel* it," Frederick said.

"Let's go back to the room."

"*'Wo die Zitronen blühn.'*"

She smiled widely at him. "Yes."

Of such stuff are his memories made. He remembers how
she learned to cook—to begin with from a cookbook, then a
friend, and how the first time she made rice she burned the pot.
He told her that it didn't matter, but Sarah said it mattered very
much, and he soaked and scraped the encrusted rice kernels
until the pot was clean. The *boeuf à la Bourguignonne* was, she
said, a disaster, and when he did not argue she enrolled in cooking school and after a series of classes became what she said was
an adequate cook. Frederick disagreed. He said she wasn't only
adequate but excellent and very fetching in that apron when she
bent above the stove. He had been reading Ian Fleming, whose

James Bond declares he likes a woman who makes love as well as sauce Béarnaise, and he repeated the line. Sarah waved him away with a long wooden spoon; he remembers how the sun came through the kitchen window and spotlit her hair. Her hair had been russet-colored; later it shaded to gray. When she lost her hair from chemotherapy she bought a wig with curls like the ones she sported as a junior in college; he knew she had known he was lying, but told her that she looked just like the girl he fell in love with way back when. It was as though no time had passed and nothing had altered between them, as though they both were young again and facing a bright future. This last he did not say.

The Oleskers will be in the lobby at six; he stands at the window and studies the traffic beneath. As he does more and more often these years, Frederick finds himself drifting—watching the Mercedes and the BMWs and Porsches and Audis file slowly towards the Tiergarten, remembering driving to Boston, and noticing the way Self-Storage Warehouses proliferated since the first such unit he had financed. In the outskirts of Hartford and Springfield he passed eleven installations where once there had been none. Opening a bottle of complimentary spring water, he pours himself a drink. His notion of a three-tiered system— plain self-storage, air-conditioned storage, and wholly insured and climate-controlled storage units—had been a success.

Success: he tries to count what others would call blessings. He has lived more than his biblical span, has money and leisure and, except for minor predictable problems, good health. His parents died of natural causes; his children have never known war. He leans against the windowpane and presses his head to the glass. He can remember coming back from work one night and being late for dinner, forty minutes behind schedule because of a bad accident on the Merritt Parkway, a traffic jam policemen untangled into a single slow-moving line, the pickup truck and two sedans smashed by the side of the road, the police-car beacons rotating, blinding him. When Frederick reached home at last, the members of his family were seated already—John and Daniel with their plastic plates and cups full of chocolate milk—at the kitchen table set with a platter of corn on the cob and the roast Sarah was starting to slice. The ambulance had carried off the bodies of the dead or maimed he'd inched past in the breakdown lane, having avoided disaster, having arrived safely home.

He remembers now the way the boys took turns lighting the menorah in holiday season, the ceremony of Hanukkah candles, the lessons he gave them in building a fire—*triangulate* trapped air, he explained, make a tent out of logs so the flame stays enclosed—and how on starlit nights they'd take their telescope outside and name constellations, the Big Dipper, the Little Dipper, then the more elaborate and abstract figures: first John, then Daniel, who was better at it, naming names. *Cassiopeia*, the crab. *Orion*, the mighty hunter. He remembers the strawberry birthmark on the neck of Sarah's oncologist who told him, "We'll do whatever we can."

In the morning their driver arrives; his name is Michael Kay. After breakfast, he collects his clients in the lobby; they have scheduled a four-hour tour. Michael has been in this business privately for six years, he says, and earlier worked for a tour-bus company and the Tourism Bureau. He therefore knows—he smiles—everything about the city, they must only ask him and he will have an answer.

Tall, wearing a gray suit and red striped shirt, he checks his watch. "You are from where?" he asks. He has a wife and daughter who desire to go to America, but only as tourists, *Gott sei dank*; he himself has been to Los Angeles for a Tourism Bureau Convention, and once to Chicago.

In a Mercedes limousine he pilots them down crowded streets, negotiating traffic jams and inching past pedestrians or men and women on bikes and motorbikes. He drives them by the Jewish Museum and declares they must visit it later; he shows them the river that runs through Berlin and explains the substrate of the city is marsh and therefore there are pumps extracting water everywhere; otherwise, and if we pay no attention, we sink. He points to the site where John Kennedy stood, explaining "*ein Berliner*" is both a person from Berlin and a kind of local pastry, so all the peoples of Berlin was both a lot happy and little bit laughing when their visitor pronounced his famous sentence: "*Ich bin ein Berliner.*" I am not yet fifty years old, he says, too young to have been listening when he spoke it but my parents remember the speech. Then also there is the famous sentence later by President Ronald Reagan: "Mr. Gorbachev, tear down this wall."

Michael talks unstoppably, telling jokes about the airlift when the city was surrounded, and how you Americans dropped manna from the sky for which everybodies were grateful. Driving towards the remnants of a stretch of wall, he shows lines marked out along the streets where once the structure divided the city. "Here is a painting"—he points—"of a Stasi car and here a portrait made by a graffiti artist of the Russian Leonid Brezhnev kissing Erich Honecker." He shows them the large Memorial to the Murdered Jews of Europe and the Information Centre; he says the architects Peter Eisemann and Daniel Liebeskind are very popular here, very much, how do you put it, à la mode. Then he drives past a department store with the letters KDW and says you can buy everything, anything; if for example you want furniture or knives or perfume or the very best crab cakes and chocolate in all of Germany you can purchase your merchandise inside this building. There is nothing that is not for sale.

"They came, they saw, they did a little shopping," Michael says. He shows them the statue of Press Baron Axel Springer and a park where Turks and gypsies have been permitted to sleep. "Ah, the Romanis"—he bursts into song—"*Du schwartzer Zigeuner*," and when Judy asks for a translation he says, "You dark-skinned gypsy, you stole my heart away."

Frederick has written down the address of his father's house, and he hands the slip of paper to the driver—who enters it into his GPS. "Charlottenburg," Michael informs them. "A nice part of the city, if you would like to see. Not far away, we can manage, and if this is your wish, it is of course my command."

They proceed for some minutes in silence. Then Michael commences his prattle again. "You know the song, perhaps, "Unter den Linden." Well, these are linden trees, very famous in Berlin, and here where we are driving through is for artists and people in theater, and soon we come to where expensive houses are and the street where your father calls home."

"*Called* home," Frederick wants to correct him, "it's an important difference," but usage of the proper tense does not now seem important, and as they approach his father's house he feels himself surrounded by the presence of the past. The streets grow wide. Several buildings have a security detail standing at attention, and national flags on poles by their gates; these are Embassies, Michael explains. They take a wrong left turn, and he apologizes, reversing, and then they take two sharp right turns and enter a small park—a street that rings a circle of grass, with four or five houses on the perimeter, facing it. Number 5 is his. *Was* his, Frederick tells himself, *would have been* his.

The house is large, imposing. He steps out of the Mercedes and approaches a gap in the hedge. He can see only a section of stone, a verandah and a portico with columns and a gray tiled roof. There is a solid iron gate with the brass number 5 and high thick greenery he cannot see beyond; he peers through the lattice of eye-level bars at white stone walls of what had been the Hochmann home and wonders, should he ring the bell? What would he say if the buzzer were answered; how could he explain himself? He stands staring for a minute, then makes his way back to the car.

Michael has turned off the ignition and is polishing the chrome. The Oleskers wait on the pavement, watching a girl with two leashed Dalmatians in the circle of the park. She is speed-walking, striding away.

Judy asks him, "Don't you want to go inside?"

"There's no one there," says Frederick, and Sam, who has been watching, says, "How can you tell?"

"I've seen enough," he tells them, and Judy says, "Let's try anyway," and approaches the entrance and presses the bell.

Then there is silence. She rings it again. After an interval a woman appears—stout, wearing a crucifix, holding a broom. She asks, "What do you want?" in German, and his German fails. She repeats, "*Was wollen Sie?*" and he stammers out an answer, explaining this was the house his father lived in, and his father's father before him, while she stands there, her face like a box. Her wig is yellow and her apron pink and her nose looks broken; she is, he thinks, exactly the kind of Teutonic *Hausfrau* his parents had taught him to fear. Or, if not fear, detest. He asks if the present owner is home and she says "*Nay*, nobody" and makes sweeping motions with her broom.

He turns to go.

But Michael stands beside him now, holding the rag with which he was polishing brightwork, and waves it at the limousine and speaks in rapid dialect which Frederick can only partly follow, discoursing on his clients' consequence, *diese gnädigen Personen*, these noble people, how far they have traveled, and how they are staying at the Hotel Adlon and will be disappointed and it would be a shame to turn this gentleman away when he asks for *nur einen Augenblick*, an instant only at his father's birthplace, where his family lived, is this too much to ask?

"*Doch, doch*," she says at last, and shambles up the high stone steps to the door of the mansion behind her, and enters, and after a long minute that door opens for a second time and an elegant woman emerges and descends to where he waits.

"*Mein Name ist Hochmann*," Frederick says. "My name is Hochmann."

"Of the family who lived here?" she inquires in English, and he tells her, "Yes."

She is wearing a pantsuit, a pink satin blouse, and double string of pearls. "There are, as you know, many Hochmanns, and we cannot be certain which one owned this house."

"My father was born at this address. My grandparents built it. Rebuilt it."

"Your grandfather's name?"

"Benno. Benno Hochmann."

Perceptibly, the woman softens. "Yes, I have the plans. Designed for *Der Herr* Benno Hochmann in 1928."

"My grandfather . . ."

"He was a banker, no? The house stood here before, but that was the year they rebuilt."

This accords with the little he knows. There were concerts in the garden, which is where his parents met. His mother had come with a cousin, and after the concert there were refreshments; then his mother and his father went walking in the park. His mother Gisela loved the theater, and kept a pocket diary of plays attended and the programs of concerts she heard; in 1931, the year they were engaged, she attended such performances more than sixty times. When Peter made his bid for freedom and a change of lifestyle, she told him he was doing nothing that had not been done before: the Berlin of her youth, she declared, made New York seem tame.

"I am pleased to meet you." Speaking with a heavy accent but with great precision, Elke von Stroheim introduces herself. When Frederick looks askance she says, "Like the film director, yes, except there's no relation. It is in any case my husband's name," she offers, unlocking the gate.

Now the spring sun is warm, and he finds himself perspiring; the cleaning lady has exchanged her broom for a dust mop and pail and brandishes these instruments at him reproachfully and disappears.

"When did your family leave?" Madame von Stroheim inquires, and he tells her, in the 1930s, and she says, "Yes, but exactly which year?"

"They sold in 1936," he says, and an expression of relief crosses his interlocutor's face. When she smiles she looks younger, a young woman nearly—forty, perhaps forty-five. She had feared, he understands, that he arrived to lodge a claim of ownership—but 1936 was before the Jews were forced to sell, and he would have small legal standing. In any case, he wants to assure her, he has no desire to return or any designs on the family house. His brother Peter would feel the same way, and no doubt even more strongly.

"You and your friends are welcome. Please come in."

They follow her down the path and climb stone stairs to a vestibule.

The driver remains with the car.

"We come from America," Judy offers. "Connecticut. You know it?"

"I have been," she says, nodding. "To Yale University; there my husband gave a speech."

Her husband, Wolfgang, she explains, is a lawyer for the government, and they bought this house—it had been almost a ruin, in great need of repair—when unification came, and the government moved from Bonn to Berlin. They have three children: girls.

"This is the kitchen," she says—"please, you must call me Elke—but of course in your grandparents' time the kitchen was below." She points to a dumbwaiter: "The maids would fetch the meal. I myself enjoy cooking and have made the kitchen on the level where we eat—and here is the study and here are Wolfgang's books. I myself was once an archaeologist, but when you have three girls at home"—she shrugs her shoulders winningly—"it's not so easy to be a professional person."

"It was Albert Speer," Frederick tells her, "who had been clerk of the works. You probably know this already. My grandfather said—or so my father told me—'This young man is very talented. But he has a bad character.'"

Elke von Stroheim waves her hand. "But your construction project was finished long before Speer started working for der Führer . . ."

The Oleskers drift away. They stand at the window and admire the rear gardens—formal, with tiers of stone steps. As an archeologist, continues Madame Stroheim, she is of course interested in what went before, what is buried, and if he has any photographs of the house as his father and grandparents knew it she would be very grateful; they are trying to be faithful to the original structure, which is why she studies the architect Tessenow's drawings, and the notes from Albert Speer, but there were bombs on the north terrace and a good deal of damage and the previous owner did nothing; they have only last summer completed the roof. When—she pauses briefly—the government required a listing of occupants in the late 1930s for the census, there were thirteen persons in the house, and we are only five, but five seems—how do you say?—sufficient for a family, and of course there are no maids. Or not anyone who lives in. The girls are still in school.

She continues in this fashion, showing him the drawing room and dining room and where the front reception hall had been halved to make way for the pantry and kitchen. The rooms are large, the ceilings high, the plasterwork ornate. There are family photographs on the shelves and brightly colored landscapes and oil portraits on the walls. She points to a curved stairwell and marble banister, but does not take him upstairs. Then she says she is sorry, she has an appointment, she was planning to go out the very moment he arrived, and she must not be late. If he wishes to return he will of course be welcome, but now, she says, she has to go and after a look in the garden he will have to let himself out.

"This was important to me," Frederick says. "Thank you. *Danke vielmals.*"

"*Bitte*," says Elke von Stroheim, "you are very welcome," and he thinks how *bitte* and *bitter* sound alike. He thinks of the book *Bitter Lemons*, and tries to remember who wrote it and which island it describes. He tries to remember, and cannot, when Goethe made his southern pilgrimage and how the poem and the song about flowering lemon trees ends.

The lady of the house ushers her visitors into the garden again. She carries a handbag, a hat. "Please take whatever time you wish, the gate will lock behind you."

He turns to watch her leaving, and the gate clangs shut.

Sam and Judy wait for him; they stand beneath the trellis of a small stone gazebo at the foot of the lawn. Shaped conifers march in a line. A reflecting pool with ornamental shrubbery surrounding it sits at the base of a raised stone patio, and there are koi in the pool. They swim in circles. Imagining his second self—the one who would have lived here if history were otherwise—he walks back to the living room and tries once more to see.

Frederick looks at himself in the window. He sees an old man staring back, well-dressed and slightly plump. His reflection is shadowed, a little, and blurred; the trees behind him waver in the mild spring breeze. He places his hand in his pocket and rocks back on his heels. His grandfather would stand that way, right hand holding a cigar or walking stick, and in the slanting light he sees their silhouettes blur, merge. He is his own ancestry in the formal garden, and *gnädige Frau* is the phrase he would use if speaking to the shadow at his side. It bends; it takes his arm in hers; it smiles at him, half-rueful, and then disappears.

Cuba
1936

HE HAS BEEN called "distinguished gentleman" and "filthy Jew"; the former is better, of course. He has been treated turn by turn with civility or contempt. "*Der gnädige Herr*" was how they had referred to Benno in the office, but lately in the street he has been "pig" and "dog." Respect or disdain is his lot. His own behavior does not change; what changes is the attitude of those whom he must deal with, the officials and the harbormaster and the porters and the maids.

The last are the least likely to refuse his proffered tip. The porters too will carry bags for whoever hires them, though he foresees a moment when no porter will be willing to carry bags for Jews. This too will come to pass. It has not happened yet. He makes a habit of providing a *pourboire* to those who offer assistance, and it's remarkable, he thinks, how even those who scorn him have a pocket for the folded bill and palm for the bright coin.

The man Benno now approaches is wearing a clean uniform, and his pants are pressed. The shoes could profit from polish; the cap could have its braid improved, and there is a weariness about the eyes and broken nose and ill-trimmed beard of the customs official. Upright in a wooden chair, he holds a clipboard and pen. He is perhaps forty years old and has a brown complexion with a yellow tinge. He sits at the side of a desk. Another customs officer—an older man, but not, it would seem, senior in the hierarchy of harbor administration—stands

26

two feet behind. This one smokes a cheroot. He has a sheaf of paperwork, a pile of forms, and scrutinizes every document requested, then passes it with a flourish to his superior. It is two o'clock.

The room is full. They have weighed anchor at the harbor's mouth; tenders wait below. Gently, the *S.S. Lohengrin* rocks. The authorities in Cuba have, he understands, an elaborate entrance procedure, and though it is an anxious moment he himself is calm. This is the sort of negotiation at which Benno has long been an expert; the steamship's upper deck has been transformed to an immigration office, where passengers are screened. Second Class and the poor people in steerage crowd the hallways in long lines. The family Hochmann, by contrast, has been sitting in the First Class lounge awaiting inspection, their luggage at their side. His wife Ilse and their son Johann and Johann's wife Gisela and their two-year-old boy Peter, who holds a lollipop with which he has been bribed, *cajoled* into silence—these form his traveling party. The ship's manifest has listed them as *Familie Hochmann*, and they are listed that way also in the ledger the official consults: five persons with visas in order, four adults and one child. They have sailed from Hamburg without incident and are wearing not their best because one must avoid display but proper clothes.

The air is warm. Their suitcases and steamer trunks and hat boxes and briefcases make an imposing pile. The steward has arranged them and, at the command of a third customs official—a younger man who smiles at Gisela flirtatiously—opens a suitcase and three steamer trunks and one hat box for inspection. This procedure takes some time. He pokes through the shirts and the boxes of books and closely examines the jewelry and Gisela's white peignoir.

Benno wishes his Spanish were better, or that they might speak English here, of which he has an adequate command. Nonetheless he understands what the officials are asking, and in a respectful manner deals with their requests. He produces the family passports and visas, the customs declaration forms, the photographs and letters that announce his profession as banker and, from his cousin, promise sponsorship; he has medical letters also, a file of attestations, and between the letter from his cousin and the letter from his doctor he has inserted a sheaf of bills as if for the purpose of storage. The official sitting at the desk does not examine him further or alter his professional demeanor but stamps the papers loudly, systematically, and when he hands back the folder there is no money inside.

"*Gracias, señor*," says Benno, and the man says, "*De nada*," and waves him and his suitcases and family out of the salon, two porters shouldering their luggage, and down towards the gangplank where liberty awaits.

"*Muchas gracias*," he repeats.

Past the line of those awaiting permission to disembark or, instead, refusal, the five of them proceed in single file. One woman reaches out to touch his sleeve, as though he might confer on her the power of acceptance, the gift of immigration, and she has, he notices, dark brown eyes like his Ilse and a body not yet bent from toil, but he shakes her off.

Bright coinage, he tells himself, the coin of the realm. The pfennig and the peso and the dollar and the pound. The franc and Rentenmark and lire and ruble and krone and bank draft and letter of credit and gold. When inflation was rampant in Berlin, his dog Till—named for Till Eulenspiegel because of his high spirits and his way of getting into and then getting out of trouble—killed the neighbor's hen. A hen is expensive, of course, because of the eggs it delivers, and in any case a dog cannot be permitted to forage in the neighborhood without liability. Eulenspiegel's pranks were merry; this one cost his master dearly, and was not a prank.

So in order to be beyond reproach, Benno offered compensation for the bird. He and his neighbor, the patent lawyer Otto Wohl, settled on a value of six hundred thousand Deutschmark, and he filled a wheelbarrow with the money and told Johann to wheel it down the street and deliver payment. Johann obliged.

But twenty minutes later he was home again, his mission not accomplished, because he said Herr Wohl claimed the price of eggs and chickens had doubled in the interval, since last night when the hen was killed, and now the proper payment must be one million two hundred thousand. This amount he would accept.

Benno remembers feeling handled, *dealt* with, but he told his son "We have no choice" and added six hundred thousand additional marks to the sum in the wheelbarrow, covering it with a sheet so the money would not blow away and no one in the street or park would see what bulked beneath. Again, Johann returned—with a long face this time, saying, "Papa, he wants *two* million now, he says that is the rate." During the lunch hour, therefore, he filled the car's boot with money and drove the two doors to Wohl's gate and said, "My final offer." His neighbor knew he meant it, and accepted the two million marks for a single chicken, and while he was delivering packets of bills and watching the man count them Benno decided, and remembers, now, deciding, he would leave. It was not so much the sum itself—two million marks were worthless and would be four million in the morning—as the insult of the thing.

Like any other Jew, he has grown used to such behavior, the little and large humiliations in the daily course of business—the levies and the household taxes and the papers he must carry and, as of Hitler's ascendancy, the brown shirts and the boots. More and more there is suspicion and paperwork and, once the Third Reich is established, a set of procedures to follow and the sense of no longer belonging to a world where he until this moment had felt welcome. The family Hochmann lived in Berlin since the middle 1600s, and they have grown prosperous; a great-uncle was a tax collector and also a deputy mayor. The banking business proved excellent, the house was large and well appointed, his parents and then he himself went to the opera weekly and, if not the opera, to concerts.

Throughout his life he had wanted for nothing, and the cook and chauffeur and the two gardeners had been very well behaved, until one winter morning the cook refused to cook for them and the chauffeur would not drive. It is a common story, not one that needs repeating, but Benno can remember standing by the servants' entrance of the Wohl *Residenz* and handing over stacks of bills and telling himself, *Das ist genug. Enough.* This is a family saying, having to do with chocolate cake and the amount of cream it is proper to serve, but the tedious business of watching Herr Otto Wohl tally Deutschmark while he stood at attention is something he cannot forget. Why this should be the case is not entirely clear to him, but that his poodle Till should be thus fined and penalized—why the dog should be treated as a criminal for behavior that could have been predicted, and was wholly normal—seemed like a warning: *It is enough. You must leave.*

This of course has taken time. The incident with Till took place in 1923, and it is many years later. The Rentenmark stabilized matters, and hyperinflation came to an end. But as of 1930, with the kind of patient planning that had made him, once, successful, and is now required not so much for success as survival, Benno made his preparations for escape. The dog is dead. His parents too have died. That had been a great sorrow, but they passed on in the fullness of time, at eighty-three and eighty-four, and would not have countenanced departure; in some sense, therefore, the death of his parents was a blessing in disguise. Had his father stayed alive, who believed that everything was still in order and the Führer would grow moderate, he himself could not have left.

In May of 1932, Johann married Gisela Lefchinsky from the Bing family in Hamburg. They have a child now, the boy Peter, and lovely Gisela has promised that, once they settle down again, she plans to have another. Her people are in the import-export business, furs from Russia and bristles from China, and therefore have wide commercial dealings; a connection in Havana has made it possible for the Hochmanns to depart for Cuba with the aim of America later. It is their promised land. They could all perhaps have sailed for America directly, but the *Lohengrin* was bound for Cuba and then Brazil and Argentina, and it seemed advisable, once they secured a passage, to take what was on offer and not wait. What funds he could transfer have been transferred to correspondent bankers in New York; what furniture and plate and paintings he could send are sent.

The house is sold. Benno regrets the sale but not the transaction, which had been properly managed. To have retained the house, he knew, would be impossible in exile, and it is better to have completed a sale at no great loss than to have been foreclosed. There is writing on the wall, he told his partners in the bank, and although not precisely the biblical sentence it is much in the same vein. In the Book of Daniel the prophet declares, "*Mene, mene, tekel, upharsin*: You have been weighed in the balance and found wanting."

In the Third Reich, however, they weigh you in the balance and place a finger on the scale; they are the ones who are wanting and what the government now wants is everything, all the ownership papers and entitlements and property he so carefully amassed. They will not be content, he knows, till there is nothing left. For the whole of the Atlantic crossing, leaning above the endless waves and watching them gather, rise and fall, he told himself "*Mene, mene*" and then, "It is enough."

On the dock his cousin waits. There is also Ilse's cousin, with a white straw hat and cane. There is Ilse's uncle, who has brought an additional driver and car. They have not seen each other for years, and the reunion is glad. His cousin Rudolf wears a thin mustache and pomaded hair as if he is a native, a citizen of southern climes.

"*Willkommen, willkommen*," he says.

There are tears and handshakes and embraces and introductions; there is general rejoicing on the dock. He hears laughter and weeping as if from a distance, although those who greet him crowd near. They are all together in Havana's harbor now at last, and the sky is blue and weather warm and Benno allows himself to breathe the fragrant inrushing compound of flowers, salt water, and smoke. He feels a strange unsteadiness, as if while he is standing still the paving stones beneath his feet are nonetheless in motion, like the constant waves.

With his handkerchief, he wipes his face. The family has landed, the family is safe.

"A good trip?" Rudolf inquires.

"*Ein gute Reise, ja,*" says Johann.

"You must speak Spanish in this country," Ilse's cousin offers. "Or, if you prefer it, English."

"My name is Rodolfo," says Rudolf merrily. "It's what they call me here."

Young Peter has managed to retain his lollipop, although diminished by sucking. Rudolf-Rodolfo pats him on the shoulder.

"You cannot imagine," says Benno, "how relieved we are to be in Cuba. And to have left Germany."

"We will return," his wife declares, "when this madness is over. When the madman has finished."

He does not tell her what he knows, and she perhaps has also understood but refuses to acknowledge: the *Wahnsinn* will not be over soon and the madman not be finished. This is clear as clear can be. There will come a time, perhaps, when all will be forgotten and therefore all forgiven, but that time is in the distant future and they are not young.

"A cigar?" Rodolfo offers. "We have good tobacco here."

"*Ganz gern,*" says Benno. "With pleasure."

Ilse's cousin produces a light. They are standing in this place, he tells himself, as though the world were normal, as though things have not changed. Inhaling, he feels once again that his balance is uncertain, that he remains on deck unbalanced and should be holding the guard rail, except there is no guard rail, and the cobblestones beneath his feet are solid and unmoving although he feels them move. He studies his cigar. When the first ships came from Europe to Havana, they brought cobblestones as ballast and left them at the harbor while they loaded up again for the homeward journey with cotton and sugar and tobacco and, later on, rum. The cargo on the outward journey was slaves; the cargo on the trip back home was cotton and produce for profit; this is the way of import-export, and it has always been so.

He puts his arm around his wife, who does not know, or pretends to ignorance—it is Ilse's way, her habitual procedure with a subject that causes confusion—about the slave trade and its misery, and thinks these thick-armed men with ropes, who are making fast the tender and have long poles and grappling hooks, are happy, happy, happy, as he himself is happy now to be standing on this paving in what William Shakespeare called the Brave New World.

Benno puffs. The smoke settles his stomach, a little; it is, as Rudolf promised, a very good cigar. Peter points at the black men with wonder; he has not seen negroes before. He asks his mother why they look the way they look, what costume they are wearing, and she leans down to explain to him that this is not a costume but the color of their skin, and the red bandanas at their neck are what they wear to keep themselves cool in the sun. While he is listening and looking, gazing idly at the crowd and the small boats at the harbor mouth, the head of the family feels—no better word for it—*flooded*, awash with relief. Benno has not recognized, had not permitted himself to recognize for the two weeks of the journey (and here, he knows, he is much like his wife, a fist clenched against confusion) how difficult the trip has been, how nervous although outwardly calm he had felt with the customs officials and men who examined their luggage, and is seized now by the need—an overmastering desire—to leave the port behind. He tips the porters lavishly.

"*Gehen wir doch*," he urges his cousin. "Let us by all means proceed."

This they do. The three automobiles await them, and after the bags have been loaded there is barely room for the party, but they squeeze together hotly and make a slow processional through the place he must now call home, Havana not Berlin. The fort above the harbor is hewn from what looks like white rock.

"Morro Castle"—Rodolfo points. "It is very well positioned, *nein*? There is also one in Cartagena and, of course, San Juan.

Everywhere in South America and on these islands at the harbor's mouth they built a fort."

Benno yawns. He is, he understands, exhausted and though he can manage to keep his eyes open he does not fully register the things he sees, the palm trees and the men on donkeys and the women attired in black and shoeless children everywhere, the roof-tiles and the fastened wooden shutters and delicate filigreed balcony ironwork as though they were in the Alhambra, or perhaps Madrid, the pink and yellow buildings in the late afternoon sun. There is a smell he cannot place, beyond the smell of horse droppings and dead fish and drying ocean-spawn, and Ilse's uncle tells him, "Sugar cane."

The sea wall is called Malecón; it has been recently built. Waves batter it, but gently, and Rudolf-Rodolfo says before this wall was put in place there were daily floods. They discuss the voyage out, the hardships of the journey, and though there were in truth few hardships and a sense, now, of deliverance, it is also true that this small town with men in sombreros and women in shawls and a three-legged dog now limping past is not where Benno planned to be or, arriving, plans to stay. When his papers have been processed and his turn comes for the trip to New York, he will take an additional trip. He is not so old or weak, he tells himself, he cannot start anew; he is sixty-three years old, and though his means have been diminished he remains a man of means.

They make their way through town. His wife says, "I rejoice." He himself does not rejoice; he is not feeling fortunate; he remembers keenly the pantry of the house he sold, with its hanging sausages and wheels of cheese and jars of herring and bottles of beer, the abundance left behind. In the library there were bound red-leather volumes of Goethe and Schiller and Lessing and Schopenhauer and Winckelmann and Fichte and Heine and Nietzsche and Schelling and Kant, and they repose there, still, for the new owners to open, while Benno and Ilse and Johann and his wife and child bounce jarringly out of the center of the city to an area called Miramar that Rodolfo tells him is welcoming to Jews.

"Thanks be to God," says Ilse.

Benno takes a final puff and extinguishes his Upmann.

"We have landed," says Ilse. "Safe, safe."

"How is *Tante* Lotte?" asks Rodolfo.

"Well."

"How is that foolish son of hers? What is his name, Fritz?"

"No longer so foolish. They are in Paris."

"And who remains?"

"*Niemand*, no one. Or only a few. Only those who cannot leave. Who are too sick or old to travel, or who still believe there can be an accommodation . . ."

Rodolfo shakes his head. "Your house?" he asks.

"Was sold."

The architect Tessenow had been a friend or, if not a friend precisely, someone with whom Benno felt comfortable and would take a schnapps. Eight years ago he and Ilse decided their home could be improved, and therefore he hired Walter Tessenow to make suggestions and drawings and also to install new terraces and a proper portico and a fountain on the grounds. In 1928 they made enlargements to the property; the work had taken months. There were men whose expertise was stone and others who were good with wood and others who were plasterers and painters; the young man Tessenow employed as clerk of the works now works as an architect for the Third Reich. His name is Albert Speer. Benno can remember still the steely gaze, the nimble hands, the way the upstairs maid Frederika fluttered and was flustered each time young Albert drank a coffee from the kitchen and returned his cup. Always, he had pencils in his shirt pocket, sticking out of it; always the clerk of the works wore a brown cloth cap. He can remember asking Speer why he consulted the drawings so seldom, and can remember the

clerk's answer, not pronounced with insolence but an unnerv-
ing confidence: "There are plans and plans. The world is a map
in your head, *mein Herr*, a garden to walk through with every
pond an ocean and each stone bench a mountain range and the
porte-cochère a continent. I do not need," said Speer, "to look at
Herr Tessenow's drawings when I have them all"—he touched
his fingers to his eyes—"right here. Inside."

This had seemed remarkable, but now that they are driving
through the streets of Miramar and seeing palm trees and smell-
ing salt water it is as though the map in his own head has been
inscribed in actuality upon the actual world. Young Speer had
had a point. What Benno sees around him is the city of Havana
and men driving carts; what he sees in his mind's eye is Berlin
and the district of Charlottenburg, the linden trees in snow. He
sees his office in the early morning, clerks standing at attention,
the lamps lit. At dusk when the day's work is done the clerks
line up again to await his departure, hats in hand, while he
extinguishes the desk lamp and is helped into his overcoat and
bids them each good night.

A donkey brays; a rooster crows. *Here* is a country where
they do not threaten you, Rodolfo says, and if you start out selling *schmattes* and are a rag collector or a peddler sooner or later
you open a shop and then you start a business and purchase the
building the business sits in and then you can be prosperous in
Cuba. The day after tomorrow, says Rodolfo, when you have
had a little rest I have arranged a meeting in the Hotel Presidente, where we lunch with several bankers hoping to make your
acquaintance, and the *ambiente* is good. It is important that you
meet these men, and the Hotel Presidente is the place to meet.

He wants to sleep. He had slept well enough on the *Lohengrin*, or at least for a few fitful hours each night, but whenever
he awakened he sensed Ilse also wakeful, her eyes open on the
pillow and staring at the stateroom wall as though it were a cell.
Benno takes her hand. He repeats what she said, soothingly,
"We have landed. We are safe." She smiles at him, as no doubt
in the next car Gisela smiles at Johann, and their son Peter, who
will finally have finished the lollipop he's been sucking on and

who therefore asks for another. In the third car follow their belongings, the books and clothes with which they will begin once more, for it is passing strange to have been from a family that for three centuries were residents of Germany and to be once more a wandering Jew.

In Rodolfo's house there are beds for them all, and the luggage is distributed. The house is stone and stucco, and the courtyard in its center has a shade tree beneath which a long table has been laid for celebration, with a white lace cloth. Rodolfo's wife, Elizabeth, has also grown older and stately in the fashion of a Southern lady—plump and dressed in this hot weather as if she might instead catch cold, or feel a chill; she wears a scarf around her shoulders they call here a *mantilla*, and in Spanish she orders the servants to offer up refreshments.

She and Ilse are happy together, talking about the old days and the school they both attended, and a shopping trip they took together to the city of Bremen, although Ilse is two years older, and they had known each other only glancingly before. Benno sighs. Tomorrow perhaps, says Rodolfo, I will show you a nearby apartment, but tonight of course and as long as you wish you are our guests. On the verandah in the garden, as the preparations for the meal are being completed, he lights a second Upmann: firmly packed. While the children and their cousins gather in the living room and discuss in animated fashion whatever it is they discuss, he finds himself adrift again, as though still on the *Lohengrin*'s deck and seeing on the wide Atlantic Ocean only the tops and the white spume of waves. Because he is a prudent man, and needs to know the strengths and weaknesses of those he deals with, and who deal with him, he has read Hitler's *Mein Kampf.*

It is *furchtbar*, awful. It is very clear what Hitler plans, and his plans are mad. Rodolfo smokes beside him, and Benno tries to explain. He misses the home in Charlottenburg, the comfort and solidity of what he left behind, the concerts and music lessons and *schul* for Johann and the Sunday breakfasts, but he is not deluded: it was time, even past time, to go. *Herr* Schickelgruber is the very devil, and he will make of Germany a hell.

Days pass. Months pass. A whole year passes while they wait, and what news they have from home grows worse. The laws and the levies increase, and he thanks his lucky stars that passage on the *Lohengrin* had been available, because it is less easy now to leave. The mail comes only rarely, and the letters confirm his worst fears and suspicions; the bank is declared by the authorities bankrupt, and his partner Robert Strasfogel has disappeared. The Strasfogel family moved to their house in the country, and then the house burned down. By the second year in Havana, there are rumors of forced liquidation of assets; there are stories of Hitler's police.

Benno tries to take pleasure in freedom. He tells himself that what he lost is insubstantial, unimportant; what he has gained is liberty, which cannot be bought. He revels in the summer rains and ripe fruit from the garden, the music the Cuban people seem always to be making, the way they smile and salute him with no seeming irony when he takes his constitutional after the morning meal. As the weeks and months proceed, he does a little business in trade. His heart is not in it, truly, but Rodolfo's friends are much involved with the Sugar Stabilization Institute and the Sugar Coordination Act, and they assure him of the importance of planning and, by the government, control. Sugar is the crucial thing; the export of sugar is central to prosperity. In the period of Prohibition, rum became impossible, but the people of America, he knows, all have sweet teeth. They require cane sugar for breakfast, and in everything they cook and the packaged food they buy, and for their cakes and tea.

Maria Fuentes who now cooks for them is an island beauty. He is past the age where such things matter, but if he were not sixty-four and soon to have his sixty-fifth birthday he would no doubt have pinched her bottom or caressed the soft curve of her breast. He watches Johann watching her with a kind of curiosity; does his son, he wonders, take Maria into bed?

It would be no surprise. She is laughter-loving, it appears, and generous with butter, and if she were an upstairs maid in the old days in Berlin it would have been expected that she serve her young master also at night so he would be a practiced husband later on. That had been Benno's own form of instruction, his way of learning the ways of the world, and it would have been a pleasure to be seventeen again and embracing this Maria in the watches of the night. But all such thoughts now are, he knows, mere idle speculation, and whom he lies next to is Ilse instead, lightly snoring when she sleeps.

"*Mehr Shakespeare als Shakespeare*" is what they say of Schlegel and Tieck, who have translated the playwright; "It is more Shakespeare than Shakespeare." So he finds himself repeating, "Brave new world, that hath such creatures in it," in silence while watching Maria slice onions or dice fruit. She does so with an abandon that is somehow also precision, her black hair flipping wantonly with the movements of her neck. The apartment they have rented is a pleasant one, with views of the water and shade from low trees, and when she arrives each morning to prepare the midday meal she smiles at him becomingly and makes a little curtsey. His Spanish has improved, of course, but the rapid-fire Spanish in which she converses with others in the family's employ, or with those tradesmen who come to the door, is not something he can understand; the sing-song lilt of it and the way she hums while washing and drying the dishes is an enchantment for Benno, a reason to be grateful every day.

Nonetheless he mourns the old cold country he was forced to leave. The family Hochmann makes excursions to the countryside of Cuba—to Matanzas and Villa Clara and Ciego de Ávila, to Artemisa and Mayabeque and Cienfuegos and Sancti Spíritus—where there are farmers and cane fields and a sense that nothing changes or will change. They do this out of restlessness but also from curiosity; it is wise to know the place they now call home.

This is a sizeable island. There are hills and even mountains and dark groves of trees—not like those of the Alps or the Schwarzwald, of course—and a rocky shore reminding him of the North Sea and the beach at Worpswede, except the water is warm. They picnic by a river and watch women in bright yellow clothes immerse themselves in the current and listen to them chant what sound like spells from Africa; at ceremony's end there are dead chickens everywhere, their heads and feet ready to be picked over by crows. He thinks of his dead poodle, Till, and how the single hen Till killed has brought them to this place.

Reports from Germany grow worse and worse—so bad at times he does not want to hear them, for the persecution seems like a bad dream to Ilse, and to Johann and Gisela and everyone who learns about brutality at home. There are new rules to obey. Soon enough there are rumors of camps where Jews are conscripted for labor, and where the slogan falsely claims, *Arbeit macht frei.* His own work, yes, has made him free, but this is instead conscription and the Jews who now are forced to work have not been granted freedom and will not attain it. Sleepless, Benno thinks of his ancestors, the ones who first arrived in Germany from Italy, wearing furs and skullcaps, holding books and prayer shawls, the scholars and the moneylenders who by the eighteenth century could call themselves bankers and be received by men of consequence when they required loans. There have always been ghettos, always pogroms, but a man of business was treated with propriety and also a grudging respect. Now every Jew in commerce—even a Rothschild, even a Warburg—has forfeited respect. Albert Speer, he thinks, has planned it, and though he knows this is untrue he cannot rid himself of the memory of Speer, long fingers pressed to his eyelids, saying of the drawings and constructions in the garden, "I have it all inside . . ."

His father, dying, had declared, "*Ich glaube, dass ich keine Feinde habe,*" and Benno did not dissuade him. "I think I have no enemies" is a comforting thing to declare to yourself when you are dying, eighty-four, but it is not the truth. The Hochmann family, and all Jews in the neighborhood—as well as those who converted, the *conversos*—have enemies. Their enemies prevail.

One day he discusses with Johann the situation in Cuba and

the fact that cousins Bing and Bleichroeder have opened up an office of the import-export business in New York. They have guaranteed employment, and written him to say his name has been submitted and his application now at last approved. It is an opportunity, and the question is of course if the family feels ready to be uprooted and relinquish what has grown familiar for something once more new.

They are sitting on the porch. It is mid-afternoon. Palm fronds rattle in the breeze. Maria brings them mangoes and papaya and a plate of fried plantains and a saucer full of olives. With the exception of green olives, he thinks, all these foods were strange to him two years ago, and when she bends to inquire if he wishes one more cup of tea or perhaps a cup of coffee or a glass of beer or rum the edge of her left hip comes up against his arm. He does not withdraw his arm. Her hip is both bone-firm and softly sheathed. He looks at Johann looking and understands his son as well will miss the comforts of this island haven, the good humor of its people, the way that they have settled in and been received. Gisela is pregnant again. She will have, Benno hopes, a second son but a daughter too would please him in this brave new world.

"Señor?" Maria asks.

He shakes his head. He tells her with his now nearly fluent Spanish that he will continue drinking tea and requires nothing else. From the lemon tree behind him comes a rustling; birds alight. There they settle, preening, and call to each other repeatedly, with always the same notes of the same song. The cook need not take off her clothes in order to stand naked; she is the very picture of warm yieldingness while she lifts the teapot and, for the two men, pours. The image, Benno tells himself, is straight out of a canvas by the painter Paul Gauguin; it is a woman in the tropics, *of* the tropics, and fecundity is everywhere; he wishes he were young again, except he is not young.

In Havana there are churches where the bells toll loudly, and the Presidential Palace is always, when he goes to town for business, loud with sound: music and laughter and traffic and the cries of hawkers in the streets. Dogs bark; the donkeys bray; the roosters greet the dawn. But there is silence also while he takes his constitutional and walks to the sea wall, then back to the apartment, considering the bulletins and headlines in the paper and what the other refugees discuss in the cafés.

On November 8, 1938—this news travels quickly, for once—he learns of the death of a German Embassy Official, Ernst vom Rath, in Paris, and learns the name as well of the Polish Jew Herschel Grynszpan who shot him, who then took two days to die. After November 9 and 10, they hear of *Kristallnacht*. It is *furchtbar*, it is *Wahnsinn*, but the terror and the madness are what Benno has for years predicted, and the shattered glass and shattered lives come somehow as no surprise. Hundreds of synagogues and thousands of places of commerce are burned to the ground; in Berlin and in Vienna there is nearly nothing left.

So once again he tells himself he must continue traveling and remove to the safe haven of New York. At sixty-five, he knows, there will be little further opportunity; he must take what is on offer, a third country to call home. Rodolfo and Elizabeth and the others who made them welcome in Cuba urge the Hochmanns not to leave; there is no danger here, they say, or at any rate small danger, and a minister has promised that every enterprising gentleman who helps with the investment and supports the infrastructure will be protected by the government they help. There is a man called Lansky—Meyer Lansky from America—with plans for casinos and nightclubs, and the future of Havana is a future of prosperity; why not, asks Rodolfo, remain?

Again they embark from the dock by the fort; again the Morro Castle looks down upon them whitely, mutely; again there are high waves. This time, however, the journey is rapid; they are going not a hundred miles to the city of Miami and, above it, the port of Fort Lauderdale, where they will land and go through customs with, he is told, no trouble. This he in part believes. Again Benno stands by the railing, staring at the sea-foam and the green declivities where wave-tops crash upon themselves and fall and recover and rise. The waters of the Caribbean in hurricane season are fierce, but today is a calm crossing, although he feels in his stomach the familiar pitch and the roiling tumble of motion at sea.

He prepares but then thinks better of it and does not light his cigar. Birds follow the wake of the vessel, feeding on the food-scraps tossed from portholes or the galley-waste; fish leap in the near distance, and he sees a school of what a sailor tells him are dolphins: ballerinas of the deep.

Johann stands beside him. "The promised land," muses his son. "At last."

"*Endlich*," Benno repeats. "Those fish are marvelous."

"Are you looking forward to it, *vati?*"

He spreads his hands. He studies them. The fingernails are yellow, and the veins are prominent, with liver spots everywhere above the knuckles: an old man's hands. "It is your promised land," he says. "For me, it is the place I hope to die."

Johann is shocked. "Don't say such things."

"Why not? It is only the truth. Even Moses made accommodations, yes?"

"Except he did not reach the promised land. He pointed the way only, but you have brought us here. And tomorrow we will be in America, and sooner or later they enter the war."

He touches his boy's shoulder, his boy who is a man and has now a son of his own. "We must hope they do not wait too long. Till the moment when no Jews are left to save."

"Franklin Roosevelt will help us."

"Are you certain?"

"*Doch, doch,*" says Johann, "of course." But his voice registers no certainty, and they look out at the water together and watch the dolphins leap.

In America they have, as predicted, no trouble with authorities, and the paperwork does not require a bribe. In Fort Lauderdale there are many stevedores working with a practiced urgency, a sense of organized bustle that Benno finds consoling although Ilse is alarmed by it, and soon enough they are established on a train that hurries north. The Hochmanns have reserved a car, and their luggage travels in a separate compartment; the porter is an old black man who speaks to him in English he can barely understand. But the man is affable; beneath his dark blue cap he has white hair. Gisela has grown big with child, and her face is moist with the exertions of the journey, but she does not complain or make difficulties for her husband, and Peter, who is five years old, amuses himself by making faces in the window, nose pressed against the glass.

The villages and towns and cities succeed each other rapidly; the scale of this new

country is, he understands, a large one and the size of it enormous; by the time they reach

New York, he has made up his mind to be grateful, and though the rush and press of people makes him weary they have been correct to come.

At the end of May 1939, the *S.S. St. Louis*, having come from Hamburg with a thousand refugees, is refused permission to dock in the port of Havana. Permission is also denied in Miami, and the liner must return to Europe with its human cargo. This means, for Jewish passengers, an almost certain death. From his safe haven in America, Benno follows the fate of those who followed after and tells himself, if only they had sailed before, they would have been safe. *If only, if only*, he tells himself: the two saddest words in the language and, if not the saddest, most useless; there is nothing to be done.

They settle in Westchester County and the town of New Rochelle. He and Ilse need no more than an apartment, but Johann and his family desire a house, and the houses in Manhattan are for a young man expensive, with no garden or clean air to breathe. In America the firm of Bing and Bleichroeder is prosperous already, but he has grown too old to work and his arrangements for the transferred funds from Berlin years before have been successful, so he can sit and listen to music and watch his son and grandson and, soon enough, his two grandchildren with no fear of penury; he has, he knows, enough.

There are Mozart and Haydn and Brahms. There are Schubert and Schumann and Bach. There are Mendelssohn, Beethoven, Mahler, Handel, Telemann to listen to each afternoon, after the midday meal. He will not listen to Wagner, although of course he still feels fond of the good ship *Lohengrin*, but the Ring Cycle fairly reeks of savagery: oaths and spears and vows of revenge and evil scheming elves. After the bombing of Pearl Harbor, America enters the war. It has been a long time coming, and Benno was from time to time impatient, because every day and every month America did not support the Allied cause was time lost to the devil's party, the little house painter from Munich and his madman plans. But as of 1942 the balances are shifting; there is new weight in the balance, and it is instead the Axis powers who will be found wanting. This he understands.

Johann and Gisela and their two sons Peter and Frederick move to a new house in Larchmont, not far away from New Rochelle, and he and Ilse move as well to an apartment in Larchmont, which will be their final home. He sits in the Stonecrest Apartments, in the south-facing window, and sometimes when he shuts his eyes he sees the cook Maria with her brown cheeks and black hair approaching, her arms outstretched and hands full of fruit. Her smile is the smile of satiety, her neck wet with sweat. He has enjoyed the years in Cuba, the safe haven of Havana, but with the clarity that from time to time still comes to him, Benno knows his family belongs now in this country, where they will have a future that is in some ways better than had been the past. It was an effort to settle, it was a large risk and wager, but the risk was worth it and the bet has paid off handsomely, even though he has grown old and weary with the effort of escape. On the profits of this particular wager, he himself cannot collect.

For himself it is too late, of course; he will live in exile with Ilse, listening to music and drinking his schnapps while she takes a Campari and soda, a pair of refugees. But when they ask him—and people ask him, often, in the library or at the bank—if he will return to Germany when the war is over, he tells them he has no such plan or any such desire. His grand-children are Americans, not Germans, and that is a good thing. In this country everyone has been an immigrant, and the Statue of Liberty holds up her torch in the harbor like a beacon for the free.

The war goes on. He listens to the radio and reads the paper carefully, and with Johann discusses the progress of the Allied force. Because bristles are declared a necessary commodity for the military effort, since they clean and polish the barrels of guns, Bing and Bleichroeder enlarge their staff and Johann is promoted; when D-Day comes and General Dwight David Eisenhower lands with the annihilating power of the American army, Benno is elated and knows the war will end. Though it is not of course correct to view initials in this fashion, he thinks of D-Day as Dwight David-day, and likes to make a joke of it, and he repeats the joke to his grandsons although they do not laugh. More and more he can hear himself laughing at the sheer relief of it, the unlikely result of survival when it did not seem likely that the members of his family could prosper or survive. Spooning sugar in his morning tea, and stirring it, he thinks how fortunate he was to sail to Cuba before the near-total embargo, and when he and Ilse if it is fine weather walk the paths of Manor Park and look at the Long Island Sound, its sailboats and motorboats and circling ducks, he tells himself that they are lucky, lucky, lucky to have escaped from Germany when the *Wahnsinn* was not yet total, and his good wife reminds him it was foresight in addition to just luck.

They learn about the camps. They read about Bergen-Belsen, Dachau, Auschwitz and the liberation of those few who survived them; the horror stays with Benno for his final years. He cannot close his eyes at night without the image of a pile of shoes, or gold from teeth, or bodies flung against a wire fence to leave for the foraging dogs. He will live this way years longer, wearing vests and suits that have grown too large for him, and on his wrist the watch from Patek Philippe he can only now with difficulty wind and read. Rodolfo and Colonel Battista, he learns, have learned to trust each other, and have good business dealings, and with a flash of his old insight Benno knows his cousin is making a mistake.

Marriage
1949

HER FATHER IS a stubborn man, but finally he dies. It has taken a long time, a small eternity, thinks Gisela, and although he had been vain about his looks he grew in the end bent and old. In the end there had been nothing left but white wisps of hair, the waxen lips, the long patrician nose. He died at eighty-five. For the final weeks, although he lay at home in bed, he drank only a few sips of water through the straw she held, and did not speak, and kept his blue eyes closed. Those eyes had been trained blazingly upon her for so long she could not get used to his eyelids instead, the blank and shuttered stare. *Glare* is more like it, Gisela thinks; all during her childhood, and later on serving her father, she shrank beneath his watchful condescension and always-present disapproval. For her mother it was worse.

Theirs is, she knows, a history like other family histories, and when you live it your whole life it does not seem peculiar. But sometimes when she sees her boys, first Peter and then Frederick, so normal in America, she thinks it an astonishment that who they are and how they are is part of her strange history, the family they come from and the place from which they came. Someday, she thinks, she must write it all down. Someday her children and her children's children when they are born will want to know the circumstance that drove them out of Hamburg to Berlin and then to Havana and New York. This is a story in only her keeping—even Johann does not know it all—so she should write or type it out and then bind it as a book. Her typing skills are adequate and her handwriting is good.

It is a long story. It reports on her parents' intimate wrangle—marriage and divorce and separation and reunion—the way they lived together but apart. To tell it properly would take a proper writer, but her children will forgive her if—in the old expression, *after all these years and all these tears*—she gets a detail wrong. The tale is one of unrequited passion, ambition and atonement, her mother's romantic devotion and her broken heart. It has to do with scandal, the women her father would bring to his office, the unbroken silence of her parents and the way she had been made to serve as go-between between them. Although they both spoke German, she had had to translate—from *Plattdeutsch* to *Hochdeutsch* and back again, from dialect to dialect for two adult adversaries in agreement only on a warring truce. Her father had forbidden his ex-wife Miriam *née* Bing to speak to him directly, and in any case she refused to, so Gisela would act as intermediary at the table.

"Would you tell your mother, please, to pass the salt?"

"Mama, papa please would like some salt."

"Ask him if the brisket is not sufficiently salted?"

"Mama wants to know if you don't find the meat sufficiently salty?"

"I do. Please tell your mother that the salt is for the vegetables."

"He wants it for the carrots, mama."

"They were intended to be sweet. They were glazed with sugar."

"She meant them to be sweet, papa. They were glazed with sugar."

"If I require salt, Gizi,"—this had been his nickname for her—"that is the taste I'm looking for. I don't need cooking lessons."

"Tell him to take his own salt, then. And with my compliments."

"She doesn't wish to pass you the salt cellar, papa."

"Very well. Tell her this food is inedible. I will go outside to eat. I will be better served elsewhere, you can be certain."

"We know that, don't we," said her mother. "He is very welcome to enjoy the service of others."

"I heard that," said her father. "Please tell her I intend to."

Her mother raised her napkin to her eyes—this would happen often—and pushed back her chair unseeingly, sobbing, and stormed out of the room.

It is difficult to write all this, but something she feels she must do. Now that her parents are both dead, and she is living in Larchmont, New York, with *Gott sei Dank!* a husband who is not a monster, with two children of their own and peaceful conversation at the dinner table, Gisela feels a duty to preserve the story of her parents' marriage and, in the end, her part in it. When Johann Hochmann asked for her hand, and she consented gladly, she did not tell him everything about her parents' courtship or the sorrows of her mother's *mésalliance* with Simon Lefchinsky from Lübeck. The details would have concerned him, no doubt, and though her Johann is a steady man and one who does not change his mind, he might have changed his mind. This thought is one that frightens Gisela, and so she held her tongue.

Her father had been very handsome when young, but he had had few prospects. *Her* family was in the import-export business, and in the fourth generation; *his* family were rag-pickers and, although educated, poor. By the Baltic Sea there was little to bring his dreams to fruition, for he dreamed of becoming a doctor and even perhaps of a clinic for which he would serve as director. In his childhood, once, he went to such a clinic, and it was something he never forgot. His own father while delivering a load of linen to the hospital dispensary suffered a seizure and required immediate treatment, and the dismissive, prideful way the doctors received their impoverished patient but nonetheless attended to and healed him made an impression on the boy. He decided early on that this would be his calling, and his calling it remained.

Medicine is a respectable profession, and if that were the end of the matter there would be nothing to tell. But Lefchinsky had expensive tastes, or so it would seem, from the cradle, and since the cradle was not lined with silk, and the spoon he spooned his gruel with was made of tin not silver, he determined early on that what he required was an advantageous match. Blue-eyed and intelligent, he was also studious, with only the fault of empty pockets he had determined to fill. To succeed as a doctor he needed fine clothes, or so he told himself. To indulge in luxurious habits—caviar, a game of cards—was also his intention, and from the start he understood he must marry well.

Accordingly, when Simon Lefchinsky arrived in Hamburg from Lübeck, he came as an adventurer intent on a good marriage. Soon enough he set his sights on poor rich Miriam Bing. Gisela's mother was the perfect match, a girl with wealthy parents and little else to commend her; she had no beauty or distinctive wit and was going to be a spinster who had already lost the charm of youth. Her sister—aunt Susanna—had married and was living with her husband the lawyer in Strasbourg; her two older brothers both had families and established homes.

Of the four Bing children, therefore, there was only one who remained to be married, and if it were going to happen it had better happen soon. Gisela's mother Miriam was living with her parents and by her own admission long in the tooth and resigned to a life of celibacy in the house on Blumenstrasse, where she had been born. Never having acquired a taste for large gatherings or dances, she did not miss society; the living room and dining room and drawing room and gardens were where she passed her days. First her bedroom was a nursery, and then her hopeful girlhood's room, and now an old maid's room. On the third floor she maintained this space and dreamed of great adventures, but rarely ventured forth into the street and town. Staring when distracted at the walls or out the window at the garden, Miriam read books or did her needlepoint or watercolors but did not expect to speak of literature or display her handiwork to admiring strangers. She spent her nights alone.

There is a saying, Gisela knows, "beggars can't be choosers." But it is equally the case that rich plain aging women cannot have their choice of suitors, since suitors are not numerous. Therefore when the young man from Lübeck—whose uncle was a Rabbi and whose name was Simon Lefchinsky—appeared at the door of the Bing mansion, having seen and briefly spoken to Miriam twice at Temple, and closeted himself with her father and emerged with a nuptial agreement, it seemed as though kind Providence at last had found an answer to her maiden prayers and given her a handsome companion. This was 1893. He was twenty-nine years old, she twenty-eight. Miriam adored the man: his blue eyes and intelligence, his well-cut suits and fondness for fine wine; until her dying day, unfortunately, he was the love of her life.

To begin with, everything was roses and champagne. Simon completed his medical studies, and the Bing family provided the newlyweds with a furnished house to inhabit. His manners were a little rough, a little common to begin with—he said "don't" for "does not," for example, and "ground floor" for "*rez de chaussée.*" Over time, however, he learned to comply with the patterns of speech and fashionable deportment of wealthy Jews in the city. Miriam's was a large dowry, and soon enough there were children, which made her parents happy and made her happy as well. How it made *him* feel, the old man told Gisela in his charming way at the end of his life, was trapped.

There were Thomas, Henry, and—many years later, the last one—Gisela herself. She was born in 1909, with the century no longer young, and by that time her mother was exhausted and her father rarely at home. Having studied hard, he flourished as a doctor; Hamburg ladies in particular were fond of him, and solicited his service. Simon became a specialist in fainting fits, diseases of the nervous system, and feminine disorders of the legs and lower spine; in particular what Sigmund Freud would later call hysteria was an illness he learned how to treat. He cultivated and soon enough perfected a winning bedside manner. The women who flocked to his office were not always married, or not always happily married, and because he dealt in troubles of the female body he was expert in these matters and consulted, often as not, when the office door was locked or the office empty in the middle of the night. Miriam had her suspicions, of course, and her sorrows also, but her husband gave her children and, in the course of time, fur coats and pearls, and she did not complain.

This went on for years. The boys grew up and then away, while little Gisela spent long days with her mother, learning to crochet and play the piano. They read books together in silence; they worked on needlepoint. She knew, of course, the difference between her own home and her grandparents' house, where the halls would ring with laughter and the bustling servants' chatter; she lived her own childhood in silence except for the sound of the piano and, from time to time, the exultant cries of women in the adjoining office or the sound of her father's automobile on the cobblestones at midnight and then the loud rattle of keys and the sound of his boots on the stairs. He was fond of her, or so it seemed, and liked to cuff her ears and give her marzipan at breakfast, but did not express a similar teasing fondness for Miriam, his wife. Towards her mother, the doctor's behavior was proper but cold, as if he were discharging an old debt.

Then, when the gentleman from Lübeck was well enough established and no longer in need of her family money, he commenced an affair with an actress. He arranged to be caught with the woman *in flagrante delicto* in the Hotel Atlantic in Hamburg, and there were articles and photographs and a very public disgrace. This outraged the Bing family, and once again there was an interview, and the upshot was that Herr Doktor Lefchinsky was given a sum of money and told never to darken their doorstep again and granted a divorce.

It had been, he told his daughter in his charming way, his intention all along. "Your mother Miriam and I," he explained to Gisela, "do not see eye to eye, and never have, and it was always my intention to be free. So now I am my own master, and with your grandfather's encouragement I have decided to leave provincial Hamburg and establish myself in Berlin. You must meet my lovely Eliane."

Lovely Eliane had red hair. She came from the city of Strasbourg, and was known by *Tante* Susanna to be a dangerous

woman, one whose morals were so loose it was impossible to
call them morals, or to judge her by the standards of behavior
to which proper people subscribe. No doubt she had been paid
for her performance in the Hotel Atlantic; no doubt she used
her skill in fainting and the notoriety of photographs made *in
flagrante delicto* to good advantage in her career on the stage.
And it was of course the case that she and Doctor Lefchinsky
soon parted company, or came together only sometimes, when
she had medical troubles or he had bodily needs. Soon enough
she died in Paris, after a performance of *La Dame aux Camélias*,
and the ingestion of pernod and laudanum taken in too great a
quantity together. When the news arrived of the actress's death
there was no rejoicing in Hamburg, but only a sense of the
wheel come full circle and of just desserts.

Still, Miriam nursed hopes. The divorce was never her idea,
nor her expressed desire; she pined for her ex-husband Simon
and hoped he might return. Although she had consented to
the separation and had had, in truth, no say in it, the image
of the handsome boy from Lübeck continued to compel her.
She did not destroy the wedding photos in their ornate silver
frames, but turned them instead to the wall. For minutes on
end she examined her face in the mirror, making eyes at herself
and practicing expressions—little movements of the mouth and
cheeks—she hoped might render her attractive. They did not.
Her hair went gray; her chin found its own double at the neck.

Little Gisela would be a beauty—that much was clear already; she had inherited her father's good looks. Thomas and
Henry were gone. Her aunt Susanna, in the first of their family's great misfortunes, died of influenza in faraway Alsace-Lor-
raine. Susanna's daughter too—Gisela's cousin Gertrude—was
by that all-leveling pandemic killed. For years the two surviving
women lived together, the daughter growing tall and slender,
the mother short and plump. At night, in the family house on
Blumenstrasse to which they had returned, staring at the river
Alster from her bedroom window (with a few oil paintings and
the wedding silver, but nothing of the furniture or drapes and
certainly not the wedding bed from the house she had shared

with the doctor), Miriam would tell Gisela that perhaps the story was not over and the page would turn. "Such is life," she said. By this she meant—and used the phrase often—that the unexpected is to be expected and you never know until it is ended how a tale will end.

This proved to be the case. At a certain moment, when Gisela was still at home—ten years old, and living in the family mansion with her spinster-mother—the two of them were summoned to Berlin. Herr Doktor Lefchinsky had had an accident, a result of high blood pressure and overwork and a fall down the stairs (though there were rumors that he had in fact been thrown downstairs in his boarding house by men an irate husband hired to disfigure him). An arm and leg were broken, and his skull badly concussed. The nose of which he was so proud had been badly broken as well. It was not clear, the authorities informed the Bings, that the patient would recover, but they promised to keep Herr Doktor Lefchinsky's ex-wife and daughter up to date as to the patient's progress. "Such is life," said Miriam, and wept.

Over time, however, the injuries did heal, and in the third month of his convalescence it grew clear there was no lasting insult to the nose or brain. On August 27, 1919—Gisela has kept the letter, so she knows the date precisely—the doctor wrote his relatives and in excellent handwriting and dark blue ink on unlined stationery with the address of his lodgings suggested they share his apartment because he needed company in his weakened condition and what else is family for?

There were many tearful interviews with the Bing relatives—Miriam's brothers and her father and mother—who counseled against such a step. But Miriam herself proved adamant, reminding her parents of the Christian virtues of forgiveness, even if they were not Christian, and reminding them as well that the divorce had not, had never been her own hoped-for solution to her husband's infidelity. Now at last, as a result of his own suffering, perhaps he understood the error of his ways. Little Gizi *should* have a father, she said, and though she would not share a room and certainly not share a bed or live together as husband and wife it was her, Miriam's, duty to succor the man who had given her children and be of what service she could. Over the objections of her parents, and without any further financial support, she left the large family establishment on the *Ausser Alster* (where there were canoes at the base of the garden, by the summerhouse) and moved in with her ex-husband in Berlin.

Then began a chapter of unequaled strangeness in the story of their lives. At this time, in general, the German people, having suffered through the war and with the imposition of the stringent terms of peace, were impoverished. Food was difficult to come by; coal was scarce in winter, and payment uncertain for services rendered, if there were payment at all. The doctor himself had certainly not prospered, and his flat was small. It needed airing, badly; it smelled of chicken fat and too-sweet tea and fish. Gisela and her mother slept together in the living room, on the daybed by the window, and Lefchinsky—who would not relinquish his old expensive habits, his taste for wine and good cigars—slept by himself in the bedroom while his health improved.

Miriam had not, of course, had any training as a nurse, but her ex-husband could and did instruct her in the skills of bandage wrapping and which ointments to apply to him where. Gisela too grew expert in the niceties of how to change bed linen and, when her father felt too weak to walk, emptied the bedpan of slops. From time to time he helped her with her schoolwork, correcting her Latin and sums. Once, as in the old days, from the pocket of his dressing gown he produced wrapped marzipan.

Doctor Lefchinsky had no interest, seemingly, in the sons who had repudiated him when the article about the actress in the Hotel Atlantic appeared. Her brothers had their own careers; they would not countenance association with a publicly shamed scoundrel. And the elder Bings in Hamburg—though they made it clear she and her mother could always return to the family fold—made it equally clear that, while away, there must be no contact nor any expectation of assistance. For months and then for years the three of them inhabited the cold small rooms, the man and the woman not speaking to each other unless absolutely necessary, and Gisela therefore the one who talked to both.

"Good morning, Gizi."

"Good morning, papa."

"Good morning, my darling."

"Good morning, mama."

"*Hast gut geschlafen*? Did you sleep well?"

"Yes, thank you."

"Good. Breakfast is ready."

"I'm hungry."

"Tell your father he may sit."

"Breakfast is ready, papa."

"And about time, too. I am busy this morning."

"Might I inquire," Miriam asked, "with what your father is busy?"

"When is your first appointment, papa?"

"Soon enough," he said. "I'm hungry."

"Tell your father to sit down."

"Tell your mother I am ready to be served."

This became their habitual procedure. It was an arrangement, no matter how strange, that suited the ex-wife and husband, because her pride would not permit her without an apology to forgive the man who had disgraced her, and his pride would not permit him to apologize. The adults managed to accommodate each other—the one with no love lost, the other with love overflowing, the one dry-eyed, the other in tears—while the child moved back and forth between them like a shuttlecock in badminton or ball batted over the tennis court net.

For Gisela the situation was torture; in pleasing her mother she displeased her father, in obeying her father insulted her mother. And always she felt insufficient, as though the fault were hers and the difficulty of the marriage was of her own making. The doctor somehow made her feel—this was the case throughout her life—as if his troubles could be solved if only she were less a disappointment. When he turned to look at her, it was always, she thought, in reproof. Her mother made no such accusation, but the very fact of their confinement in the small reeking apartment (which did not lose the smell of fish, no matter how she aired and scrubbed it) loomed as a reproach.

Miriam gave piano lessons to the children of the bourgeoisie, and also sold some needlepoint. This small income supplemented that of Simon Lefchinsky, who still kept a very few patients. Together they scraped by. After four years had passed in this manner, on her fourteenth birthday, when Gisela herself had set the table with their most festive linen—old and soiled and torn as it was—and helped bake the Sachertorte and lit the candles and then blew them out; at the end of the meal, just as she stood to clear the plates and stack them for washing at the sink, her father turned to her:

"Would you ask your mother a question, please?"

"Of course," said Gisela.

"It's an important question, and I want her to consider— very carefully—the answer."

"Ask it, *noch*," said Miriam.

"Carefully, carefully, yes?"

"Yes."

"Would she consent to marry me?"

"Excuse me, papa, can you repeat yourself?"

"Gizi, you heard me."

"Except I am not certain what I heard."

"*Dummkopf*," she heard him mutter under his breath. "Imbecile. All right, I will repeat it."

"Thank you."

"Will your mother marry me?"

"Again? A second time?"

"Enough! Will she marry me now?"

Miriam had been, as usual, at her end of the table throughout this conversation. She was listening. Her eyes glistened. "Tell your father, yes."

"Her answer is 'Yes.'"

"It would be my honor," he said.

"And mine as well."

"She accepts you," said Gisela.

"Good. And now perhaps you will leave us alone together?"

"*Ganz gern*," said Miriam. "Gladly."

"You may go," the doctor said.

In this fashion the marriage resumed.

The family in Hamburg had an interest in art. Gisela's grandmother patronized artists, sometimes going so far as to invite them to her famous Sunday breakfast—Karl Schmidt-Rottluff and Ernst Haeckel and Ludwig Kirchner and peculiar Emil Nolde—and hung their bright oil paintings on the living room and library walls. She liked the work also of Paula Modersohn-Becker and Käthe Kollwitz, though of the latter she liked only the black-and-white graphics, so when finally Gisela was of an age to go to university, and Miriam and Simon Lefchinsky were no longer forbidden, *strengst verboten*, to cross the threshold of the house on Blumenstrasse, it was natural enough that she attend a lecture course on the History of Art. The promise of her beauty was now a promise delivered, and she grew accustomed to, if never wholly at ease with, the attentions of men. Although she played the piano she did not know much about music, and had no talent for it, but one afternoon in Berlin, where she was a student, she was invited to a concert in the Hochmann house. A string quartet in the garden was performing chamber music of Franz Schubert. "Can you believe," a young man standing at her side exclaimed, "that Schubert died at thirty-one? Can you imagine what else he would do? Have done, I mean, if given the chance . . ."

"He would have kept on working."

"Yes. *Mein Name ist Hochmann*," the young man introduced himself. "We have not properly met."

He was the son of the house. Of medium height, and with light brown hair, he was graceful in his movements; when he pulled out a chair for her and invited her to sit, it was as though the invitation meant more than "Please sit down." His hands were shapely, his eyes brown. There was, for Gisela, an immediate attraction, and later Johann said the same, which is why he had approached her and made the remark about Schubert. They discussed the composer's unhappy fate and, of course, the fate of Wolfgang Amadeus Mozart, and perhaps most of all the death of Felix Mendelssohn, great artists expiring young. At a certain point she told him her father was a doctor and he need not be embarrassed to mention the word syphilis, because it was an affliction that laid Schubert low and with which she was familiar. "Not"—Gisela colored—"familiar in personal terms, but it is a word I've often heard and one you need not avoid."

Later Johann told her that her willingness to entertain such a discussion, her readiness to walk with him after the concert without a chaperone in the park adjoining his family's house, signaled to him that she was no ordinary creature but a girl who would take risks. "You have no idea," she did not tell him, "how safe this seems to me, how ordinary such a conversation feels." By comparison with what she had endured in childhood, a walk without a chaperone or the use of the word "syphilis" was hardly shocking behavior, and she felt, with Johann, free. The two of them continued talking, for the subject was of interest: why some artists persist in their labor, others die young, and why those who die in the fullness of age—consider, for example, the example of great Goethe!—know some things it is impossible for youthful composers and painters and poets to know.

Soon enough it developed that the families Hochmann and Bing were acquainted and had a collateral cousin in Vienna, and even once went walking on the same trails in the Tyrol. There were many similarities of substance and style, and the families could understand each other in a way they had not understood the dreams of a young man from Lübeck who was born with not a silver but a tin spoon in his mouth. In the house of Benno and Ilse Hochmann, Gisela felt at home. So it was only natural to put her past behind her and share a present and a future with this young man she met at a concert. She did not continue her studies but accepted his hand gladly, and in short order they were married by the Rabbi in her grandparents' garden, which had been newly designed and planted, underneath a *chuppah* on a fine morning in May.

The wedding was a small one but managed in high style. Her parents were on good behavior; her brothers came with their children, the Hochmanns from Berlin all arrived with lavish gifts arrayed on the hall table and in the music room. It was a splendid affair. But already there were limits to the kind of display a Jew should make, and therefore the splendor was hidden and the celebration quiet. She remembered, clearly, the feel of Johann's hand when he placed the ring on her finger, then the sound of the glass breaking when he stepped on the wrapped glass. She remembered the guests' laughter and a bird above them in the trees and the way her new mother-in-law blessed the union and her grandfather Bing, in praising the bride's beauty, made her blush. She, Gisela *née* Lefchinsky, was now Gisela Hochmann and could leave the past behind.

Johann's father Benno in particular was kind to her, neither severe nor judgmental; he did not turn paternal eyes upon her as if always dissatisfied, but approved of what he saw. By comparison she came to think of her own father's few proffered pieces of wrapped marzipan as not so much a signal of affection as a bribe. She and Benno would take walks together, admiring the swans or sailboats, and at a certain point he broached the matter of her mother and Doctor Lefchinsky, saying that he hoped and trusted they were reconciled.

"You know about their difficulties?" Gisela dared to ask this kindly man, her new father-in-law.

"Certainly. *Gewiss.* All Hamburg knows, and many of us in Berlin. In any case I made some inquiries."

"They are happy, yes," she dared to say, and wondered, was this true?

"Your grandfather Bing and I have been discussing the matter."

"Yes?"

"And your father wishes—so he has informed us—to travel

to America and start a practice there."

"With my mother?"

"Yes." Benno was watching her closely. "*Liebchen*, would that bother you?"

It was now the winter of 1933. She wanted, she told her father-in-law, nothing so much as to put all this behind her and to start a life with Johann other than the one she'd lived, and if he could arrange to send the Lefchinskys to America she would be grateful, truly. She smiled up at her protector. She would of course miss her parents, her mother in particular, but what she wanted most of all was to begin again alone—or not so much alone as with her bridegroom Johann in this new life they shared. Johann's father said he understood, and, returning from the park by the river, pointed to a pair of nesting swans.

The Bing and Hochmann families were therefore in agreement, and between them arrangements were made. In 1933 it was still a relatively simple thing to leave the country, if there were sufficient funds, and Simon and Miriam welcomed assistance; they too wished to start anew. "Out of sight," her father said, "is out of mind."

Gisela saw her parents off at the dock in Bremen, where already Herr Doktor Lefchinsky was in close conversation with a woman not her mother, offering his elbow on the gangplank and smiling graciously at all the world except his wife. When her parents landed in New York, and telegrammed that they were safe and later wrote to say the New World was a pleasant one, she felt both relieved and reprieved. Her servitude was over, she told herself, the duty of a go-between was no longer one she would have to perform, and Gisela relinquished the role of daughter and became a wife and mother with what later on she would remember as untrammeled joy.

But no joy is untrammeled and no carefree time can last. Miriam had caught a cold on the transatlantic crossing, and her doctor-husband was too busy attending to the desires of others to attend to the needs of his wife. This, at least, was what their child believed when she learned of her mother's pneumonia and the damage it did to her lungs. The woman did not die immediately, but her health was compromised, and in Forest Hills in New York City where the couple settled she became an invalid. Turn by turnabout is fair play, and Simon did take care of her, but he was often at the office after dark or during the lunch hour, with the doors locked to prevent interruption. In America his clientele continued to be women whose problems were located in the chest and lower back and pelvis, and Simon focused his attentions on those regions in his work. He remained a handsome man, and courtly with the ladies. His income, however, was meager—sufficient for good suits and wine and soon enough a Packard convertible, but not for an apartment where his wife might take her ease. Always, in the Lefchinsky household, it was the husband who gratified appetites first.

In the last two years of life, therefore, Miriam was once again consigned to solitude, living in a single room and staring at the walls. She wrote long letters to her children, and in those to her daughter remembered fondly the days in Berlin when the three of them would share a table and Gisela would act as go-between. Gisela did not share those memories as happy ones, but she wrote her mother long letters as well, describing the birth of young Peter, the apartment she and Johann furnished, the growing difficulties at home, the men in the streets in brown shirts. When it was clear Benno intended to take the family away from the Third Reich, and planned to settle in America, his daughter-in-law had the hope and expectation of seeing her mother again. But on October 27, 1935, Miriam *née* Bing Lefchinsky passed away.

Gisela was informed of this by letter from her father. His handwriting had coarsened, and it wavered on the page, but the message was the same as the one she had received on August 27, 1919: he required company, and what else is family for? He seemed to have no notion that her world had changed, her life had changed; he was, as always, thinking only of himself and those who would see to his comfort.

So it was almost a relief to her when Benno booked passage to Cuba instead of the United States, and she did not have to deal with her widowed father. The years in Havana were happy ones for Gisela, with her family now safe and Peter on her knee. Often, however, she thought of her mother, lying and dying alone. This image of Miriam haunted her: a woman breathing heavily yet faintly, wearing black and with no relatives except a faithless husband to attend to her, far from the place where she was born and waiting to be buried in a grave in Forest Hills. "Such is life," she told herself, repeating her mother's old saying. "Such is life."

Therefore, in 1939, when the family did travel north and settle in America, it took her several weeks to visit with Simon Lefchinsky. She was glad to be an ocean away from der Führer's monstrous reach and grateful to the country whose sea walls were a fortress. Having arrived in New Rochelle, she was so busy settling in and settling down that she put aside the question of her father and focused instead on her husband and their child. Further, she was pregnant, and the pregnancy was hard. When finally she asked Johann one Saturday if he would mind driving her to Forest Hills and the address she had for *der Herr Doktor* Lefchinsky, he—with his usual grave sweetness—complied. He would not let her make the journey by herself, and for an hour they were lost together in the crisscrossing streets and avenues of the endless city. At long last they did find the building, and Johann—with his usual tact—said he would remain downstairs while she went up to visit with her father. There was, he said, and pointed to, an open coffee shop across the street where he would read his newspaper and wait.

Gisela climbed the stairs. She felt herself a child again, although she reassured herself, by catching her big-bellied reflection in a stairwell window, that she was a grown woman now and no longer her mother's go-between or her father's maid. She had written Simon, who had no telephone, and told him when to expect her. The stairs were steep.

On the second landing a child's bicycle lay, wheels in the air, and from the third-floor landing came a smell of frying food.

At the top of the house was a door painted blue and a tarnished mezuzah at the entrance to the furnished room where her mother lived and died.

She knocked.

There was silence.

She knocked again, uncertain the doctor had heard her. "It's Gizi, papa."

"*Come!*" he called. "It's open."

She tried the door. Creakingly, the door did open, and past a pile of newspapers and empty seltzer bottles she saw her father sitting by an open window, in an upholstered chair. The shock of it was immediate, although she had prepared herself; the man in the chair was indeed her father but also a near-total stranger. He tried to rise, then subsided; she stepped into the room.

"Come here and kiss me, child."

Obedient, she did. "Hello, papa."

"It's about time. I've been waiting."

"Yes."

"How do I look?" he asked.

This was such an habitual question with him that Gisela smiled. Always, in the old days, in Germany, he had asked it as he strode towards the door, straightening his shirt cuffs or tilting the brim of his hat. Always, regarding himself in the mirror, he had solicited praise.

"Tip-top," she said. "Not a day older."

Gratified, he smiled. She smiled down at him also, for neither of her compliments was true. His suit was still the old elegant suit, but threadbare now, and with missing buttons, and his shirt collar had stains. The hair in his ears needed trimming, the hair on his head had grown thin. There was water at the edges of his red-rimmed eyes. Simon began to speak—not asking her a single thing about her husband and their child, her pregnancy, the house in New Rochelle or how they had liked Cuba—about his own condition, speaking with a medical man's detailed knowledge and detachment, listing the symptoms that were not in his case serious and the ones that were. For five minutes and more Doctor Lefchinsky discoursed on blood pressure and oxygen levels, the piles and gout he suffered from, the ache in his left side that was, he was certain, rheumatic, the trouble with his spleen.

It was, she thought, astonishing: this old man in the chair and the young gallant from Lübeck who stole her mother's heart away could not be the same person but were nonetheless the same. He had altered but not changed. At seventy-five the man remained that monster of proud self-regard who hired a photographer to capture him *in flagrante delicto* with an actress from Strasbourg in his suite in the Hotel Atlantic. He told her to make tea. He said he detested his neighbors, whose music was too loud. He inquired if she had brought him something, anything of interest to eat. By the time the interview was over, and submitting to his will as usual, Gisela invited her father to move to New Rochelle.

And so began the final chapter in the sad tale of her childhood, because although an adult she became his child once more. Johann's parents lived together in the Stonecrest Apartments in Larchmont, and *der Herr Doktor* Simon Lefchinsky took an apartment nearby. He did not need as large a space, and in any case could not afford it; she and Johann paid for his accommodation in the Hillview Cottages where he lived, this time with an elevator, again on the fourth floor. When her husband had suggested—not meaning it, of course, but because of his sweet decency compelled to make the offer—that her father move into their home with their two sons, Gisela refused. "There must be a limit," she said.

"To what?"

"To what I ask of you."

"We can manage, dearest, if you wish . . ."

"If it had been my mother . . ."

She left the rest unsaid. Had Miriam been a widow, not Simon a widower, she would have welcomed her remaining parent and made space in the house. But her father was not and would not for the next decade be someone to accommodate, because—in an expression she learned—if you gave Simon Lefchinsky an inch he would take a mile.

Gisela's English was poor. She had spoken French, of course, and Italian when she lived in Germany, and had acquired Spanish in the years in Cuba. Now English would be necessary in New York, so she enlarged her schoolgirl knowledge and became, if never fluent, rapid in her speech. After some years she lost her accent, although native speakers of English knew at once she was not native to the tongue. This all took time, *natürlich*, and once she had a second child there was little time to spare; to begin with, Frederick was sickly, and required close attention, but by his second birthday was a healthy and a happy child.

For their first years in New Rochelle, her father came often for dinner. He could not afford an automobile, and no longer had a driver's license, so she or Johann fetched him from the Hillview Cottages to share their evening meal. Nonetheless, while Gisela was driving, he told her to drive faster or for heavens' sake slow down; he told her when to stop at a stop sign and, although he did not know the neighborhood, where to make a turn. She chauffeured him to Gristedes so that he could buy his groceries, and then she carried in the paper bags to his apartment kitchen and distributed the food. On Thursday mornings, as a treat, when Johann was at work and the children at school she invited him to Brodersen's Delicatessen in Larchmont and helped him choose the delicacies that reminded him of home.

He very much liked a sausage that would remind him not of Berlin or Hamburg but his native Lübeck, where he said this particular variety of sausage and roast potatoes with mustard made a Sunday feast. She drove him to the dentist and optometrist and barber and, when he needed them, doctors. Emerging from each medical appointment Simon told her, always, the new doctor was a fool.

And, strange to say, near the end of his life, her father returned not to his own childhood but hers. He began to speak to her as though she were, again, a ten-year-old translating for her mother; it was as if there were, again, a third person in the room.

"How did you sleep?"

"Quite well, papa. And you?"

"I had my dream."

"Your dream?"

"*Doch*. We were riding through the Schwarzwald. We were planning a picnic—potato salad, pumpernickel, cheese, and the wild strawberries you were fond of."

She never had liked strawberries. It was her mother who was fond of *fraises des bois*, not Gisela, and she could not remember having driven through the Schwarzwald.

"At a certain point you said—remember?—'Here let us have our picnic. It is better not to let *Kartoffelsalat* get warm.'"

"Did I say that? *Would* I say that?"

"*Doch, doch.*"

"Do you want breakfast, papa?"

"Yes. And then I have an appointment."

"Do you want sausage with your eggs?"

"With salt, of course. *Dummkopf*," he growled.

She never knew what he was seeing when he with an unblinking stare examined himself in the mirror. She rarely knew what he was saying, although he spoke with urgency to someone on the ceiling or the floor. Over time she came to understand he was addressing her mother, for Miriam lived on in Simon's memory as he had done in hers. She spent long hours hearing her father complain about the library in Lübeck and how it was inadequate if someone needed to study, how anybody not a fool would understand the need for privacy, which is why he kept his office locked, and would not be interrupted, and if you don't believe me, *Liebchen*, it simply can't be helped. I have nothing to hide or disclose. You may listen at the keyhole, if you wish.

Das Ewig-Weibliche Zieht uns hinan, was something he said often. The last line of Goethe's *Faust*—when, Gisela wondered, had her father made time to read Goethe's *Faust*?—praises "eternal womanhood," and says "we will be led" by it. "Raised" by it, rather, she found herself vulgarly thinking, *drawn on, pulled up, aroused.* The old poet too had been a skirt-chaser, and "eternal womanhood" for Goethe meant a line of chambermaids. In his dotage, what the poet doted on were pretty maidens, just as did the doctor, and they led him on. *"Mehr Licht,"* were Goethe's final words, and though her teachers had insisted Goethe's phrase was praise for the Enlightenment, a restless intelligence stating its claim, she herself believed the dying man was shouting at the chambermaid to bring another light . . .

In the end there had been nearly nothing left. Simon Lefchinsky coughed and coughed up nothing; he drank only a few sips of water, though his tongue was always moistening his lips. Neither Thomas nor Henry, her brothers, lived through the Second World War, and their children too were dead. Because of Benno Hochmann's foresight, Gisela alone of all her family survived the Holocaust that claimed the Lefchinskys and Bings. Alone, she watched her father breathe—his sunken chest, his fingers on the blanket-rim, his bright blue eyes now pale and gray—trying to forgive him and finally succeeding, and thinking back to what it must have felt like for her mother Miriam, when she received the first bouquet of roses and was asked to share a first glass of champagne. "Such is life," she told her sons, the day her father died.

Family
1954

THE HOCHMANN FAMILY, by general agreement, prefers their house in Larchmont to the one in New Rochelle. The street has fewer houses, and the plantings are mature. The lawn is wider, better kempt, and not pitched down a slope. Their new home boasts a library called by the real estate agent a den, and a two-car garage. Most importantly, perhaps, the boys have separate bedrooms, and—given the age differential between them—this has been long overdue. In truth, it does not matter much, since Peter now has left the house, and Frederick could well have claimed sole ownership of what was their shared bedroom. On the ladder of advancement, this is only a small step. Yet the move six miles away brings a feeling of expansiveness that pleases Gisela, a sense of space evoking the grand homes their families left. The Hochmanns in Berlin and Bings in Hamburg lived on a scale much larger than that of their descendants, but Johann is a good provider, and they are free from want. Free also from a sense of danger in this village and state and country where Jews are protected by law.

For much of her childhood, indeed, Gisela knew something like privation, living in a one-room flat with silent warring parents and the odor of stale fish. Her mother has been dead for nineteen years, her father five, but their life-long wrangle still can make her grieve. In America, however—with an elder son now twenty and a younger one just turned fifteen—she feels safe. "Our life here is not nothing," Johann says, and reaches for her hand.

There is of course Joseph McCarthy. For the last years, increasingly, the junior Senator from Wisconsin has captured the nation's attention and dominated the news. His hunt for Communists is unrelenting; his chairmanship of the Senate Permanent Subcommittee on Investigations into what he calls "un-American activities," his accusations and waved lists of spies in the government and Hollywood, have made him greatly feared. His thinning hair and stubbled cheeks are studied by Gisela daily on the television screen; his voice is more familiar than the President's own voice. Benno Hochmann used to call "D-Day" "Dwight David-day" in honor of Eisenhower's military leadership, which he much admires. But the aging President now seems withdrawn and passive, not speaking out against the Senator but playing rounds of golf. McCarthy and his henchmen, Roy Cohn and David Schine—two Jews who ought to know better, says Benno—are busy all day long. According to their statements they are ferreting out treachery, disloyalty, and plots against America. According to her father-in-law, however, they are telling lies.

The family owns a Philco television set, nineteen inches on the diagonal, and they discuss the purchase of a larger model so as to see things more clearly. Every night they watch the evening news and, each day when they are televised, the Army–McCarthy hearings. In spring, when the hearings air and Frederick comes home from school, he likes to watch ABC also, joining his mother in the den and doing his homework beside her. Joseph McCarthy and Roy Cohn take turns accusing witnesses and asking them to name the names of others in "the Party." It is not a party in the sense of "enjoyable gathering." It is, according to the Senator, a widespread conspiracy to overthrow the government of the United States. His high-pitched voice, the way he gestures with his glasses, the reptilian stare of his henchman, Cohn—all these make the Hochmann family uneasy and, more than uneasy, afraid.

Throughout the week the television flickers in the background of Gisela's vision; all afternoon long, from April to June, in the course of household duties—cooking and cleaning and ironing shirts—she watches the proceedings on the screen. The committee chairman, Senator Karl Mundt from South Dakota, and other Senators like John L. McClellan and handsome Stuart Symington are men she comes to recognize and feel she can predict. The Senator from Georgia, Sam Ervin, whom at first she could not understand—his Southern accent was so thick—is someone she has learned to like, and the lawyer for the Army, Joseph Welch, reminds her of her grandfather, dead white-haired Morris Bing.

There are men and women from the entertainment industry and Department of Defense; there are educators who, McCarthy claims, are brainwashing the young. They have lawyers at their sides, and when they confer with their lawyers they do so, it seems, out of fear. Many in the witness stand take the Fifth Amendment, refusing to "incriminate myself." The phrase perplexes Gisela, since Joseph McCarthy suggests—by his disgusted expression, always—that the taking of the Fifth Amendment is itself an admission of guilt. And those who sit in front of him, sweating in the camera's glare, somehow do seem guilty: their lives at risk, and if not their lives their livelihoods. Often, they drink water from a pitcher on the table by the microphone, and when they pour the water their hands shake.

She and Johann discuss this at night, in bed. "Point of order, Mr. Chairman," is another phrase that puzzles her, since it seems a disruption of order, a way to interrupt. She believes that what is happening has happened to them elsewhere, and he says No, McCarthy is not hunting Jews in particular, and Cohn and Schine are after all both Jews. It is perhaps about homosexuals, but there are rumors that Roy Cohn himself is homosexual, and David Schine possibly also, and if that is the case he cannot understand why homosexuals or "fairies" would be singled out. Gisela reminds her husband this is how the terror started twenty years ago, with laws and legal maneuvers, and men insisting other men were enemies of the Third Reich and putting them in jail.

"You exaggerate," says Benno Hochmann, when he comes

to dinner.

"How, papa?"

"This is," he says, "America. There are decent people here."

Gisela trusts her father-in-law. Even in his eighties he retains his lifelong clarity of perception, and an awareness of danger, and she hopes he is correct. He understood when it was time to take the family from Germany, and she would like to think his present calm is therefore justified. Benno points to the lawyer, Joseph Welch; he says "This man is a good man and will not let bad things happen."

"*Hoffentlich!*" says Johann. "Let us devoutly hope."

"Agreed," says Gisela. Her in-laws come to Sunday dinner always, and she has made a *coq au vin*, which pleases the old couple. Throughout this conversation, Ilse has been silent, but—as is no longer the usual case—finished her full portion. Now her eyelids droop.

"I am not saying," Benno says, "there is nothing to fear from McCarthy. Only that he's Irish and, so it seems, a drunk. In the end he will undo himself."

"You think so?" says Johann.

"I think so, yes," says the old man. "I cannot imagine the *Kerl* will succeed."

"*Vati*, how is he different from Hitler?"

Benno pats Gisela's hand. "The mustache is different, of course. He hasn't yet grown a mustache."

Pleased with himself, Benno laughs. His wife, however, does not smile; no doubt she has heard this before. Lately Ilse has grown distant, inattentive; she will die of congestive heart failure on December 31. Frederick helps clear the dinner plates, and Gisela brings out—she has prepared it in honor of the family's sojourn in Cuba—a dish of banana flambé. She lights the long wooden match for her husband and hands it to him where he sits. Johann ignites the pool of brandy, and everyone at table watches the blue flame flare up and consume itself, subsiding.

"He *would* be Hitler if he could," says Benno, still thinking of Joseph McCarthy, "but he plans to run for President and does not dare a *Putsch*."

Gisela wants to believe him. She hopes what keeps the old man calm is not a form of denial or his unwillingness to pack and move again. She hopes that what transpires daily on the television screen is proof sufficient of their freedom in this country, since it goes on in front of the ABC camera and not behind locked doors. Still, "contempt of Congress" is a phrase that worries her, and sometimes at night she imagines herself being asked by Cohn or McCarthy or Schine if she knows anyone who is a Communist or a fellow-traveler, and although the answer is *No, no, no*, she fears she would get it wrong and have to take the Fifth Amendment or be thrown in jail.

The family admires Arthur Miller. They have seen *Death of a Salesman*, and they know he is an honorable person who refuses to incriminate his friends. There are others who name names. Gisela hopes she would be brave enough to refuse all such temptation and to hold her tongue. On bright crisp May mornings, when Frederick is off at school and Johann has taken the train to New York, she practices taking the Fifth Amendment and saying, in front of the mirror, "On the advice of counsel, I must respectfully decline . . ." The look on her face as she looks in the mirror is one of cold determination: a martyr's look. She is being disobedient, she tells her enemy the Senator, because she knows of higher standards of behavior to obey.

Frederick attends the Fieldston School. The local grade schools and the high school in Mamaroneck are first-rate, but when the time arrives for Peter and then Frederick to go to junior high school their parents enroll them in Fieldston instead. Gisela's faith in the value of good education remains unshakeable. "It is," she says, "the one thing they can't take from you when they take away your paintings and your house." Johann says let's not exaggerate, they have lost the paintings already and won't now lose their home; the mortgage is secure. But Gisela is adamant about the importance of schooling; she insists that she would rather have a boy who studies Latin than a new car or fur coat.

Frederick, this year, is taking a third year of Latin; Peter too studied the language, but dropped it as soon as he could. "*Amo, amas, amat*," he said, before he left for college, when the family was sitting at their last shared breakfast. "It's all I need to know."

"*Veni, vidi, vici*," said his father, who is rarely jocular. "That too is useful in the courts of love . . ."

"I know what *that* means," Peter said. "'I came, I saw, I conquered.'"

"Yes. Render unto Caesar what is Caesar's," said Johann.

"'*Alea iacta est*,'" pronounced Frederick. "That's something else Caesar declared. When he crossed the Rubicon."

"And something about all of Gaul being divided into parts," said his elder brother, not to be outdone. "Three parts. *Amo, amas, amat*."

Their mother said, "Finish your orange juice, please."

The Fieldston School is located in Riverdale, a twenty-minute drive away, but other students are enrolled from Westchester, and a driver's service is available for an additional fee. Two brothers run the business: Frank and Joe Fish. Because the Hochmann house in Larchmont is an early stop on the car-service route, Frederick must be collected a full hour before school. On winter mornings, if the snow is serious, they come even sooner, and the drive through Westchester and then on the Cross County Highway feels funereal; by the time they reach the dark stone buildings and the congested parking lot of Fieldston, Frederick is ready to go home.

Joe drives a Cadillac limousine and wears gray suits; Frank, the younger brother, drives a station wagon with wood trim and wears checked flannel shirts and a pilot's black leather jacket. He is a burly man who likes to laugh; by contrast Joe—the senior partner—is a chain-smoker, severe. Waiting for one of the cars to arrive—he never knows, beforehand, which of the brothers will come to collect him—Frederick sits in the kitchen, finishing his toast and orange juice and zipped into his coat already, watching the street. In the spring and early fall, he can wait outside.

Seven students fit inside the Cadillac, or in the Dodge station wagon. The students range in age from First to Sixth Form, hailing from Mamaroneck and Eastchester and Rye and Larchmont and New Rochelle. If someone calls in sick, or someone's parent is driving to Manhattan and taking along his own child, the passenger list varies, but most mornings Frederick gets to sit behind a girl called Nancy Castro, whose family makes sofas, and who—already in the Second Form—wears braces and a bra.

He and Tony Koch—the other Fourth-Form boy to be collected on the Fish brothers' route—are Yankee fans, and they discuss the pitching rotation and score of last night's game. Mickey Mantle in particular compels the pair's attention, and they memorize his daily batting average and the number of walks and strike-outs and "the Mick's" slugging percentage and, of course, home-runs. They know the name of the town where he was born in Oklahoma; they know the Latin name for what's wrong with his knees, *osteochondritis dissecans*. This, Frederick jokes, is the major value of Latin, and also the knowledge that *E pluribus unum* means "Out of many, one."

"It's what happens when you have a kid," says Tony Koch. "Two people get together and then a third one comes."

"You mean, after the first two have come?" says Frederick.

"Nine months after conjugation, yup."

The boys chortle noisily. Sitting in the trundle seat in front of them, Nancy Castro stares out the car's frosted window, and her ears turn red.

In Fourth Form—the equivalent of tenth grade in a public school—Frederick pursues his Latin and also studies French. He takes English and World History and Math and, once a week, a class in Ethics, since the Fieldston School was founded by members of The Ethical Culture Society. Every Thursday afternoon, before sports practice or chess club, questions of morality and justice are presented by the teachers and debated by the students. If someone drowns beside you on a beach, for example, are you more or less affected than if that person drowns ten thousand miles away? If ten thousand people drown ten thousand miles away, does "social distance" enter in, and if you could have saved your neighbor on the beach towel but instead were buying popsicles from the Good Humor Man, does that make you more or less affected by the death?

Peter, when a senior, said he'd figured out what sort of people are members of The Ethical Culture Society, and when his father asked him, said "They're Jews who don't believe in God."

"Don't be fresh," Gisela said.

She says this with some frequency to her elder son. He has had a streak of rebelliousness in him, or so it seems, from the start. And now that he is off in college in Ann Arbor, only rarely returning her phone calls or returning for vacation, his mother fears she has lost him. The younger boy at home is well behaved, and scrupulous with homework, but Peter is a restless spirit and she no longer has any notion of how he spends his days. Or nights—it is the nights that worry Gisela, the things he does or doesn't do when no longer under her roof. Johann tells her not to worry, that boys will be boys and men will be men and there are wild oats to sow. She says, "*You* didn't, did you?" and he smiles and spreads his hands.

Her fears are not misplaced. Peter is a junior at the University of Michigan, but his attendance at class is fitful and infrequent; he goes mainly to stare at the girls. The lectures bore him; the professors mumble and repeat themselves. He fails to complete his assignments on time or take scheduled tests. Those he takes he does not pass. He would rather read *Zorba the Greek* than what has been assigned for class, a study of democracy in Greece. *The War of the Worlds* by H. G. Wells, and then the movie made of it with Gene Barry and Ann Robinson, is something he reads and sees often. Pursuing his own course of study, he will not last the year.

Ann Arbor, however, is a town he prefers to the village of Larchmont, and he wants to stay. The "diag" on the campus where the students congregate, the River Huron where he walks, the movie theaters and the concert halls and a lecture series on the history of Labor Movements turn by turn compel him. He spends most of his time in a beer hall he likes, or wandering the streets, half drunk, and falling asleep in strange rooms. He likes to argue politics with men who hold up JESUS placards and women in post-office lines. What has gotten him excited is a theory about galaxies, how in another universe a shadow self enacts precisely the history that he, Peter Ernest Hochmann, enacts here and now, but in a parallel world. It is—he uses this word often—*asymptotic*, the lines are parallel but destined only at the outer edge of space to meet. There, if he could be bodily transported (though he does not delude himself, he knows it is not possible in this historical moment), he could embrace his own simulacrum as a being altogether other than the being he inhabits, because each of us is multiple and waiting to be made complete, inhabiting what Plato called "The Cave."

This doctrine he espouses to any and all who will listen, and there are those who do. There is "Catfish" down in Kerrytown, a black man with a ukulele, and a girl called Angelica who insists it is her actual name, though she is not, is anything but angelic, and she likes to steal. At night she shows him what she took or, as she likes to say, *borrowed* that day—a notebook, a pair of sunglasses with rhinestone frames, a hat on sale in the Nichols Arcade while she was passing through. In September of his sophomore year he heard Catfish singing "Old Black Joe" and doing a three-step shuffle on a fire escape at a party. He was wearing a hat and a zoot suit and high sneakers and called himself a troubadour, the right-thinking man's Arthur Godfrey; after a chorus of "My Old Kentucky Home," Catfish passed the hat. That night too, he met Angelica, and she said he could come home with her, and they argued over—she had been born in Grand Rapids, some two hours west—the definition of home.

Angelica is twenty-three, with brown hair falling thickly to her waist. She is tall—as tall as Peter—and bone-thin. She carries a white powder she calls "Angel's Dust," and when he sniffs or swallows it he knows his theory about parallax and asymptotes is deeply true. The value of a college town, he has come to understand, is how ideas are taken *seriously*; you can argue with a person about the nature of reality, the nature of subject and object, and the problem *counts*. In such discussions, always—as when he debated a graduate student on the matter of causality, the solar system, and the likelihood of cosmic clash—Peter takes delight. It is a pleasure to be proved correct, a pleasure to demolish your opponent with the rigor of your logic and to triumph in debate.

Angelica has introduced him also to the pleasure of sex standing up. It is her preferred position, and on the few occasions when she lets him fuck her—mostly she says he should leave her alone, she's not in the mood or is seeing someone else—she lifts her skirt and is not wearing panties and Peter holds her in his arms, thrusting and panting and after a few minutes sending gouts of sperm into the wet receptacle between her legs. She stands there, legs akimbo, silent, while the come runs down.

It is an education. Catfish and Angelica and the others of their circle—brother Andrew who smilingly proclaims himself a devotee of Satan, brother Tom who went to Law School but, in the third year, dropped out, sister Susan who talks constantly about her weight and how if she could lose ten pounds she'd be a happy person, happy *and* fulfilled because the body is the marker of the lightsome soul—live together in a brown dilapidated clapboard house on Ann Street near the old brick Armory. These five have established themselves as the core of a kind of collective, a not-so-much-commune as community of fellow travelers who travel, they insist, by standing still. Andrew has a trust fund and they do not go hungry; Susan likes to cook. Catfish and Angelica move in and out according to a rhythm Peter cannot follow; sometime she is absolutely *present*, lying on the couch or drawing her arcane designs on butcher paper and taping them to the windows or walls, engaged with local politics or the neighbor's cat. And sometimes she is absolutely *absent*, gone for days. She lines her stolen objects up on a bookcase in the living room, and declares she will return them by and by.

The shelf accumulates trophies. Returning from her forays, Angelica deposits a Motorola console, a pair of tortoiseshell hairbrushes, a copy of the *Kama Sutra*, and a scarf. Her draw-ings are of dogs and cats and what she tells Peter is a mandala, a Tibetan prayer wheel with men and women embracing and a monkey god called Hanuman and an elephant god, Ganesh. The Animal Kingdom compels him. When he goes to study in his third-floor dormitory room he feels he is a caterpillar in a silk cocoon; when he visits the house on Ann Street he feels himself a butterfly, aloft. The denizens of Plato's caves are each and every one of them a part of a collective whole, and incom-plete alone. Tall thin unwashed Angelica, Peter tells himself, has taught him more about the world than all his courses on the history of Europe, and when she beckons him and lifts her skirt he feels himself an adept in the ways of lust.

Johann Hochmann too is troubled by the demagogue's as-cendancy. He cannot quite accept that such a sweating bully's claims will be taken at face value. It seems unlikely, somehow, that his sweeping accusations can dominate the news. But there are many men with newspapers on the commuter train each morning who appear to share McCarthy's views, who talk about the Communist menace and agree that the man has a point. The trial of Julius and Ethel Rosenberg is one such case in point. When they were accused as spies and, on June 19, 1953, executed for espionage, Johann was certain of their in-nocence—and also that there had been anti-Semitism involved. Had the Rosenbergs been members of the English-speaking up-per crust—as, for example, Alger Hiss in 1950—they would not have lost their lives.

But he did not as a refugee dare to join the protests. He tells himself his absence from the picket lines is not a mark of cow-ardice but proof of the instinct for self-preservation. He signs no collective letters and attends no meetings and writes no per-sonal checks in support of the dead Rosenbergs or even Alger Hiss. What he wants is to be left alone; what he dreams of is privacy after this madness, this *Wahnsinn*, is done. In the American History course at Fieldston his son studies the Federalist papers, the faith that Alexander Hamilton and John Adams and John Hay expressed in the idea of democracy, together with the recognition that democracy requires educated people. Without an educated populace—so Thomas Jefferson argued, and therefore designed the University of Virginia—nothing is agreed on or agreed to that is for "the greater good."

"But Jefferson kept slaves," says Frederick.

"He was a man of his time."

"And do you still admire him?"

"I do."

The plot against America, of which Senator McCarthy speaks, is a plot of doctored photographs and false accusations and forged papers, and Johann believes the truth will out. Why he should feel this way about his new adopted country—when he felt otherwise about the country he was born in—puzzles him. If it happened once in Germany, says Gisela, it can happen here. Yet Johann carries with him everywhere the sense of great good fortune that his family escaped the Nazis, and has begun again. The Army–McCarthy hearings give him cause for hope, not fear; he would like to stay home from the office and watch and, like the members of the gallery when Joseph Welch departs the room, burst into applause.

In Grand Central Station, as he disembarks, or, later, when the day is over and he waits in the crowd of commuters for the return trip to Larchmont, Johann feels anonymous, part of a moving mass of travelers in overcoats, with briefcases, yet somehow singled out. The storm of accusation, he believes, will blow away, the insanity will dissipate and he can get on with his work. He loves his wife (her fine brown hair now just beginning to go gray, her sturdy legs, her breasts with their dark aureoles) and trusts her (her cleverness, her quicksilver reaction to his moods) but does not share Gisela's anxious foreboding; like his father he believes that sooner or later Joseph McCarthy will collapse like a punctured balloon. The day the lawyer Joseph Welch says, "Have you no sense of decency, sir? At long last, have you left no sense of decency?" he knows the time has come. The end is foreordained.

When Senator Ralph Flanders of Vermont introduces a resolution of censure against his colleague in the Senate, the Hochmann family elders—as they do only rarely—drink a bottle of champagne. Although Ilse now lies dying and at best half conscious, they gather by her bedside and raise their glasses to her and say—*Do you hear me, mama? Are you listening, Liebchen?*—she can be proud. And when, on December 2, 1954, the Senate votes 67 to 22 to censure Joseph McCarthy, although they do not expel him, the career of the demagogue is finished and the lawyer from Boston has won.

Gisela watches her boys growing up with a mixture of sorrow and pride. She worries about Peter, so rebellious and so far away, and keeps a wary eye on Frederick, her remaining home-bound child. Although she tries, of course, to be impartial, even-handed as a mother, she feels a special closeness to her second son—has felt that way from the time he was ill as an infant and she nursed him back to health. Every morning when he leaves for school she watches from the window while he opens the door of the Cadillac or station wagon at the curb. Each afternoon when he comes home she asks him how the day has gone and if she can help with his homework or prepare something to eat. He tells her "Fine," and "No," and "Yes"; he is polite to her, always, but he has nothing to say.

So more and more as time goes by, she finds herself alone in the house and wonders what would happen if she tried to make a change. The term for it is "empty nest," and she tells herself her sons are taking wing. It is something to be pleased with, to expect, but it is necessary also to find something more than motherhood with which to pass the time. She is not qualified, she knows, to join the American work-force or to pursue a career. For years she attempted to manage the garden, but she has always had a brown thumb with lilies and roses and lilacs; no sooner does she plant them than they die. Even the rhododendron bush—resplendent when they bought the place and flourishing, the real estate agent said, because it liked the acid soil behind the brick garage—has withered and turned brown.

There was the period of watercolor classes in the Larchmont Public Library. A dozen or so housewives gathered in the reading room and studied a live model or a vase of flowers, and she enjoyed the sessions and, little by little, improved. But she knows enough about excellent art—remembering her grandparents' collection of Kirchners and Noldes and Schmidt-Rottluffs—to know she has no gift for it, and to give it up. There was the afternoon ten years ago when she had been tempted to start an affair with Johann's friend Pink Pincussohn, but thought better of it when he picked his nose repeatedly—a habit she found disgusting—and then examined his finger. To tell the truth it had been easy not to compromise her husband's friendship with the lawyer, or her own with Felicia, Pink's wife. About Pink Pincussohn, who propositioned her almost as a courtesy, Gisela has no regrets.

This is less true of Henry Mayer, Johann's senior partner in the import-export firm. On meeting Henry Mayer, she was shocked by his resemblance to the photos of her father when he himself was young. Later, in his wedding photos and for the first years in Hamburg, her father faced the camera with just the same up-tilted chin and sharp patrician nose—with just the same conviction that the camera would be kind.

Henry Mayer also is, according to Johann, a man-about-town who squires glamorous women to dances and has a special table at the Stork Club. On the wall behind his office desk there is a photograph of the eligible bachelor in a tuxedo and the blond singer Peggy Lee standing next to each other near the stage of the Copacabana. These are establishments she would not dream of visiting, but, when Henry Mayer comes to dinner at the house in Larchmont, Gisela makes certain that he sits at her right side. When she serves him, at meal's end, with whipped cream and Sachertorte—her famous Sachertorte, as good as the original from Demil's, or so her guests declare—she offers him a second helping and he says he shouldn't, mustn't, but he will.

On his second visit, the two of them play chess. She is very good at it—far better than Johann and her two sons—because she played chess with her parents for much of her childhood, and has not lost her board-sense or ability to see three, four, and even five moves in advance. Her adversary too is an accomplished player and, saying "Please take this as a compliment," opens with a Queen's Gambit. She knows the opening by heart and, half an hour later, forces him to lose a rook with a discovered check. At the end of the game, when he gently knocks over his king as a gesture of surrender, she understands it is not mere politeness on Henry's part. He understands, he tells her, it will be forced mate in three. And when he flatters Gisela, saying she looks just like Rita Gam or Cyd Charisse or a dark-haired Ginger Rogers, she welcomes the attention. "I surrender," Henry says.

But—as had been the case with Pincussohn—the attention is not serious, a form of courtesy. A hostess is supposed to make her guest feel welcome; a guest is supposed to compliment his hostess, her figure and the dress she is wearing and the excellent taste of her food. It's what goes on between a man and woman who are almost strangers, and the name for it in good society is manners. Another name for manners is flirtation, and her husband's senior partner is practiced at flirtation. Her father, she knows to her sorrow, was skillful at it also, her mother not, but Gisela has had little practice and cannot decide if she wishes to learn.

She thinks of the repeated phrase at Passover, *Dayenu: It would have been enough*. It would have been enough for Henry Mayer to lose at chess and look at her admiringly. *Dayenu*. It would have been enough to brush against his body when handing him his overcoat and would have been enough for him to kiss her hand, departing, and say how much he has enjoyed the evening and hopes to see her soon again. *Dayenu*. It would have been enough to see him enter his sleek car, a gleaming black convertible he drives with the top down. It would have been enough to think of him at night while drawing down her stockings or to imagine him next morning in the bathroom standing next to her while she brushed her teeth. *Dayenu*. But when he calls her the next day and suggests that possibly they might have lunch, and how about next Thursday when he knows Johann is out of town, it is too much, too much.

She tells him, No, she is sorry, she has a hairdresser's appointment. Henry Mayer says, "Well, cancel it," and when she asks him why he says "You're beautiful without a hairdresser," and she says That's very kind of you, and he says "It isn't kind, it's accurate."

"You flatter me," says Gisela, and Henry tells her, "Nonsense, I'm telling the truth."

She has had no practice at this back-and-forth, this *badinage*, and Gisela is blushing even on the telephone as, seeing herself in the hall mirror, she hangs up. It was, she remembers, a forced mate in three when he acknowledged he was beaten and gently toppled his king . . .

In chess a practiced player will resign. If you see your position is hopeless and the game beyond retrieval, then you do not pursue it but congratulate your opponent and say "I resign." The inexperienced player, by contrast, will insist on playing out the game until its bitter end, when checkmate is declared. These are judgment calls. She is not inexperienced, she knows when she will win or lose, but that is true of chess not love and Gisela does not in this case trust her judgment; what should she do, she asks herself, when Henry Mayer calls again and says he meant nothing improper, only that she had beautiful hair and did not need a hairdresser but should come to lunch. She thanked him and hung up again and, seven years later, regrets the decision; her son Peter is in Michigan, her husband on the homebound train, her son Frederick is upstairs on the telephone talking endlessly with a girl called Penny Dean he hopes to be dating, and her life is dull, dull, dull.

The firm of Bing & Bleichroeder has offices in Chambers Street and a warehouse for its merchandise-in-transit on Duane Street near the fire station. The main office occupies the second floor, and there are cubicles on the third floor where clerks and secretaries store the files. With the closing of the China trade—now that America no longer permits commercial transactions with Mao Tse-Tung's mainland China, though there continue to be contacts via Taipei and Hong Kong—the bristle business has suffered. When Johann first entered the firm, there were crates of bristles everywhere—Kolinsky and Chunking 2 ¾—sent by suppliers in China; the warehouse had been full to overflowing with supplies for house-painter's brushes and hairbrushes and artist's paintbrushes and brooms. Sisal and jute are products for brooms, and there are tall bundles of piassava stacked against the walls.

Now, however, all orders of bristles from China must be re-routed through England, and the Manhattan branch of the import-export firm looks elsewhere for its profit. He has turned his attention to furs and, for the last year, wigs. Bing & Bleichroeder compete with Kazaranov & Sons, whose family is Russian, and who therefore have a competitive advantage with respect to furs. Walter Davis in the office down the hall from Johann's comes from missionary parents who spent decades in China, and his Mandarin and Cantonese are therefore fluent; this is an expertise, unfortunately, that no longer has much business value, and Walter—whose language skills are excellent—tries to acquire Russian.

Johann's secretary, Miss Upjohn, has a smattering of Russian, because she once was married to a trader from Moscow, or claims to have been married, though three years ago the man disappeared and she now claims to be divorced. Miss Upjohn has black hair and high pointed breasts, and the men in the office believe that she is sleeping with Executive Vice President Henry Mayer, which is why she remains in the firm. Her typing skills are minimal, her transcriptions from the Dictaphone are slow. She lives in Queens.

The other unmarried men in the office—the accountant, the business manager, the assistant business manager—all envy

Henry Mayer for his dalliance with Miss Upjohn. But they envy even more his photograph of Peggy Lee and his mention, once, in Walter Winchell's column as having been seen together with Rita Hayworth and Douglas Fairbanks Jr. at a table in Toots Shor's. The foreman of the warehouse, Richard Green, is short, black, and heavily muscled; he keeps a bottle of Four Roses in his locker, and after work each evening unscrews the bottle and pours himself a two-inch drink of whiskey and says, to the workers punching out at the time-clock by the top of the stair-well, "Bottoms up."

He has, he tells Johann, two families: one in Staten Island and one in the Bronx. Between his wives he has eight children, and he loves them all. It's why he works so hard, he says; ten mouths are a whole lot of trouble to feed, and the mouth on his first wife is—you should see it—*wide*; that woman never stops.

"Did you divorce her?"

"Yessir. No question of it. But you don't, you never get divorced from kids."

"Agreed," says Vice President Hochmann, and wonders, is that true?

"Far as I'm concerned," says Richard Green, "the woman could die on the street. And far as I'm concerned that'd be the end of it and there'd be no funeral. Nothing *I'd* pay for any-ways. But her and I got five kids together, and so she gets my paycheck just the same."

"Your present wife accepts this?"

Green sighs. Having put his glass away, he shrugs himself into his pea coat. "Yessir."

Johann likes his senior partners and the rhythm of the work-ing day, the telephone calls and the lunches and bills of lading from the docks with pink and yellow and white copies on a spindle on his desk. He likes visiting his clients or having clients visit, and he likes the convention of Bristle Merchants, which he must attend. Once he took Gisela along, and there were many compliments, and he believes it resulted in an increase in busi-ness from Hollander & Sons, because when Philip Hollander called to place an order on behalf of the brush-maker Windsor

& Newton the man made a point of inquiring after his children and his beautiful wife's health.

More often he travels alone. Last year, for example, at the Greenbriar Resort and Country Club, he found himself wishing he understood golf, because so many of his customers and business associates enjoyed the game and played it all day long. Henry Mayer is adept at golf, and has an eight-stroke handicap, which someone tells Johann is very good, respectable. On the final night of the convention, there's a banquet and a dance. He wishes Gisela were with him, so that he could dance with her as they had done at their wedding, the fox-trot and the waltz. Henry Mayer on the dance floor is squiring Philip Hollander's wife, and the two of them do the tango together with intricate steps and maneuvers, seeming to know in advance what the band will play and when to dip or twirl. When he comes back to the table at last, Mayer is perspiring, and he tells Johann, "It's exercise. The tango," he says, "can't be beat."

For consolation in his solitude, Benno Hochmann listens to music. He has a first-rate system by a man called Avery Fisher which is far more faithful to the sound of a performance—they call it high fidelity—than his old RCA. It can be a piano sonata, performed by Claudio Arrau or Artur Rubinstein or Vladimir Horowitz, and he can tell which one is which by the precision of the playing and the expressive intonation of a passage or even a phrase. So too, if he is listening to a violinist, he can tell if it is Joseph Szigeti or Mischa Elman or, the greatest of them all, Jascha Heifetz by the time a cadenza is finished and the concerto resumes.

He and Ilse would listen together, but now he must do so alone. He and she would share a cocktail, and it is still a shock to Benno that he pours a single portion now and must consume it solo. With some embarrassment but no sense of irony, when the ice is ready in his glass and the aquavit or whisky has been poured, he raises his drink to the empty seat across from him and says, to Ilse, "Your health."

She died quietly. She was lying in her own bed, underneath good blankets, and though he has in his time witnessed the deaths of men convulsing or children in an agony, though he knows it is not usual to be peaceful in one's final moments, Ilse had been calm. One minute she was breathing and then she was not breathing and he had not known for certain—his attention had wandered, perhaps, or he had risen from her bedside for a breath of air or to go to the toilet, and in any case his eyesight has been failing now for years and he therefore cannot tell if a sheet is rising or falling across a person's chest from a distance of four feet away—the instant Ilse died. To record the event he and the nurse he hired had to make a guess; it had been 3:27 p.m. or perhaps 3:28 or even possibly 3:26 or 3:29 p.m. on the thirty-first of December, 1954.

Benno blames himself for this uncertainty; he is a man who admires precision and distrusts the inexact. He would of course have wished to *know* and not guess the minute Ilse died. But it is only a small uncertainty, and in the end he managed to persuade himself that it was a blessing, a *mitzvah*, because it means his wife succumbed so peacefully to her congestive heart failure that he thought she continued to live.

She does so, in his heart. She is with him in Berlin and then Havana and now Larchmont, in his youth and middle and old age; they remain the best of friends and intimate companions even though he buried her in Ferncliff Cemetery in Hartsdale, not thirty minutes away. He goes to visit when he can, when Johann or Gisela drives him, and then they have lunch. There is an Italian restaurant in the center of the village, and he orders minestrone and perhaps a veal cutlet or dish of pasta and always, at the end of the meal, a gelato and cup of espresso with a slice of lemon peel. Always, on this occasion, whether his companion is his son or his daughter-in-law, or both, Benno insists he must pay.

His eyes are bad; he barely can read, but has been rereading—with a magnifying instrument, a glass held in place with a light below it shining on the open page—*Buddenbrooks* by

Thomas Mann. It is Mann's first novel, written when the author was young, and published in 1901. The decline of the Buddenbrook family through its several generations is a book he has admired since the first time he read it—in German, of course, and Germany—when he himself was young. He believes that Mann's family story is the tale of his family also, except there had been Hitler and Dwight Eisenhower and Winston Churchill to defeat him, and Johann has not been a disappointment but good son. Benno has confidence also not so much in his charming grandson Peter as in studious young Frederick, and he thinks the Hochmann fortunes are not wholly in decline.

Geh zum Deifi—"Go to the Devil!"—is the shocking thing that Permaneder says in the book to his wife Antonie *née* Buddenbrook, when in Munich he calls her a cow. Not once in their long life together did Benno speak to Ilse in this fashion, or even need to raise his voice, and standing by the urn with her ashes in Ferncliff he says softly not "Go to the Devil," but "May you be at peace."

Flyaway
1968

IT'S THE BITCH of a problem, he says to himself, the trouble with the turning world and how he has to turn with it in order to stand still; *Down boy, heel*, thinks Peter, and is there still a television program called *As the World Turns*? Or was it *The Days of Our Lives*? They show women in trouble and doctors who help them and husbands who are losing jobs or getting promoted because of some ideal upheld or compromised, some love affair begun or ended or exposed, and always in close-up the actresses and actors speak their soap-opera lines, *Oh darling, don't ever leave me, Oh I'll make myself try to forget you, Oh no I won't ever forget.* Their mouths should be washed out with soap. They are idiots, he thinks, they speak bourgeois inanity and parrot on a daily basis nonsense, non-sense; the bored restless housewives with ironing boards who never miss a session, and the men who marry them, are—he understands this now—exactly what's wrong with America, exactly the reason he needs to be standing on this street corner today. The bitch of a problem, the cartwheeling world, and maybe it's an inner ear or vertigo or even standing on his head which is a thing he used to do, but topsy-turvy, inside-out, and upside-down are how he feels inside his head which is, to tell the truth, the whole unvarnished and nothing but truth, the one place on this fucked-up planet it feels safe to be. Not at the end of Navy Pier, not out there on the waterfront, not yet on Michigan Avenue where the traffic is unstoppable and he will go to rid himself of an effluvium of company but in his, Peter Hochmann's, mind where there are pretty colors, *pretty* colors, beautiful colors, extravagant rainbows of color because of the pill he just swallowed, the echoing arch of his skull.

Hello, hello out there. The men wearing suits, the women heels, the police in their parked cruisers, *oink-oink* or is it instead *honk-honk*? But that's the sound geese make, not pigs, and the men in suits and women in heels pass him for the most part by on this sidewalk with its curbs and windows reflecting, *refracting* dark light without so much as a by-your-leave, a second look, a lingering or malingering glance because he feels invisible, impervious, fairly *wreathed* in his bright solitude, the pot of gold at fucking rainbow's end. Saluting Mayor Daley and his storm troops, Mayor Daley and his thugs. Mayor jackbooted jackass Richard Daley where the trains and the El run on time.

And although he is too old for this—at thirty-four, which is, he knows, older than, if not Methuselah, Jesus (though he cannot quite remember if Jesus died at thirty-three or thirty-seven and in any case the calendar was different then, the toll of years, for if you think about it *everybody* dies at thirty-three or thirty-seven or in the end regardless), although of course in the instance of Jesus there's the issue of eternal life if you happen to believe in it which Peter doesn't, can't, and won't—he's in Chicago anyhow to join the party in Grant Park, the Happy Birthday party for the rebirth of our cherished lost and found democracy, fist raised in a protest for freedom, *Freedom*, highday, ho-die, and then at the jackbooted thugs. The Nazis his parents and grandparents feared and fled from are these Nazis once again in combat gear with gas masks and tear-gas canisters and body armor and bulletproof vests and truncheons clearing protestors out from where we have a right to be, storm troopers with bullhorns and Mace and squad cars in their serried ranks encircling the convention hall where Hubert Humphrey reigns. It can happen, is happening here.

Therefore fatigue is what he feels on the hot pavement, peering down at the slow water and wondering whether to jump. Oh Chicago you city of cities, you cradle of democracy now rocking in the busy wind, the tempest and teapot of politics, you place of the jackbooted thugs. How many people, Peter wonders, have been thrown or threw themselves with despairing certainty under these ramparts and off of this high bridge?

It would be excellent to know. It would be *excellent* to know. The Democratic National Convention is about to be—well, what's the phrase? *consigned* to the *dustbin* of—*history*, the rules of fair play and the right of free speech have been, ah, what's the term? *suspended* and are dangling midair like the legs of a hanged man from, oh, what's the word? a *gibbet* in the wind.

It is August 28. There are fifteen thousand people who will not be dissuaded, who carry him along with them in the great tide of good feeling, there are sticks and stones and broken bones yet a joyousness abounding in the fellowship of those who all together march towards if not Jerusalem the International Amphitheater and the Conrad Hilton Hotel. There are a hundred thousand protestors petitioning the court. We will overcome. We *will* overcome. And if not prevail on the instant, if not in this very confrontation then surely in the near and not far distant future when the tide of history, the great tide of good feeling will have turned and swept mere tyranny before it like those waves that break upon a lakefront's shore and where the people march. *Oh darling, don't ever leave me, Oh no I won't ever forget.*

For just around the corner comes the sound of a guitar. And its plangent chords. Someone is singing, badly, *If I had the wings of a turtle dove*, and someone else is joining in, *I'd fly cross the river, to the one I love.* These are children, most of them, while he himself is thirty-four and not to be trusted because you mustn't, Peter likes to tell them—particularly the wide-eyed girls, the wide-legged girls, the wide-hipped girls—trust anybody over thirty, and likes to say it best of all when he is inside them and about to come.

Fly away, oh darling, fly away. We have no business there. There being Vietnam, or Laos, or Cambodia, or any of the countries we so much like to bomb. Those targets of our target practice and occasions for national shame. Instead, we have business *here*.

What he is doing with these children is of course conjectural, a question to be answered at some other time and place, because right now the press of flesh, the confluence of bodies with their torn shirts and their Toxin caps and *Hell No I Won't Go* in black letters on their backs and *Make Love, Not War* on t-shirts on their braless if uplifted chests has something of an urgency, a rush and even panic to withdraw from the horses, the pigs. What am I doing here, he asks again, but receives of course no answer; and where will I go?

The heat of late summer, the sluiced-down-with-hoses streets. The white horse rearing by the fire hydrant and the car with its front windows shattered and its fenders battered and the shards of glass. The hubcap someone lifted and is using as a shield. *Get the fuck off of me, pig.* And is there safety in numbers or, by contrast, danger in the press of them, the rush and even panic, because the motion all around him is also a collective motion of which Peter forms a small yet individual component, a part of the inchoate whole, because the strange thing is the black man with the two-day growth of beard and the muscles of a laborer or, perhaps, a body-builder now embracing and calling him "Brother" does comport himself as though he were his brother although his own and actual newly married brother Freddy—remember that series of children's books, bro, the adventures of *Freddy the Pig?*—is a thousand miles away and not remotely a part of the party, not likely to approve of it but safely established in Riverdale and maybe, though he cannot bring himself to believe it, even of his long-lost sib, his kid brother, a *Republican*. With a wife he'd like to fuck. With her come-hither glance that is all the more exciting because it says please stay away.

Except that on this battlement there appears a blonde beside him with a red bandana and legs that won't quit and right hand upraised who would be very welcome as a substitute: But this is a party he's not asked to join, asked not to join, so is reduced again to fly cross the river to the one I love, the turtle dove, the by-the-waters-of Babylon baby, or is it the Chicago River? Let us therefore raise a fist in protest and, if not a fist, a glass.

Oh-oh Freedom. Oh-ah Freedom. Oh Freedom over me. The flunkeys of the middle class, the elected non-representatives, the fat cats with portfolios we send to City Hall and in this state to Springfield and in this nation Washington, D.C., are inside the Convention Center and slapping each other on backs. They have nominated Hubert Humphrey, they have made fools of themselves. They have picked the one man in America who can't beat Tricky Dick. *Humphrey Dumb-free sat on a wall, Hump-free Dumphrey won't have a great fall.* And certainly no glad Election Day. Because with whatever shards and shreds of self-respect cling still to the American voter, not to mention the American dream or its Democratic remnant, the self-negating self-affrighting fact of it is clear: we have taken a wrong turning, friends, and swallowed a difficult pill. Heigh-ho, the acid he dropped. Heigh-ho, the coke and the lude. But must digest it now or be clubbed into submission by yonder pig who's whistling Dixie and beating the air with a stick. His non-observant parents do not themselves keep kosher but would not eat pigs in blankets, or swallow shrimp, or soft-shelled crab; there's a limit, says his mother, Gisela, there are some things we don't countenance or do. Oh yes, he wants to ask her, what won't we do, what sky's the limit, Mom?

"Hey."

"Hey."

"How you doin'?"

"Good."

"Looks like you had a hard night of it, brother."

"Don't *brother* me."

"Buddy. *Compañero*. Comrade."

"Fine."

"That better?"

Peter nods.

"We've had it, we're calling it quits."

"A day."

"What?"

"You heard me. Calling it a day, not quits."

"Call it a night, brother."

"*Don't.*"

"Don't what?"

"'Am I my brother's keeper?'"

"Enough already. We're going to Lakeside. Wanna come?"

"Where's Lakeside?"

"Michigan."

"Not Michigan Avenue?"

"No way, *José.*"

"*Compuesta, no hay mujer fea.*"

"What the fuck does that mean?"

"'Made up, no woman is ugly.'"

"You can say that again."

"*Compuesta, no hay mujer fea.*"

"Come off it, bro. We're into equality here."

"Where the fuck's Lakeside?"

"Not far."

And so they go and went. Somehow his newfound company has managed to withdraw, to inch in single file down side streets and out of the storm-trooping center and hurricane's eye into a providential alley where, hey presto, waits a vehicle that is the very vehicle, the *deus in machina* with which to effect their escape. There is a man with a key. There is Old King Cole who's a jolly old soul and these are his fiddlers three. Peter finds himself surrounded by or at least in momentary league with strangers in the soul's dark night, beneath the street lamp's flickering, beside the garbage bins.

They slap each other on backs. They run and are not weary and seem to know each other if not him. But who are these who travel, Sammy with his pony-tail and White Sox cap and camouflage pants, and Tim or is it Tom or Jim with his black beard and tattoo? *Get your ass into the car, man. We got to get out of this shithole town.* Who with his head in a bandage that is blood-stained but not badly drives an old hard-used sedan, a turquoise blue and white Oldsmobile 88, *annus dei* 1959, this year-of-the-revolution-and-its-triumph-automobile, the one whose back seat where our hero sits is ripped and taped and patched together with black tape, and who now sits beside him but the selfsame blonde with her plaid cloth coat and blue jeans fetchingly—oh *fetchingly*—unraveled at the knee?

Peter considers this. How do we ravel out in time, and why do the words ravel and unravel mean the same, why does *sanction* mean *support, approve of* and its opposite, and what is your name, babycakes, because now we ravel-travel together and I should *know* you, yes. Except that she is sleeping and since he can look more closely and examine with impunity his fellow female traveler he sees a scar that winds in corkscrew fashion down her neck and where her plaid cloth coat encloses it continues but how far he cannot tell. They are mostly out of traffic now, having maneuvered through the streets and through Hyde Park and up onto the Skyway and having attained Indiana, the godforsaken back of beyond and ass-end of the universe, *Gary*, for chrissakes, Gary Indiana, a name like an old porn star's stage name or that guy Robert ditto who paints LOVE. Whose real name is Robert Clark. Nonetheless they have escaped the confines of Grant Park, of Lincoln Park, those Civil War memorials where he has been uncivil and it turns out Tim or Tom or Jim has a family house in this Lakeside which is, he says, a downshift and a stop sign and a place to hang while waiting for the shit storm to blow over and then out. How long, how long, asks Sammy, and Tim-Tom-Jim says your guess is good as mine. As long as it fucking takes, bro.

What Peter asks himself is this: how could things go so wrong? The white breast of the tormented lake, the heartland and the meadowland, our dear dream of equality, the decision to drop napalm on our enemies who have no reason to be enemies but used to be and maybe sometime in the future will again be friends. *Hell, no, we won't go,* is what they sang in Lincoln Park, arms linked, and *Hey, hey, LBJ, how many kids did you kill today?* He's coming down, is Peter, coming back to earth from what had been a sky-high high, a trip to the moon on gossamer wings, a free-fall of mock gravity through universal flux. The shooting stars, the meteors, and all the ships at sea. He can feel it in his stomach, in his ears.

Turns out the girl beside him on the torn seat of the Oldsmobile is Kate, or so she calls herself, offering a stick of gum which he accepts but does not chew, and she and the driver are sister and brother; two halves of the family whole. He doesn't ask them, doesn't want or need to know, but asks himself and promises to try to answer how is it possible that he, Peter Ernest Hochmann, born in Berlin, raised in Havana and New Rochelle and Larchmont, should find himself now driving past the barbed-wire fences and hellish chimneys' indifferent smoke of Gary, Indiana; how has he come to this pass? And why did they offer him and equally inscrutably why in God's unsayable name has he accepted their offer to come along for the ride? Heigh-ho, the fiddle and cat.

They stop for gas. He is definitely sober now, and the neon light above the gas pump that is pouring down upon them hurts his fucking ayes. His fucking eyes. But in this particular instance and for the foreseeable future he is the senior citizen who was rescued by these children and therefore he offers to pay. From his pocket he extracts a twenty-dollar bill, and a soiled but serviceable handkerchief, also a Swiss army knife he carries with him everywhere, a talisman, a good companion with a toothpick and tweezer and file. Kate with the corkscrew scar is talking; she is saying Rennie Davis, she is saying Bobby Seale. Someone else says David Dellinger, Tom Hayden, and John Froines. They are naming names together and remembering a speech they heard, a speech that they assure each other was, yes, dynamite, but what he wants and needs to do is take a piss. So he goes inside the—what's the word—*emporium* and visits the *facilities*; might a soul bathe in these rushing waters and thereby slake its thirst? It feels excellent to piss. It feels *excellent* to piss. And lay his burdens down.

In the bathroom mirror he peers blearily at his own stone face, his own *stoned* face, the three-day growth of stubble on his chin. When he steps outside again and rubs his eyes, his ayes, the midnight mist has settled wetly and it's August 29. "Let's get a move on, man," says Tom-Tim-Jim, and they resume positions two-by-two in the by-now-familiar refueled and waiting chariot, the ark, this Oldsmobile that carries them back to if not old Virginny or Mt. Ararat to Lakeside in not Illinois or Indiana but Michigan, *Michigan, Michigan* where it will be dawn.

A highway called Red Arrow is the highway they traverse. It's Michigan City and New Buffalo and Union Pier and potholes that require fixing and motels with Vacancy signs. There's a roadhouse and an eatery called Redamak's where they do not pause. I'm just not hungry, man. Sammy descants on the things he saw, the things he heard, the violence policemen did; can you *believe* it, man? At least, says Tom-Tim-Jim, they gassed the photographers too. The journalists will tell it like it is, because they got an eyeful and a mouthful of the stuff. Let's listen to the radio or buy a paper later, I bet you dollars to doughnuts what happened is the front-page story and all over all the news. Except what does "dollars to doughnuts" signify, Peter wonders, what does the expression convey? The girl beside him reaches out and touches Sammy's shoulder, and he wonders if they know each other well, how well, and in what capacity and for how long? One of these boys is her brother, the other one not; he tries to recall which is which.

"Daley's an asshole," says Kate.

Ah child, he wants to tell her, eight years ago when you were in your training bra, or maybe didn't need one yet, when you were barely sentient—presuming, that is, you qualify today for what we might call sentience—we *loved* the man for letting dead men vote, and twice, and delivering the city of Chicago and therefore the state's electoral numbers to John Fitzgerald Kennedy. It was Tricky Dick that time as well, and Daley to the rescue, and though we could of course not countenance or even admit to all those dead men voting, all those precincts under the mayoral thumb, it was a comfort and a kind of consolation to know *hiz honor* knew the way to rig things, and we were in his debt.

Except of course we were deluded then as well, we thought the President would be the last best hope, that JFK and RMN were polar opposites, the former fair, the latter foul, the former warm, the latter cold, and learned the hard way what Lord Acton knew, that absolute power corrupts absolutely, so you can be a Democrat and not Republican, like my brother and his sexy wife, but maybe they aren't quite that bad—not, I mean, Republican—and maybe the come-hither look means what it says and not the opposite, *get lost*, and still fuck up in Cuba and then Vietnam and bring us to this crossroads because your asshole Mayor Daley delivered all those precincts where dead men voted twice. He would, he *could* go on in this vein, but a great weariness has settled in; Peter cannot remember the last time he slept, for this has been a three-day blow and in the cocoon-like warmth of the car, the gently rocking motion of it, fights to stay awake.

Kate and who-he-assumes-is her brother and who-he-assumes-is her lover are keeping their own counsel, so he also keeps his counsel, and the silence in the car encloses him like one of those blankets Maria produced and his grandmother spread over him in his bed in Havana at night. *Aye aye aye aye aye, querida*, and is that a deer in the headlights or am I just seeing things, love?

What he sees when he wakes up is a dark blue house among the pines. It is sizeable: six windows and, counting the dormers, eight. It has gables and a front porch and a driveway that's a weed patch with remnants of spread gravel, a chimney with ivy clustered thickly on it and purple climbing vines. It's Hansel and Gretel time, a cottage in the forest where these children take their ease. *In the pines in the pines*, don't you lie to me;

by Marshall Field's emporium I and the black girl sat down and wept, except because it's August I failed to shiver the whole night through or sing along with Mitch. So it has been a decent trip, Peter tells himself, *excellent*, a source of clarification as well as fruitful confusion, and now that he is coming down, has *come* down altogether from his high he asks himself in chill sobriety if the protest movement is a good thing or a bad thing or indifferent, if it makes any difference, if it made any difference, if we have the slightest fucking chance of changing the country's direction and muting the drumbeats of war?

Not likely, he tells Kate, who doesn't seem to hear him, who is standing by the car door and leaning on the fender and stretching and rubbing her eyes. A warm dawn, a hot day to come. Behind the trees he hears two things: a train's whistle in the distance, then the rat-a-tat-tat of the engineer's horn, the nearing approach of it, louder and louder, the warning tattoo of the whistle and then its worn and fading repetition, the chorus and the echo and the freight train gone. Did they cross tracks, he asks himself, or were they driving parallel, and—what's the word he used to use?—along an *asymptote* and from which direction therefore does the sound arrive?

It is in the middle distance and then far far away. When he can hear it no longer, Peter hears instead the sough and rustle of wind on water, waves on a beach, and remembers—*Lakeside*, remember, he says to himself—they are by a beach. Lake fucking Michigan, man.

Turns out there is shit in the trunk. Turns out there's a blanket and a leather case and Colt pistol nestled inside it and a pair of rifles Sammy lifts out lovingly, and when he notices that Peter notices he shrugs and says, "Protection," and carries heat into the house. Kate has a suitcase of her own, a blue duffel and a cardboard box of groceries: a box of cereal, some cans of soup, spaghetti, powdered milk. She tells him it's their parents' place, their family vacation home, and her folks were here this summer but now are back in what he thinks she says is Madison; Kate has a key and has been coming here forever, and no one in the neighborhood will notice their arrival except to say, "Hello."

"You can stay with us," says Tim-Tom-Jim, "or split. Your call."

"Easy come and easy go," says Peter. "Thanks for the ride."

"Take care," says Sammy.

"*Adelante, juventud.*"

"What the fuck does that mean?"

"Take care," Sammy says again. And, standing on the porch, Kate waves.

"You too, my children. Go with God."

This last he does not say. Instead, he walks away. It is the moment he lives for, the farewell without prolonged goodbye, the by your leave I'm leaving and the so long, I'm outta here waltz. It's what he tells his women when he tells them he has had enough, what he told his teachers when they said there were more tests to take, what he told his parents when they asked him to get serious and to get a job. It's the high wine of independence, the liberated man, man. For there's certain comfort in departure, and he has gotten good at it; a hundred yards along the road he sees signs for "Murphy Hollow" and then "Gottlieb Grove" and then the beach.

At some point in the coming day he will have to find something to eat. At some point in the coming night he will have to find somewhere to sleep. But it is August 29, and happy families will soon enough approach the shore, their pails in hand, their beach chairs and umbrellas and beach towels at the ready.

The wandering Jew, thinks Peter, and thinks about a tune from awful Lawrence Welk, "The Happy Wanderer." The pursed lips and the fixed smile and those women with their bouffant hairdos and their girdles, the radical innocence of early television entertainment, the whistle and yodel and yap. Which brings him back to *As the World Turns, Days of Our Lives*, the doctors and the housewives and stilted dialogue, *I'll make myself try to forget you.*

He does. Peter Ernest Hochmann, in the rising light and alone this summer morning, has the lake on his left side.

It is an astonishment. There are waves and whitecaps and no limit to the span of it, no opposing shore he can discern. Chicago and Milwaukee and other cities on the lake lie past the reach of visibility, and the beach beneath him stretches out for miles and miles. Who would believe it, he thinks; who would fucking believe what I see? Again in the near distance he hears the sound of a train whistle and its syncopated blast. This freedom, Peter thinks, is something to cherish. He does.

Family
1974

THE WATERGATE HEARINGS obsess them. The Hochmanns listen all day long and follow the proceedings. They have been doing so since the first arrests were made, but in this last year things have grown more public. The details of the break-in at Democratic National Headquarters are stage by stage revealed. What started as only an incident—a group of men who bungled a job—takes over the national news.

In July of 1973, Alexander Butterfield reveals the details of the taping system in the White House, and "deniability" is no longer possible. In September of that year, Special Prosecutor Archibald Cox is fired. In what reporters label "the Saturday night massacre," Elliot Richardson resigns. Deputy Attorney General William Ruckelshaus resigns. Those who once were members of the government—Attorney General John Mitchell, men like Jeb Stuart Magruder, Robert Mardian, Kenneth Parkinson, and Gordon Strachan—are exposed in headlines daily, and their faces grow familiar on TV. John Ehrlichman, who looks a little like dead Senator McCarthy, H. R. "Bob" Haldeman with his marine-like posture and buzz haircut, bespectacled John Dean with his blond wife behind him: the President's henchmen are often on screen, as are the Watergate thieves.

Frederick and Sarah know the names and occupations and the cover stories of Hunt and Liddy and the rest; they know the name of Richard Nixon's secretary, Rose Mary Woods, and how many minutes are missing from the Oval Office tapes. When, on August 5, 1974, the "smoking gun" tape is released, with its evidence that Nixon knew about the cover-up, both husband and wife are elated.

"It's over now," says Sarah.

"The smoking gun," says Frederick.

"The smoking gun?" asks Gisela.

"It means you're caught red-handed. Bloody-handed, really. With cordite on your hand."

"Excuse me?" asks his mother. "What are you talking about?"

"It's an expression, mama, about people caught in a crime."

"Whatever," Sarah says. "It may not be all over, but today is the beginning of the end."

"Not," Frederick explains to Gisela, "the Watergate break-in itself. Those are what they're calling 'dirty tricks.' But the cover-up makes it much worse. And now the President himself can't say he didn't know."

Charles "Chuck" Colson and the "plumbers" turn by turn engage them, and the more they learn of Nixon's paranoia and vulgarity, the more they come to understand how narrow the escape has been from national disgrace. They read the tapes with "expletives deleted"; they listen to him ranting and are shocked. It astonishes Johann that an incumbent president, facing reelection and ahead by a large margin, should still have felt it necessary to have henchmen break the law. "Tricky Dick" is what they call him, and his son wishes Benno were alive to witness what has happened to Ike's choice for Vice President, the man who promises the country "I'm not a crook." The old man admired Eisenhower as much as Franklin Roosevelt; between the two of them, he used to say, we were by America saved. But in the case of Richard Nixon, the general chose wrong.

Sarah now is thirty-five, and Frederick's birthday comes soon. They have been married seven years, and she is pregnant with their second child; Johnny has turned four. For his birthday she has baked a cake in the shape of the candy he loves best, a

Tootsie Roll. It is a chocolate log-cake, decorated like a Tootsie Roll, with his name spelled in white icing in the center, and he claps and waves at the camera. His face is smeared with icing, and Frederick makes a home movie of the birthday boy, with his conical hat and pudgy hands clenching and unclenching in childish exuberance. Sarah stands beside him, smiling, hands folded on her stomach and wearing a pink dress.

The birthday party also serves as a house-warming party, since they have settled in. The elder Hochmanns drive to New Canaan from Larchmont, and Frederick asks his wife in private if Johann still should be driving; he has watched his father park their Lincoln Continental, and the car requires washing and has recent damage on the right rear fender. Johann parks aslant. Emerging, he and Gisela stand slowly, and when they stand they bend as if against a wind. In the film the birthday boy tugs at helium balloons and bangs the tambourine one of his playmates from preschool brought to the party as a gift. The other invited children blow their paper horns.

The house had been Sarah's idea. At first they lived in Riverdale, in an apartment near the highway, and Frederick would drive to work on the Cross County and then the Hutchinson Parkway, reversing the direction of his childhood drive to Fieldston School. Sometimes, he drove past the grounds. It is, he knows, a common reaction but he finds himself surprised at the small scale of it; as a student he believed the buildings and the courtyard were enormous. Now the structures seem more modest, self-contained.

The same holds true for where they live; what seemed sufficient to start with has come over time to seem pinched. When Jonathan was born and they outgrew the apartment, they moved to a two-family dwelling in Rye, and were content with the move. But now that she is pregnant again, Sarah wants to settle in a home where the children will have "breathing room," and where they will be safe. They use the same real estate agent, and when the woman calls to inform them she has found the perfect house, they drive to visit it on a clear autumn morning and are, on the instant, convinced. As the wage-earner in the family, Frederick is cautious, but Sarah says, "It's perfect, darling. *Please.*" They have the house repainted, and move in in March.

New Canaan is a town with only a few Jews, but the Oleskers live nearby, and the office complex in Stamford is no great distance away. His job goes well; they prosper. Already he has understood and worked out a business plan for what will become his career. The Reliable Insurance Company has a subsidiary corporation of which Frederick is in charge: Reliable Warehousing Co. The logo SOS has been imprinted on his office door and in blue tile in the entrance hall; the initials adorn his briefcase also, in gold leaf. SOS—*Store Objects Safely*—is a company devoted to personal service and warehouse space; as one of three Associate Vice Presidents, his bonus comes in stock.

In America, he tells his father, everybody feels the need for personal storage units. It is, says Frederick, a universal preference and universal problem. The poor who have been dispossessed need a place to house their sticks of furniture and garbage bags of clothing while they look elsewhere for work. Every apartment dweller feels the need for additional space. The middle class and upper-middle class all own more than they can store in cellars or in attics: a couch or extra bed or table they can't quite bring themselves to give away. The rich require vaults in which to preserve their possessions, old family objects of value and antique chairs they no longer want to sit on but feel no need to sell. In a nation of planned obsolescence it's astonishing, says Frederick, how much we choose to keep, how reluctant we are to let go. And there's little difference in this desire, he says, if you're rich or poor or somewhere in between . . .

Johann listens carefully. He has, he tells his boy, questions: how do you plan to market it; how much advertising must you do and how quickly do you hope to grow? Will the company franchise its warehouses, or are they wholly owned?

Sarah serves them tea. They are sitting at the kitchen table; it is Sunday afternoon. The birthday party is over, and everyone agrees it was a great success. Gisela and her grandson have retired to the garden; she is pushing Johnny on a swing. She has, she says, no interest in grown-ups any longer but she does love this boy; he is—she smiles—*zum Fressen*, good enough to eat. The elder Hochmanns have brought bread and salt as house gifts for their son's new residence, a structure built in 1920. Frederick can tell his father is impressed. Or not so much impressed as gratified by his son's good fortune, how entrenched the family seems already in New Canaan. He will live here the rest of his life.

Johnny is a quiet child, absorbed in his construction projects and by reading books. At four, he cannot truly read but likes to turn the pages and narrate what he sees. He has his father's thoughtful mien; he was slow to crawl and slow to walk and slow to laugh at visitors who make funny faces at him or talk baby talk. Johnny has, his mother says, a mind entirely his own. He carries a Teddy bear called Pablo everywhere, and sleeps with it at night. He no longer takes an afternoon nap, but when he settles down for "quiet time," Pablo lies there also, the black button of his nose pressed up against Johnny's cheek.

These days he occupies himself with an erector set, building improbable structures. When Frederick uncovers a box of metal soldiers he himself had owned when young, Johnny makes what he calls "expeditions" of figures on parade.

"I think the word is 'exhibitions,'" says his father.

"These are expeditions," Johnny says.

He sets the redcoats out in ranked rows, their bayonets fixed to attack. He arranges the soldiers on horseback and soldiers with shields and soldiers with rifles upraised. On the white deal table in his bedroom he balances his armies, and if a metal fighter has lost a leg or arm he lays them on the tabletop and proclaims them dead. Once the soldiers are in battle formation he advances pieces one by one, until the battle-lines are joined and then he knocks them down and starts again.

At night he has bad dreams. In his sleep he calls out, "Mommy," and when she goes to comfort him he stares at her without recognition, in blank unseeing terror: "*No*," he shouts, "*I don't want to. You can't make me. Go away!*"

Concerned, the parents discuss this, and Frederick counsels patience, saying—with an authority Sarah hopes is justified—"It's just a phase. All kids go through this sort of thing," he assures her. "*I* did."

"I didn't. Do you think it's this new room of his?"

"I doubt it."

"Does he worry we can't hear him?"

Frederick shakes his head.

When he wakes the boy cannot remember crying out, or why he clung to his mother, inconsolable, the night before. He tells himself stories while falling asleep; he sings and chortles happily. All day he is unafraid, placid. But for weeks and months he cries at night, and though they tell him he is dreaming he says it isn't dreams. It is as though a second self, a body inside his own body, has witnessed a series of horrors—maiming, fire, mutilation—from which he can't shake loose. And the worst of it, thinks Sarah, is how powerless she feels to help; when she holds him, he shudders against her, convulsive, eyes open but unseeing, moaning "*Go away!*"

Their house is safe, protected. They are free from hunger and, in the winter, cold. She and Frederick do not raise their voices in anger, do not quarrel or complain. He enjoys his time in nursery school, and his teachers and playmates pose no threat. Yet it is as though, she tells herself, the world beyond the bedroom wall has crowded in on Johnny with the torments of his ancestry, the remorseless beat of boots on stairs and gloved fists on a door. Some part of him is terrified; some part of him abed at night is threatened by the dark. A night light does not help. A glass of warm milk quiets him, but only while he drinks. Then the terror commences again.

Frederick's maternal grandparents were art collectors in Hamburg, and sometimes he speaks about paintings the family owned. It's not, he says, a catalogue of grievance or an attempt to recapture the past, but when he visits a museum he finds himself wondering—idly, idly—if the pictures belonged to an ancestor once. In his own methodical way, and on a much smaller scale, he tries to restore what was lost.

From the beginning of their marriage, therefore, they buy art. Every wall has something Sarah looks at with real pleasure, and the central stairwell is something she pauses on, often, to examine what is hanging there: a lithograph by Piranesi and street-scene by Toulouse Lautrec or bull-fighting sequence by Goya, a portrait by Georges Rouault. The artist called them *portraits intimes*. He is better known for clowns and stained-glass windows with the head of Christ, but those are expensive oil paintings. As collectors, they are modest and what she and Frederick can afford are lithographs, the heads of Rouault's friends.

It's surprising, Sarah tells herself, but she feels closer to the heads of Baudelaire and Paul Verlaine, two of the "intimate portraits," than she does to women on the Library Committee and, once she joins the PTA, the PTA. She sleepwalks her way through meetings and car pools and dentist and doctor's appointments, the little daily duties of suburban life; she manages her household with the kind of care Rouault once lavished on a subject's profile. Too, when a job is over—the meal prepared, the meeting chaired—she takes pleasure in what has been done. Always she extracts a measure of satisfaction from the completion of a project, or a new color for the entrance hall, telling herself, in that phrase from *Death of a Salesman*, "Attention must be paid."

Still, it is difficult to pay attention, hard to think of anything but this new life she is carrying, this child now kicking at her fitfully. Her stomach jumps, her skin has grown taut as a drum. She makes Frederick put his hand on it while their baby kicks. He tries to understand but cannot what it means to have a second self, a body in your body, and sometimes she wonders if Johnny also feels this way—if what he fears when crying out is that he's been invaded.

This second of her pregnancies is harder than the first, because she has to deal with Johnny as though everything was just the same and nothing in their daily life will change. Like many other children, he is resistant to change. But when she grows so visible that everybody notices, and Johnny asks at lunch-time why she has grown fat, she tells him that he'll have a little brother or a sister soon.

Her explanation makes him happy. Others in his playgroup have brothers or sisters, and he announces, smiling, "I'll be like everyone else."

Gisela Lefchinsky Hochmann dies on December 10. Her illness had been brief. For some weeks, she told Johann, she has been feeling poorly, but when he suggests a trip to the doctor she says it is not necessary, there is nothing in particular to have a doctor examine: only she wishes to not be so tired and wants, all the time, to sleep. "It's called old age," she says.

"Sixty-five is not too old. To me," says Johann, "you are still young."

"An optimist," she says.

"No."

"A liar, then."

"You mustn't work so hard. You're busy all the time, you've been asking too much of yourself."

At this, she scoffs. "I do nothing."

"For me you do everything, *Liebchen.*"

"That's sweet," says Gisela. "It isn't true, but sweet."

Why, Johann wonders, should he insist on flattery; why does he try to cajole her out of her ill humor or pretend she is not ill? Her hands are claws; they shake. Her head bobbles continually on its neck, and the neck is like a chicken's, wattled. Still sometimes he can look at her and see the beautiful woman he married, but her beauty has not lasted except in his mind's eye.

He thinks perhaps that what they need is a vacation, time to rest. From his office travel agent—with a view to making a surprise of it for Gisela's birthday in October—he acquires brochures for a resort on the coast of Mexico, and also for a cruise. He cannot decide which she would prefer and discusses the prospect with Sarah; they go back and forth about the merits of a land-based or sea-borne vacation, and which would please Gisela more.

Before he can decide, however, all such plans are canceled. One Thursday morning in August, when Gisela picks up a water glass to take it to the kitchen, her fingers do not function properly and she drops the glass. She tells herself she is distracted and should pay more attention, but when she tries to lift a plate she drops it also. It breaks. The next day, attempting to stand up from her rocking chair, she cannot do so without Johann's help, and he insists they go to the doctor; the doctor examines her carefully, closely, and with a grave face when the test results arrive excludes what he at first suspected: stroke. A transient ischemic attack, he says, would have been not uncommon for a person of her age. But her difficulties are not, it seems, the result of stroke; that diagnosis is ruled out.

Now therefore there are other possibilities to consider, and he recommends a specialist. "What sort of specialist?" asks Johann, and the doctor tells him a neurologist. He says these are issues of balance and motor control, and he would like a second opinion from a specialist at P & S. "At Columbia Presbyterian Physicians and Surgeons," he says, pronouncing the full name of the Medical Center, "they have excellent facilities. And we need to rule things out, a definite diagnosis."

Johann pretends to be hopeful or, if not hopeful, unalarmed, but Gisela knows she is hearing a verdict, and that the verdict is death. Once the Manhattan specialist has met with her, and the MRI and CAT scans have been scheduled and performed and read, it is time to arrange for a biopsy and then exploratory surgery for what the surgeons tell the Hochmanns may well be benign as a brain tumor. It is not benign. These procedures are completed in the sense that they are finished but at the end of the procedures there is nothing to be done. The cancer is inoperable; the doctors make this clear.

Johann and Frederick and Sarah and, when he comes home to visit his mother, Peter, do everything they can. They ready the house for a patient, renting a hospital bed. They acquire, as well, apparatus: a wheelchair, a walker, a portable toilet and oxygen canisters and safety bars for the bath. They hire nursing help. Once the nurses and equipment are in place, they install Gisela in her bedroom where the surroundings are familiar. She sleeps more calmly at home. The glioblastoma in her brain is, moreover, positioned so she does not suffer; the swelling makes her peaceful, and she sleeps much of the day.

Johann sits for hours at her bedside, remembering the girl she was and then the woman he married, with whom he traveled to Cuba. He remembers the years and decades she tended to their sons, as well as to her father, and how adept she was at managing the household tasks, the daily business she now cannot manage and no longer even notices. She drinks water, broth, and lukewarm tea; she likes to have him rub her hands and feet with Pond's cold cream so that the skin stays moist. He hires nighttime nurses and sleeps in the next room. He does not, however, sleep.

Henry Kissinger remains at Nixon's side, as does Gerald Ford. John Ehrlichman and H. R. Haldeman and others near the Oval Office are fired or resign; they have thrown themselves, says Johann, on the sword. He relishes this expression, and also says that they are rats who flee the sinking ship. Richard Nixon does not pardon those who did his bidding, although they had believed he would. When finally the President has no recourse left, and in order to avoid impeachment chooses resignation, he is whisked away from the White House and flown to San Clemente. This happens on August 9; within a month the President is pardoned by his successor, Gerald Ford. What some call the national nightmare—though to Frederick and Sarah it seems like a good dream—concludes. The men who broke into the Watergate Office go to jail, and so do their superiors, but

Richard Nixon retires and composes his memoirs.

What Peter feels is a great wash of sorrow, a whelming in his chest and throat he proves—to his surprise—unable to control. He does his breathing exercises, and the grief remains. He does his morning meditation, and it abates a little, briefly, but once he uncrosses his legs and stands the grief returns. What happens, he wonders, to *knowledge*, what happened to erase it all from memory so when she turns her head and looks at him she does not see her son? His mother is a statue now, marmoreal, eyes closed and breathing shallowly, and although he kneels beside her bed, eyes wet and sometimes weeping, there is no recognition in her staring face.

He had planned on conversation; he intended to ask for forgiveness, and his mother would assure him there is nothing to forgive. He was going to ask for her blessing, was going to explain how everything would be all right, but there is neither conversation nor forgiveness nor a blessing; there is only silence from the woman on the bed. And nothing is all right.

Frederick, less volatile, tries to keep things in perspective; his mother is feeling no pain. She is, he thinks, aware of what is happening, but it does not seem like a painful awareness, and often in her half sleep she half smiles. His pregnant wife should not, he thinks, spend too much time by his mother's bedside or be over-exposed to the sickroom; far better to spend afternoons with Johnny who requires her attention and who, when their next child is born, will be forced to share. The three points of Frederick's compass—his parents' home in Larchmont, his office in Stamford and his new house in New Canaan—are ones he visits every day, and the effort keeps him occupied. He has no time to mourn.

Johann Hochmann's state of mind is a compound of the two. Like his older son he feels unstrung; like his younger he feels self-control is necessary now. He no longer goes to the office; they do not expect him at work. They tell him not to worry; he should take what time he needs. It is his turn to care for Gisela who always was the one to lavish care on him. His life, he fears, has no meaning without her; they have always been together and he can't and won't continue on alone. At sixty-five it is unfair; she is too young to die. But, given Johann's nature, such sentiments are left unsaid and his fears find no expression. Restraint and reticence are qualities he values, and he tries not to disturb his wife by showing her how much he himself has been disturbed. When asked how he is managing, he always answers "Fine."

Johann shaves carefully each morning and dresses himself with precision and makes certain that his shoes are shined and hair has been properly barbered; he sits for hours in the sick-room, folding and unfolding the *New York Times* and moving his lips as though he were reading the articles he stares at but fails to retain. When he comes downstairs for breakfast he cracks his soft-boiled egg with all the old delicacy, and drinks coffee and spreads butter on his toast—from the edges in to-wards the center of the slice of bread—just the way he used to, but there is no alertness in his attitude, no savor in food's taste. Silence is the order of the day. The members of the household make little conversation and their plans are practical—who will go to the pharmacy to collect prescriptions, who will go gro-cery shopping or contact the substitute nurse or arrange for the physical therapist to come for a massage. They wonder if the patient listens when they speak to her, or of her, and wonder what she hears.

Frederick pays a daily visit, and Peter has come north from North Carolina, where he is living near Asheville; they gather as a family at the dying woman's side. If nothing else, thinks Johann, the Hochmanns are united again; if there's anything to be grateful for, it's how they share this trouble. In this at least they are united: the loss is collective, and shared.

Sarah turns eight months pregnant. Her first trimester had been hard, but for the last four months she has been easy in her body. As if to reassure her, the baby kicks and kicks. Watching the brothers together in their long fraternal wrangle, she tells herself it does not involve her and is instead about a way of life.

Her new weight is all in her stomach, and from the rear she seems unaltered; Peter wants to fuck her in the ass. Her legs are long, her body ripe; he wants to lift her skirt and press himself against her, come and come. He understands this is forbidden, and he must not touch her, but the contiguity of his mother on her deathbed and his sister-in-law about to give birth is something he puzzles on, brooding. Sarah's lustrous russet hair and Gisela's white stubble appear to him as emblems of health and sickness, youth and age. He must, he tells himself, be on his best behavior, but good behavior isn't easy in this dark room where his mother lies and his sister-in-law rocks back and forth in what had been Gisela's rocking chair, her sandals off and legs apart and ankles on the bed.

It rains. While Peter watches her, rocking, Sarah grows self-conscious; she fears his rank animal presence, the disruptive force she knows is in him and can be unleashed. Openly he stares at her until she looks away. When she and her brother-in-law are alone, she knows she has to be careful, the mistress of a colonial house that could come tumbling down. "Can I do anything for you?" he asks, and she tells him "No."

"You're sure?"

"I'm sure," she says.

All through November, he and Frederick continue to bicker and his father asks him—on a daily basis, or so it seems to Peter—what he is planning to do with his life. Since there is no change in his mother's condition, no recognition in her staring eyes but only the sound of her breathing, her watery intake and gurgle, he tells himself he cannot bear it and leaves again for Asheville, wishing the others well.

That afternoon when Sarah comes to ask her blessing for the baby she is carrying, Gisela can barely raise her white head from the pillow and only half opens her eyes. Johann tries to wake her, saying "We have a visitor," until finally she rouses and places her hand on her daughter-in-law's large stomach, and smiles and says, "It will also be a boy."

"You're sure?"

She nods.

"Do you wish it?" Sarah asks.

"I wish . . ." says Gisela, and does not complete the sentence, although her tongue moves soundlessly against her lips.

Then again she shuts her eyes.

It rains. Frederick drives to the house in Larchmont from a storage unit he controls in New Rochelle. *Reliable* is the catch-word of his working life, and he wants to make the business of storage units feel like a safe haven, not a container at risk. The company's motto, *S.O.S.*, means help is at hand, or near at hand, and everything you choose to keep can later on be found. It's how to guard and monitor the past. To know that when you travel your belongings are inviolate, to know that when you retrieve them your things await you undisturbed—these are central tenets for his corporation. They are what J. C. Penney called "The Golden Rule."

In his old age J. C. Penney came to address Student Assembly at the Fieldston School, and Frederick remembers the clothier standing upright on the stage, intoning his motto into the microphone and telling children "Do Unto Others." Tony Koch, who was sitting next to Frederick, whispered, "I'd like to do Nancy Castro," and poked him in the ribs.

By the time he reaches Larchmont, skies have cleared. He pulls into his parents' driveway and, having parked, removes his tie.

Johann grows bone-weary. Even with his sleeping pills, he cannot sleep at night. Instead, he revisits his time with his wife, the years and decades they have spent together. He conjures up the garden in Berlin where he first saw her listening to music, and the walk they took and how she talked of Schubert's syphilis, impressing him with her matter-of-factness, with not so much a worldly knowledge as a knowing acquiescence in the problems of the world. He remembers what she told him of her childhood, the difficult marriage her mother endured, the disapproval of her family, the Bings, and how her grandparents and brothers and her brothers' children all died in the Second World War. He remembers making love to her on the *S.S. Lohengrin*, quietly and carefully so as not to waken Peter, who was sleeping in the alcove of their stateroom, only a few feet away. He sees her profile in the window of the Oldsmobile when he stepped from the commuter train at the Larchmont Station, the car's exhaust billowing grayly about her as though it were a halo, and the way she waved. He recollects her Sachertorte, her body in a bathing suit, her excellence at chess. When she dies, he knows—and knows she will die—there will be little left for him, and he is neither morose nor sentimental about this, only factual in the way she had been factual about Franz Schubert's death.

They have seldom been apart. There have been his business trips, and when she delivered their babies and, once, when Gisela spent three days in the hospital with an appendectomy. For the most part, however, their lives together have been peaceful, unruffled. They have had no tragedies or triumphs other than the ordinary tragedies and triumphs of life lived in private, and he has been content to go unnoticed, a part of what they call the upper middle class. To go unnoticed, ever since Hitler, has been Johann's ambition; and in America he has attained a form of anonymity; the men beside him in the train might nod and smile a moment, but they do not talk.

Predictably, Peter has left. And Frederick—who does visit faithfully, and who often brings his wife—is elsewhere occupied and therefore of limited use. The truth is, Johann understands, he must go through this by himself, and there is no one to turn to now that his parents are dead. So again he must engage the daily round of things, the coffee with two lumps of sugar and the newspaper and morning walk much like the constitutional his father used to take. But even his walk through the village of Larchmont has lost its power to refresh him; his wife is lying dying and he cannot keep himself from sitting at her side.

He clears out his desk in the office. He is old enough to re-tire, and his pension is sufficient, and he cannot bring himself any longer to care about Kolinsky brushes or Chunking two-inch bristles or what they import now from India, wigs. Henry Mayer too has plans to retire, but he has been recently married and says his young bride wants a family and what should he, Henry, do about that, he feels too old, too old. Johann remem-bers a time in the Greenbriar Resort when Henry passed him in the corridor, a redhead on his arm, and after they were in-troduced and Johann raised an eyebrow, Henry said, "*Sie sind überverheiratet*, Herr Hochmann."

He said this in German—"You are too completely married, Mr. Hochmann"—because he did not want the girl on his arm to understand the sentence, or perhaps he was reminding his co-worker of Gisela at home. In any case the lifelong bachelor has become a married man, and the devoted husband is soon to be a widower, alone. He remembers the way she would say to their sons, "I tell you, such is life."

She dies. Johann will continue for five more years and die at seventy-one. The usual case, he understands, is that a wife outlives her husband, but in the Hochmann family the reverse has proven true. Women everywhere live longer than men, but Benno was a widower as he himself has now become a widower, and though there will be several women who want to keep him company he remains *überverheiratet*. In his final years, as he himself grows elderly, he thinks of Gisela when young, and she does not grow older by his side. Instead she is the girl he wooed and won in 1931 in his parents' leafy garden and then, after the concert, when they went for a walk in the neighborhood park; she is his life's companion, stepping resolutely on to the gangplank of the *S.S. Lohengrin* and stepping bravely off again in the harbor of Havana.

Johann remembers driving to the building where her father lived, in Forest Hills, when she had been pregnant with Fred-erick. Bravely, again, she walked up the stairs; he sat in a coffee shop across the street, trying to read the newspaper, awaiting her return. When at last Gisela reappeared and threw her arms around his neck, he knew how hard the interview had been, how much she missed her mother and how little she wanted to take up the burden that was her father, Simon.

But Gisela had done so, as she took up other burdens; she was uncomplaining, always, about the household duties or the demands of homework or the daily round of grocery shopping and cleaning and cooking. Now she no longer performs them and old habits fall away, but in the evening lamplight—it grows dark by five o'clock on these late-autumn afternoons—he tells himself their forty years together were a gift. To ask for more would have been greedy, Johann knows: enough must be enough.

Still, she walks beside him in his mind, and sometimes he hears himself talking, telling Gisela the wind is colder than he had expected and she should bring a wrap. Or telling her to pay attention to the chirrup of a cardinal who built a nest in the Norfolk pine tree just beyond the dining-room window, its repeated call. Or telling her his right knee is a bother, and wondering if finally the cane he uses when he goes out walking is a help or hindrance to his knee.

In the end the difference between help and hindrance fades; the distinction does not matter, as he told Henry Mayer and the redhead in the hall. He had tried to explain it, and failed. If you live with a woman for decades, and you love her wholly, then her absence does not matter because she is not absent; you can feel her presence, always, in the room. When she dies he does not miss her in the way he had expected, because Gisela remains unspeaking at his side. He knows without her needing to tell him if the room is overheated or too cold for comfort, if the sandwich he is offered is a meal she would enjoy.

Therefore he becomes a solitary, talking to his wife. He explains to her that Richard Nixon lives a life of exile in San Clemente, and has been disgraced. He tells her that Heinz Kissinger continues in the cabinet, working with the President whose name is the name of a car. Johann's solitude is broken only by the visits of his family and, when he grows too ill to live alone, the noises of his grandsons on the second floor. He lies above them, listening; they laugh and take showers and shout. In the end he will die in New Canaan, attended by his son and daughter-in-law, and thinking of their long shared journey to America and thinking his wife lies beside him, incorporeal, as once he lay beside her in their cabin on the Atlantic crossing, wakeful and then briefly, fitfully asleep.

A Visit
1981

FREDERICK'S ELDER BROTHER does not visit often; his visits are a trial. When Peter arrives at the house in New Canaan, he carries with him somehow both a whiff of disapproval and the readiness to be disapproved of. It is as though—with his growth of beard and shabby coat, the after-odor of sweat, beer, and marijuana—he wants to provoke some suggestion that he should clean himself up. His matted hair and mismatched socks are banners he waves proudly, a declaration of independence. Your rules, he seems to be saying, aren't rules by which I play. I dare you, he seems to be saying, to tell me the way to behave . . .

In any case, it's a challenge—one Frederick tries to meet. When his prodigal brother comes to the door, he makes him welcome, always, and always invites him to stay.

Sarah is less generous; she calls a spade a spade. "You two are the same size," she says. "Why don't you give Peter some clothes?"

"He wears what he wants to," Frederick says.

"Your parents would be turning in their grave. Their graves."

"They loved him."

"Not to hear him tell it. When he talks about your childhood, it's mostly misery."

"That's *his* version, yes."

Frederick is forty-two, Peter forty-seven. Their paths have long diverged. It still shocks the younger brother to remember bygone intimacies; until he turned thirteen, he and Peter shared a room. He and Sarah share a bed, of course, but with the exception of his wife he's slept beside his brother more than anyone else in the world, and he does not like to acknowledge how distant he now feels. It is 1981. The standards of the middle class are standards Peter has renounced—a drifter, a man without a steady job and with no fixed address. The kindness of strangers, he likes to tell Frederick, is something you shouldn't depend on—but more often than not it's reliable; just stick out your thumb and you'll get where you're going to, bro.

"Uptight" and "hip" are also words he continues to use, and with no seeming irony, a Jewish boy-man whose corona of curls has grown thin and gray. In the 1960s and the early 1970s, he had been part of the protest movement—chanting "Flower Power" and "Make Love, Not War." But nearly twenty years have passed since he hitched a ride on Ken Kesey's bus, and in Ronald Reagan's America this wanderer looks lost. Peter Hochmann is—no better term for it—*peculiar*, and his jaunty refusal to shower feels like a kind of reproach. He does not praise or value what Frederick and Sarah have over time acquired: the house and art, the garden, and the cars so carefully maintained. Your brother is, says Sarah, a case of arrested development; he took one acid trip too many and never quite returned.

With their two sons, however, Peter seems at ease. John and Daniel whoop with pleasure when their uncle shambles down for lunch on Saturday—having arrived the night before and sleeping until noon. He has a deck of cards in his pocket, and he does card tricks for the boys—producing four aces or shuffling the deck with precision and guessing which card they select. He drinks coffee in great gulps and eats more than his share of the ham, but John and Daniel linger at table in a way they wouldn't otherwise, and they laugh at Peter's antics and invite him when he's finished to come up to their rooms.

"Are you all right?" asks Frederick.

"What does that mean?" asks his brother.

"I mean, are you healthy? Feeling OK?"

"What makes you ask?"

"This isn't twenty questions or some sort of inquisition. I

was—we were—hoping things are easy for you . . ."

"Easy?"

"All right. Excuse me for asking; how long are you planning to stay?"

"Planning?"

"I know, you don't like to plan . . ."

Then the engine of his brother's rhetoric kicks in. Peter says that *planning* isn't part of it, the best laid plans of mice and men gang aft agley, or hasn't Freddy kept up with his Burns, and has he noticed how—as long as we're being bookish, as long as you want me to quote things—we've got three years to go till 1984 and George Orwell's prophecy? In case you haven't noticed or maybe need reminding our country is two countries now, and one of them is starving while the other's full of fat cats skimming off the cream. In case you haven't noticed or maybe need reminding he got it just exactly right, did Orwell, Georgie-Porgie: Big Brother's watching *you*.

Myself, he continues, I've given up on the illusion—the *delusion*, really—that we can shape our future, not to mention present, and there's reality to swallow, like for example this ham—because who could have predicted yesterday how this morning I'd be eating it, be sitting here at table and with such a tasty breakfast? Lunch. A meal of meat. But the point is plans don't enter in, or not anymore for me. It's the ostrich principle, it's sticking your head in the sand trap out beyond the eighteenth tee, which is what this country's doing, or anyhow the plutocrats are, the ones who golf, a good walk spoiled, because closing your eyes in daytime, bro, doesn't make it night. Denying what you see. And if you think that actor in the White House has the slightest goddamn notion of the part that he's supposed to play you've got another think coming because the flow is all, is *everything*, you should give up pretending to *plan* . . .

Sarah wields the vacuum cleaner loudly in the living room, and the Hochmann brothers therefore sit alone.

"More coffee?" Frederick asks.

Peter advances his cup. His eyes are red-rimmed, and the cup is shaking, and he starts to cough. "I sometimes think," he says, "you don't really *hear* what I'm saying or trying to tell you: this life of yours"—with his free left hand he waves, encompassing the kitchen—"is gone. Done. Finished. Over. *Kaput.*"

"Why?"

"Can't you *hear* it?" His cup clatters on the saucer. "The Requiem Mass."

Peter stays. The autumn solstice comes and goes, the moon grows full and wanes. The maples by the driveway shed the last of their encumbrances, the flowerbeds get blanketed in mulch. Frederick drives to his office in Stamford and deals with the business of warehouse construction and leasing that enables him to pay for his sons' school tuitions, the new air-conditioning system, and the driveway paved with brick. Sarah too stays busy with domestic life—silk curtains for the dining room, a committee she chairs on the public library's expansion project, piano lessons for the boys and, when John loses interest in the piano, the clarinet. They have a cleaning lady and a handyman called Shirley Brown who helps her with the household chores—floor waxing and storm windows and the checklist of seasonal maintenance tasks. On Saturdays the Hochmanns entertain each other—going to the movies or a concert or a play.

Meantime, Peter sleeps. He stays in his bedroom under the eaves for hour after hour, sleeping more than they think possible and snoring loudly so they know he is in fact abed. In the afternoon he stumbles down in what for other men might pass for pajamas—his sweatshirt and frayed shorts and socks with holes—ransacking the refrigerator as though he were a college freshman on vacation, scarfing down great quantities of cheese and bologna and mayonnaise, then leaving his dishes unwashed. In the living room he practices his card tricks and on the lawn plays Frisbee with the boys when they come back from school, or basketball if that's what they want—dribbling heavily beneath the hoop set up by the garage door. When he comes inside again, sweat streaming down his neck and arms, he reeks.

"Do you have something against, oh I don't know"—Sarah asks—"a shower?"

"Why?"

"Isn't it working, the shower I mean?"

"Where?"

"The one next to your bedroom. We could have it fixed . . ."

He shrugs. "If cleanliness is your thing, I'd be happy to help you clean up."

"I'm fine. I took a bath this morning."

"Now you mention it," says Peter, "the stairwell could use a coat of paint."

"We weren't," says Sarah, "discussing the *house* . . ."

These are hints he refuses to take. Instead he speaks about the cleanliness and godliness that bodhisattvas represent and can even in this present day incarnate; last year, for example, he met a man in Arizona who in the hollowed-out heights of the hills was eating maize and drinking goats' milk only and who in the lotus position could wrap his beard around his ankles. Once when Peter visited they heard a jeep on the dry roadbed of Canyon de Chelly from a distance of ten, maybe twelve miles away, and the hermit-seer understood by the low pitch of the engine that a contingent of Park Rangers was coming to evict and maybe to arrest him. But the man stayed anyway, so after some discussion and, on his part, passive resistance, the three apparatchiks had to carry him—spread-eagled, arms akimbo— out. They stowed this visionary in the back seat of a jeep. The point of all our teaching is, Peter says, to hear the din approaching with its threatful music but sit still while it advances, staying poised for what is sure to happen, expectant but resigned. It was water, wasn't it, that drove the Anastasi to extinction way back when, or rather the absence of water, and so this holy man was waiting cross-legged, poised and yet resigned to it, white beard wrapped around his ankles, for the arrival of the Merry Prank- sters in their present bureaucratic guise, all these light-years later driving up into the canyon not as outlaws but Park Rangers— uniformed toadies of the government—to bathe themselves in dust and lave themselves in near-total aridity, which is what this country's come to or will come to soon enough.

"What are you *talking* about," Frederick asks, and his brother nods and smiles. He moves without interruption from common sense to nonsense, from logic to a kind of psycho-babble, and you cannot guess to start with where a discussion will end. Emerging from long silence he grows garrulous—then subsides into silence again. He has not visited Connecticut, he reminds his hosts, in two years, or nearly, and now seems in no rush to move along.

"How much longer will he stay, I wonder," Sarah asks her husband.

"I can't throw him out."

"That's not what I'm asking . . ."

"Remember the line by Robert Frost? 'Home is where they have to take you in.'"

She stares at him. Prettily, she lifts her shoulders and then lets them fall. "He helps with the boys' homework, that much we can be grateful for . . ."

"And sets them such a good example . . ."

"Don't joke," she says. "I wonder what he's teaching them. Or telling them about the world, our part in it . . ."

"Do you want me to interfere?"

"No."

Peter listens to the *Goldberg Variations* and Sly and the Family Stone. Sarah plays the piano, practicing her Mendelssohn and Chopin and Gershwin, and if she plays a tune he knows he sings along loudly, off-key. At the kitchen table, he bangs his spoon on the rim of his plate as might a two-year-old, beating out intricate rhythms, then wiping his mouth on his sleeve. At night they hear him pacing in the upstairs hallway; he sleeps with a light on, always, so they never can be certain if he sleeps. Sarah worries that the fugue-state Peter enters is one from which he won't or can't return.

Doesn't *want* to return is, Frederick suspects, closer to the truth of it. His brother seems at ease with idleness, sitting hour after hour staring at a paperback he fails to read, although his lips do move. He scans pages of the newspaper meticulously,

one by one, then folds them back into their first configuration
and sets the paper down. He is happy, he tells Frederick at dinner, for the chance to deal with *issues* he's been having, and
when Sarah asks what issues he smiles and shakes his head.

With the boys, however, Peter has no trouble talking; John
at ten and Daniel at six are on his wave-length, clearly, and
they pose no threat. The three of them spend afternoons and
evenings watching the pennant race and then the World Series—the Yankees and the Dodgers confronting each other for a
third time in five seasons—and he tells John and Daniel about
a subway series, what it was like in the 1950s when the Dodgers
and Giants and Yankees all had been based in New York. The
Polo Grounds and Ebbets Field and Yankee Stadium, says Peter,
and pauses, remembering, then shakes himself out of his reverie
and starts heckling the players on TV as though he were sitting
behind them in the bleachers or up above home plate.

The Dodgers win in six. The MVPs are Ron Cey, Pedro
Guerrero, and Steve Yeager. Watching, Peter discourses on ad-
versity, the way the team rebounded to take the series from two
down, the fact that "Guerrero" is a Federal entity in Mexico
named for Vicente Guerrero, and Acapulco is a part of it except
you want to avoid Acapulco, he could tell them stories of his
time in a hotel in the center of that tourist-trap, the mescal and
panhandlers and *Federales* everywhere, the overlay of glitter on
the misery of the people, the drug lords and the ladies in their
Maseratis and the one-armed children begging in the streets, oh
yes, *sí*, say can you *sí*—but we were talking, weren't we, about
the way Branch Rickey with his sponsorship of Jackie Robinson
made a difference, finally, to the whole system of apartheid in
America and how John and Danny had better remember what
it means for a national pastime to have excluded black athletes
from equal and full participation, but what else is new, the
black men in the stadium are those who hawk pretzels and beer.

They nod. They take his outbursts equably and pay close attention to what happens on the screen. Players knock their bats
against their cleats, settling into stances on the pitching mound
or at home plate, and cross themselves and spit. In the dugout,

watching, their teammates spit in unison and scratch at their armpits and scowl. Peter studies the signals offered by the third-base coach—a hand on chest, a twice-tugged ear, a slapped cheek or wrist or right foot scuffing dirt three times—and tells his nephews this is a code they must learn how to crack. "The whole thing's clear as clear can be if you just know how to look."

When Frederick says, "I can't read signs," his elder brother looks triumphal. "Exactly. That's what I'm trying to say."

In November he declares himself. "I want my share."

"Share?"

He nods.

"Of what?"

"You know," says Peter.

"I don't, no, know."

"Don't kid a kidder," he says.

"What are we *talking* about?"

"Our parents. What they left us."

"What did they leave us?"

"Inheritance." Peter coughs. "That's what I'm here for. My share."

"Your share of what?"

"Dad's legacy. His money and his furniture. The jewelry Mom wore."

Frederick stares at his brother. "He died two *years* ago. And the will was settled then, remember?"

"The fatted calf, bro. It's what I'm after, what you're keeping."

"Dad's last will and testament divided everything in half. Precisely. And since Mom died before him, his testament was final. You received your share of it; there wasn't all that much."

"Don't kid a kidder," Peter repeats. He scratches his stomach and yawns.

"Am I missing something here? Is there something you're not telling me? I thought you were the one who, I don't know, hates property . . ."

"But I love *justice*, bro."

Frederick restrains himself. "There was an executor. What was his name—Pincussohn? Yes, 'Pink' Pincussohn, Dad's friend. And he was a lawyer and followed the instructions to a T. I don't know how you spent your half . . ."

"I want that desk." Peter points to a brown polished Biedermeier desk in the corner of the living room—a cabinet with ivory insets for the keyholes in the drawers and black purfling at the edges of six shelves. On the wooden shelf that, folding out, becomes a writing panel with a leather blotter and a faded green felt surface there stands an inkwell and an ashtray on display. "I want to use it the way he did."

"You're serious?"

"I'm serious."

"And is there somewhere you plan to call home? A place you'll keep that desk?"

"Right on. Absolutely. *Yes.*"

Then Peter spirals off again into his seamless babble, telling Frederick their furniture is what we used to call chattel, the very emblem of ownership, the mark and curse of capitalistic endeavor, and though he has admittedly been on the road these years he's not been a true nomad, has always had a roof at least to lie beneath, a floor to lay his pallet on, has not been what you'd call a homeless person, except his homes were various, and carried with him everywhere the memory of Dad behind that desk, his ledger and the double-entry columns of figures inked in dark blue by his Parker pen, or was it maybe a Mont Blanc, doing whatever the hell he did on weekends and at tax time, the holy grail of—what's the word?—*accountability*, keeping the ship of stateliness afloat. And though it may seem strange to you, bro, I *am* in fact the first-born son, the one who by the laws of primogeniture should come into the title and the land and holdings because things change and I alone am come again to take my proper place.

"The will was a simple one. Right down the middle . . ."

"You want me to cut it? Take a chain-saw to Dad's desk?"

Frederick makes a movement of impatience. "This isn't like you, Peter."

"No?"

"Not so I've noticed."

"'Pi-ink' Pincussohn—our father's chosen instrument. His willing accomplice, more like it. What makes you think the division was fair?"

"What makes you think it wasn't?"

Peter shakes his head. He lays his index finger up along his nose and for an instant looks astonishingly like their father: the same brown eyes, the hooked nose and the wattled neck. It would have been Johann's birthday, Frederick remembers, he would have been seventy-four. Five years after the death of his wife, he died of emphysema and—so his son believes—despair. Consorting with his fellow refugees, playing chess and drinking schnapps, he kept an empty cigar case and pipe pouch always in his pocket; at his bedside there had been a pack of cigarettes, unopened and unlit. For the final months of his illness, their father lived with Frederick and Sarah in the room Peter occupies now.

"All right. Let's drop it."

"What, the desk?"

"The subject."

Peter smiles. Again, he shakes his head. Johann Hochmann kept a suitcase packed with "necessaries" in the coat closet in the downstairs entrance hall. At Temple or the dinner table he would reminisce about the time before the Third Reich and the Holocaust, the *bürgerliche* comforts of his parents' household in Berlin. His sons were raised on the assumption that their status was precarious, provisional, and could be revoked.

Johann never lost his German accent or his habit of wearing a vest. He took the train from Larchmont daily to Manhattan and then back again by dinnertime, carrying his briefcase and the newspaper and, all winter, a scarf and gloves and hat. Their mother would drive him to the train, and then again collect him, and sometimes in the early evening the brothers went along, getting out of the car and competing to see which one could spot their father first. Stepping down to the platform, he waved. Then they would hurry to his side, a race that Peter always won, and walking to the waiting car he would buy them *Sports Illustrated* or *Spiderman* and purchase a cigar.

The man who ran the newsstand was black, and blind; the boys called him "Old Black Joe." He wore knitted caps and plaid shirts and fingerless gloves. From his kiosk by the parking lot he distributed the *New York Times*, the *New York Post*, and magazines and comic books and candy. A German shepherd lay at his feet in all kinds of weather, panting and watchful or licking his paws.

"Can you imagine," Peter asks, "how easy it would be— would have been, I mean—to steal a comic book or chewing gum or any old magazine, really, from that guy in the newspaper stand? Joe. Why didn't we do it, I wonder, what kept us from simply lifting something we wanted from the rack and running off?"

"Decency?"

"The fear of being caught. That dog of his, remember?"

"I remember," Frederick says.

Peter ceases to covet the desk. Instead he focuses attention on an album of family photographs, then the chair in the upstairs hallway, then a Persian carpet from their parents' house. Turn by turn he claims half ownership or asks to take these objects with him when he goes. Yet he also says how glad he is to have secured a bed, and he wants his brother and sister-in-law to know how thankful he's been feeling for safe haven in a storm.

"Storm?"

"The universal shit storm," Peter says. He clenches his right fist. "You are weighed in the balances and found wanting."

"Excuse me?"

"'*Mene mene, tekel, upharsin.*' As grandpa used to tell us."

"Come off it, Peter," Sarah says. "You can stop speaking in tongues."

"It's the Book of Daniel."

"And?"

"We all are found wanting, OK?"

Again that night, Sarah asks her husband how long he thinks his brother is planning to remain. "Does it bother you?" he asks, and she says, "It depends what you mean by *bother*? Does he stick his tongue in my mouth when he kisses me? No."

"I haven't seen him kiss you."

"You haven't been watching," she says.

This troubles him. He spends long hours at the office, and the idea of the couple alone together in the house now suddenly feels fraught. His work requires, of an average, one out-of-town trip each week. On days he has an early flight and must be at the airport by seven o'clock, his wife remains in bed. He brings her coffee and the newspaper and strokes her sleep-rumpled hair.

"I'll miss you," Sarah says. "Come back as soon as you can."

"Take care of the children," he says.

She rouses herself to wake the boys, to make their breakfasts and prepare their lunch-bags and chauffeur them to school. She is home again by eight-fifteen, and the hours loom. Frederick pictures his brother in bed. He imagines his wife in the bathtub, and Peter walking in. He puts these thoughts out of his mind. Nonetheless the thoughts return. He imagines the pair at leisure upstairs—with no one but the maid or hired man to complicate their privacy or come between them if they choose to come together. Peter is, he likes to say, "a rake and rambling man." He never did get married but has lived with a series of women, and some of them he talks about—crazy Lucy with her thing for dogs, Rebecca with the handcuffs and the ankle ties. In a world of needy ladies, he tells Frederick, there's a world of choice . . .

He watches his wife carefully. As the weeks wear on she seems less guarded in his brother's presence, more willing to laugh at his jokes. At times she grows even a little flirtatious: prodding their guest's belly and telling him he needs more exercise, then on his birthday buying him a bottle of cologne. Frederick does not question her fidelity, but the image of the two of them in their shared solitude beleaguers him: the man half naked and shambling through rooms, the woman in her robe. John and Daniel trade punches with their uncle or slap each other's outstretched hands in a game about reaction-time: who can move faster, or feint a slapping motion and cause the other to flinch. Frederick does not play. A man's home is his castle, he reminds himself, and feels a small stirring of rage at how his brother takes their hospitality for granted. Hospitality has limits, he wants to say to Peter; get a job or get a life or get the hell out of here, *bro*.

Nonetheless he holds his tongue. He watches while their visitor scratches at his armpit, yawning, or ruffles the curls at the back of his neck, and wants to say OK, enough, I may be my brother's keeper but I'm not keeping a zoo. And indeed when Peter shuffles down to eat or join them for their evening martini he nuzzles Sarah's cheek the way a puppy or a monkey might, crowding up against her breast. Once, when Peter fondles Sarah, she looks across the table as if to say to her husband, *What are you going to do?*

The sight of the pair of them sharing a muffin or a pot of coffee makes Frederick both glad and angry, and he wants to say, *Thus far, no further, you're crossing a line.* But it is not clear to him what line his brother crosses; there's a harmlessness to Peter's antics that makes it hard to argue with him, although it is not hard to disapprove.

On the Day of the Dead in November, Peter shaves. His cheeks are pink and smooth. Then he lets his beard grow out again but persists in wearing his Halloween shirt—a black shirt with an orange pumpkin and a skull and crossbones stitched in white. He wears this shirt uninterruptedly for—Frederick counts—ten days. As Thanksgiving nears he tells himself things will have to change, and if Peter wants to rent a room somewhere in downtown New Canaan he'll subsidize the rent. He remembers how, two months ago, the doorbell rang and, opening up, he found his brother on the stoop and had not been unhappy. It had felt like the start of a chapter, a brand-new story to tell . . .

But it's the same old story, nothing new. They play their

parts over again. It's resistance and resentment and the sense that Peter can convey of having been ignored or—in the time of blessings, when their father lay on his death-bed—dismissed. That he was not there to receive them—was instead in California, living in Bolinas although Frederick had informed him their father lay dying—seems, by Peter's reckoning, someone else's fault. "You could have sent me a ticket," he says. "You should have insisted I come."

"It wasn't my business," Frederick says. "I *told* you it was nearly over."

"I'd heard that before," Peter says. "But while we're on the subject there's something else I need to know."

"What?"

"Why are you living in New Canaan? Why did you choose it, I mean?"

"Excuse me?"

"There's no *Jews* here, brother. And you're a Jew, remember?"

"Thanks for reminding me," says Frederick.

"'If I forget thee, O Jerusalem . . .'" Peter bites his fingernail.

For the Thanksgiving celebration there are five of them, and Sam and Judy Olesker, who have no children of their own, and the Masons from across the street with their two teenage daughters, Anne-Marie and Rose. Sarah therefore sets the table for eleven people; it's her favorite holiday, she tells Peter when he asks, the one without religious overtones or overmuch commercial fuss, the one where you give thanks for bounty and hope to make it through the coming winter with sufficient food.

She cooks for days. She prepares creamed onions and a puree of chestnuts and various forms of cranberry relish; she bakes pumpkin pie and apple pie and a chocolate pie for the boys. She has become a serious cook, and she brines the turkey and makes elaborate stuffing and two kinds of sweet potatoes as well as mashed potatoes, since Sam Olesker prefers them, and squash and Brussels sprouts. She bakes potato bread, and French baguettes, and when Peter says, hey wait a minute, you're not feeding *armies* here, she says that's not the point. What *is* the point, he inquires, and Sarah says the point is there's abundance and so we should give thanks.

"The hell of a thing to be grateful for . . ."

"What?"

"That Samoset brought in the sheaves and saved the pilgrims from starvation and by way of exchange they—*we*—gave him blankets infested with smallpox . . ."

"You've got it wrong," says Frederick. "It wasn't the pilgrims who did that to Samoset."

"No?"

"It was the pioneers later. New England pilgrims were grateful; they wouldn't have made it their first winter without the help of Indians who understood the land."

"I'm a vegetarian," says Peter. "You didn't know that, did you?"

They stare at him.

"I am," he insists. "I haven't tasted meat in years. Hadn't before I arrived here, I mean. It's just the ham on that first morning was so, so *evident*, so clearly what you wanted to serve. It would have been insulting to refuse."

"And everything since then?" asks Sarah.

He spreads his hands. "Politeness. But I've had enough of it—eating God's creatures, I mean. The cured pig, the fatted calf. I won't have any turkey tomorrow."

"All right."

Frederick sees an opening. "It would be simpler, wouldn't it, for you to do your eating somewhere else?"

His brother nods.

"We've run out the string here, don't you think?"

He nods again.

"If there's help we can be with your moving . . ."

"A storage bin, maybe? One of your famous warehouse units. I've got objects to store now, possessions."

"You do?"

"Amen to that, bro," says Peter. "And I won't be eating meat."

When the Oleskers and Masons arrive, Frederick lights a fire in the living room; the guests drink Bloody Marys or, in the case of the children, cider, and nibble on olives and nuts. Unaccountably, Peter has purchased and is wearing a fresh white shirt and tie. He wears a tweed jacket and dry-cleaned flannel trousers also, and has shined his shoes. Shaved, he looks respectable. "You clean up nice," says Sarah smilingly, and she pats his arm. At four o'clock, the adults and the teenagers and children gather in the dining room and, according to Sarah's seating arrangement, locate their place-cards and chairs.

Frederick proceeds to carve the turkey. He is happy to perform this task, and does it well, separating out the dark meat from the white and piling two separate platters with legs and second joints and breast meat and giblets and wings. His brother does refuse the meat but helps himself with abandon to the cranberry relish and sweet potatoes and squash. Once the company have served themselves, he calls for their attention, clicking his knife on his glass.

The table falls silent; he offers a toast. What we are doing, Peter announces, is living off the bounty of the heirs of Cesar Chavez, the legion of underpaid wetbacks and farm workers, the women abused—he gestures at the Mason daughters, *forgive me, girls, but rape is rape*—at border crossings everywhere, who are helpless to avoid that fate because they need Amerika for their measly paycheck and have to cross the border for the wages not of seeming sin but to feed their families, those children back in Mexico who do not have such access and have nothing on the table, what we call the *groaning* board, because our network of delivery does not offer to its poor and hungry and downtrodden any comfort or deliverance, the elaborate system of commerce and consumption and corruption that arrives at this house *here, now*. So what I want and need to say is thank you, thank you everyone—my brother and his beautiful wife, their boys, my friends, you neighbors—because we are the beneficiaries of the poor and the downtrodden and hungry and our ground-time here is brief.

"I'll drink to that," says Frederick.

For a moment the two brothers stare across the table at each other with such frank enmity that the Masons and Oleskers turn away. Anne-Marie wears braces on her upper teeth and her younger sister has acne; John and Daniel sit across from them and study their full plates.

Sarah raises her glass of white wine. "Happy Thanksgiving," she says.

The guests lift their glasses and drink.

"What I'm trying to tell you," Peter continues, "is there are benisons and bounty here abounding—*bounty, abounding,* ha!—and I for one am grateful for the chance to talk about it, since my mouth will soon be stuffed, ¬but have you ever asked yourselves why table manners matter, why we keep our knives with their blades facing inward-edge to the plate? The reason, I mean, why everybody here at table can assume no one will attack them with a sharpened knife, and no I haven't been drinking and am hip to what you're wondering, maybe, but do want to remind you of monks in the refectory, their manuals for gentle persons, persons of quality, *quality,* who were taught not to be boorish but comport themselves like angels which is why the word for guest in French is also the word meaning host. Welcome, welcome everyone." And Peter nods smilingly around the table as though he *were* the host.

Wildly, for an instant, Frederick wants to fight. How dare his brother spoil their meal with his nonsensical sermons, his discourse on rape and farm workers and table manners and knives? He wants to call Peter out. He wants to take him in the yard and challenge him and finish their argument once and for all. *No,* you cannot have the desk, *No,* you cannot have my wife, *No,* you cannot have the admiration of my sons or sleep here any longer; it's over, *Es ist vollbracht.* That was what their father said when finishing an argument; those were Jesus's final words upon the cross in Calvary, the end of things: *Fuck off!*

And then he remembers a spring morning when he and

Peter had been boys—six and eleven, possibly, or seven and twelve years old. They were walking into Larchmont to go to the Stonecrest Apartments where their grandparents lived; there was a family gathering, and they were allowed to walk by themselves and therefore to arrive a little late. Their mother and father had driven ahead. The day was mild. It had rained the night before, and neighborhood lawns glistened greenly; there were little pools of rain or dew in the leaves of the skunk cabbages and crabgrass unmowed by the side of the street. The walk took fifteen minutes: two rights, and then a left.

He had been, he remembers, avoiding the cracks in the paving and trying to clear the mottled gray pavement squares two at a time. Peter strode in front. He looked up at the sound of voices and saw two boys stop his brother—not quite as tall as Peter, but older and taller than Frederick, and not wearing Sunday clothes. They sported dirty baseball caps and windbreakers; one of them was fat. They were not boys he knew. Standing on the sidewalk, the pair of them blocked Peter's way, and taunted him; as Frederick neared he understood the meeting was not friendly and would maybe be a fight.

"You live here?" one of the boys was asking.

"Yes."

"Where?"

Vaguely, Peter pointed up the street.

"You got a match?"

"No."

"You got a watch?"

"It's ten o'clock."

"You got a dollar, maybe? Five?"

The fat one jostled his brother, and Frederick slipped by. He could run ahead, he told himself, and ask for help—but the village was too far away, and he saw no adults walking, so he turned and waited, hoping Peter too could somehow slip around the pair who menaced him. Forlornly, he searched for a stick. He heard his brother saying, "You don't scare me," and then something else, and the thin boy shoved at Peter, who pushed the thin boy back. There was a pause, a gathering in, a

moment he can still remember when everything seemed peril-
ous. "Get lost," said one of the assailants, and Peter said, "You
too."

A car drove by. From the opposite direction, a second car
approached. Then as if by prearrangement the two boys stepped
aside and let his brother go. He walked between them slowly,
not turning or looking behind. As he reached the point where
Frederick stood, Peter made a dismissive motion, flapping his
hand at the wrist. "Thanks for your help," he said.

They continued together unspeaking and reached the Stonecrest Apartments and took the elevator to the fourth floor
where their parents and grandparents waited and had *Lox und
Schinken* for brunch.

The shame of it returns. He had failed his brother utterly,
had managed to escape a nearing confrontation and had not
offered help. Now he looks at John and Daniel and the Masons'
daughters—the girls in ruffled dresses and his sons wearing
bowties and blazers—but what Frederick sees are ten-year-olds
in baseball caps, their blustering menace, the threat of a fight.
When Anne-Marie says "Can I have the butter, please?" he passes butter to the girl and swallows a mouthful of wine. He wants
to say to Peter, "I forgive you; will you forgive me?" but the Oleskers and the Masons are discussing *A Taste of Honey* and *This
Was Burlesque* and *The Life and Adventures of Nicholas Nickleby*
and *The World of Sholem Aleichem*—Broadway shows they have
seen or are planning to see—and whether or not it's worth it to
buy tickets for *Medea* and *Othello* and *Agnes of God*.

"I go for the fun of it," says Sam Olesker. "For an evening's
entertainment and not to be *improved*."

"Heaven knows he could use some improving," says Judy,
and reaches—fondly, caressingly, or so it seems—for her husband's hand. Her wedding ring is hammered gold, her engagement ring a diamond so large it looks like costume jewelry, and
the bracelets on her wrist complement her necklace: strands of
pearls.

"I mean it," Sam insists. "The world is difficult enough to
deal with on a daily basis so I don't need to go to the theater for

grief—*Othello, Medea*, why bother?—I've got enough trouble at home."

"'The green-eyed monster,'" Judy says. She explains this to the Mason girls: "One play's about a husband who kills his wife because he suspects her—wrongly, wrongly—of being unfaithful. And one about a wife who wants to punish her husband because he is in fact unfaithful. So in revenge she slaughters her own children."

"See, that's what I mean," says Sam. "Who needs it?"

"The punishment fitting the crime," Harriet Mason offers. "Except that's *The Mikado*. Right?"

"More stuffing?" Sarah asks.

"We're reading *Othello*," says Anne-Marie, "in Mr. D'Amelio's class. That bit about the handkerchief is *silly*, isn't it, how could anyone become a murderer because of a *handkerchief*, really?"

"'Beware, my lord, of jealousy,'" says Judy to Dick Mason, and lifts her glass and drinks.

Not for the first time Frederick wonders what she would be like in bed and whether she and Sam do have a happy marriage; their easy banter seems practiced, and he cannot tell for certain if they mean or do not mean it when they disagree.

At the end of the meal, guests disperse. He says to his brother, "I like your tie," and Peter says, "When in New Canaan, do as the Canaanites do." They have attained, Frederick tells himself, an understanding—or if not understanding at least a precarious peace. He helps Sarah with the dishes while Peter and the boys go out in the chill dark to play a spotlit game of Horse; he hears the ball dribbling, their laughter.

Sarah uses Tupperware for the leftover stuffing and turkey and yams, and between them they empty the final two bottles of wine. There is a half glass of red, a glass of white remaining, and they toast each other.

"Happy Thanksgiving," he offers.

"It's good to have your brother here. I'm glad we let him stay."

In December Peter tells them he will leave. "No one but a Puritan would winter in this climate, it's too damn cold," he says.
"I'm a Jew and used to suffering but I'm not

a godforsaken Puritan and might try Miami Beach. A little
coconut oil, a lot of rum, a suite in the Fontainebleau; what
could be bad?"

"You're not serious?" asks Frederick, and Peter tells him,
"No."

"You don't have to leave," says Sarah.

He looks at her. "I know."

"So what are you planning to do," she asks, "and where will
you go?"

Watching his wife watching Peter, Frederick feels uncertain.
There is supplication in her voice, a note he has not heard. Peter
says he's heading south to the Florida Keys, or maybe the Georgia Sea Islands, or back to Yucatan.

"And how will you get there?" she asks.

"The point is," declares his brother, "to grow easy with
rootlessness, a word we're using less and less, but I wonder as
I wander—remember that song way back when, the guy with
the high voice who sang it, what was his name, Alfred Deller,
Richard Dyer-Bennet?—why we who have so little time should
spend it sitting still. The way the two of you, the four of you"—
he ticks off their numbers on fingers—"are willing to weather
the winter when somewhere else it's spring. So what I'm after is
a porch with one good rocking chair and the chance to finish
Spengler, that laugh-out-loud book of his about the *Decline of
the West*. And to get ready to doing without . . ."

"What will you live on?" Sarah asks. "Can you afford it?"

"Yes. I'll miss the kids, though."

"They'll miss *you*," she says.

"So maybe they should come along." The glint of madness is
in his brother's eye again, the wild insouciance. "You were ter-
rific to be with"—he puts his hand on Sarah's arm—"but don't
double-knot those apron strings because boys will be boys."

"I won't," she says.

"You promise?"

"Yes."

Now, imitating Richard Dyer-Bennet, he sings in plaintive falsetto: "*Once, I wore my apron high . . .*"

They are sitting in the kitchen, drinking coffee. It is eleven o'clock. "About Dad's will," says Frederick. "He was scrupulous, I promise . . ."

"You just don't get it, do you?" Peter turns on him.

"Get what?"

"The two of us, I think, were raised to share and share alike, but something went wrong with the sharing, I never did learn to be happy with crumbs when there were sweets at table or there was cake on offer. This whole business of ownership, of having someone obey you, *serve* you . . ."

"I didn't say that," Frederick says.

Peter continues, spreading his hands and smacking his lips. "For me it's something else again, it has nothing to do with possessions or how much we pay for a fine pair of shoes. It's knowing I can't keep the things and people I most want to keep. They take your shoes, bro, or haven't you noticed, they take away the houses and the paintings and the cars."

"We have paintings here," says Sarah. "And you can use the car."

"Darling, that isn't the point. And you know it anyhow, you damn well know what I'm talking about."

She nods.

Now, urgently, he addresses his brother; he is wearing his Halloween t-shirt and a Yankee cap. "This business of legacy. You believe you can hoard the family album, the shares of General Motors and IBM and such. But it isn't what he left us, it's what Dad *didn't* leave. Those readers of the Talmud, those old men nodding over cups of tea with maybe one lump sugar and pulling at their *payis* knew the right questions to ask. *Know* the right questions, I mean."

"What questions?" Frederick asks.

"About the way to live this life. How not to be a hoarder

since there's nothing we can keep. How not to covet thy neighbor's possessions or"—he stands, then bows to Sarah—"wife."

She puts her hand over her mouth. Peter walks to the bay window. There is snow on the ground and light flakes drift down; in the low wintry light he peers at the garden, the yew trees and the bayberry and the leafless shrubs. He turns back again. There are tears in his eyes.

"Your boys are excellent," he says. "My blessing on this house."

He sits. It comes to Frederick, finally, that his brother and wife are in league. Their companionable intimacy has been a form of revenge. In the argument he and his brother engaged in all fall, she and Peter have become confederates—shoulder to shoulder and arm against arm. They may not in fact be lovers, but they have made an alliance. Sarah will not travel south or leave him for this vagabond; she has left him nonetheless.

"I've packed my bag," says his brother. "I'll be on the two o'clock bus."

"We'll miss you," says his wife.

"Goodbye. Goodbye. Goodbye."

The Drive
1993

RETURNING, SHE TAKES secondary roads. She is in no rush to reach her house; an extra hour's driving is nothing to regret. The day is bright and clear. Sarah knows that on arrival she will be alone in the echoing space; she wants only to get home by dark. It is Monday afternoon. Her husband is off on a business trip and won't be back till Thursday; who she misses are their sons. John is twenty-two years old, and Daniel has just turned eighteen. Her older child is a senior in Dartmouth, and she has grown resigned if not accustomed to his absence, but coming back from Williamstown and Danny's first weekend in college, she finds herself fighting back tears.

It is 1993. Her son is the light of her life. Having dropped him off on campus, Sarah found a motel in Bennington, not all that far away across the Pownal Valley. There were no rooms in Williamstown, so she had had to drive. Returning, she met his new roommates—one from Boston, one from Charlottesville—and helped Danny settle in, unpacking, hanging curtains and fitting liner paper to his shelves and making his low narrow bed, though he of course protested he could make the bed himself. She bought him things he needed—an extra lamp, a microwave, an overpriced Hudson's Bay blanket. They took a campus tour. After the next day's orientation program for incoming students and parents, they ate dinner at a restaurant where he ordered "Surf 'n' Turf" and fidgeted until she said goodnight; then Danny went to a Freshman Mixer and she drove back without him to the motel in Vermont. The roads were dark.

Now on Route 7, driving south, Sarah passes a chair-lift and ski-slope; there are shuttered restaurants and neglected fields. Her solitude is sharp-edged, and her sorrow keen. She is fifty-four years old. During the "Welcome to Williams" sessions she found herself looking at much younger parents from New York and Los Angeles—the trim brunettes and windblown blondes who kissed their sons or daughters and left them with alacrity, with no seeming sense of loss. The other parents of freshmen were tooting horns and waving, driving off, eyes straight ahead, while she stayed an additional day and went to the Clark Art Institute at the edge of campus. The Renoirs were a consolation, and the small portrait by Memling, and the Botticelli—all those young men and women who retain the bloom of youth.

Some of them no doubt were street girls or apprentices who served as painter's models; some had been self-portraits or imagined not actual figures; all of them are dead. For a long time she studied their faces, the bright eyes and effulgent skin of children—the artists' own children, possibly—their painted permanence who now are ash and bone. One child by a sixteenth-century Italian painter resembles the girl next to Daniel that morning, except the girl had been wearing a sweatshirt with the name of her high school, *New Trier*, and had a purple backpack and chewed gum.

"We met at the mixer," he explained.

"Hi, I'm Annabelle."

"Me and her are in English together," he said.

She smiled up at her boy. It was starting already, the long procession of girls by his side, the ones he will find to replace her. Her husband is a handsome man, and John too is good-looking, but Daniel has a sheen that causes you to notice, a kind of light that brightens space he enters. And it's all the more attractive because he himself does not appear to recognize how girls and women turn to him like flowers to the sun—their necks like stalks, their bodies bending . . .

"Maybe European history too," said Annabelle.

"*I'm* taking it," said Danny.

"I'm still deciding," said the girl, "but the professor's way cool."

Annabelle has braces on her bottom teeth. Danny has had his removed. In years to come, she tells herself, he will advance from Annabelle to Zöe, with twenty-four letters between. College students now live side by side, and who knows what they do at night or did with each other after the dance; there is no trial period, no mystery to sex. When she and Frederick met at the beginning of the 1960s—before Flower Power and Love-ins—romance had taken time. It was weeks before she let him kiss her, months before they went to bed, taking each other's virginity, and years before they wed. Sometimes Sarah asks herself what would have happened instead to her life if the night she first met Frederick she had slept with him and said goodbye next morning, walking what they called "the walk of shame" out of his dormitory room, dressed in last evening's finery and going back to her own space and changing clothes for class. If he had been one of a series of lovers, and not the first boy-man she slept with, would anything—would *everything*—have changed?

The town of Pittsfield looks forlorn, its Main Street derelict. She drives through Stockbridge and Great Barrington, where she fills the tank. At a roadside farm-stand on the Connecticut border, she buys tomatoes and jam. The man tending the register is fat and wearing coveralls and a John Deere cap; his arms are covered with tattoos of anchors and mermaids. She hands him twenty dollars and he counts out her change with deliberation, placing single dollar bills one by one on the counter between them.

"Fine day," he says.

She nods. As an afterthought and with two of the dollars he hands her, she buys a quart of cider and, drinking in the parking lot, waits for the grief-tide to ebb. She does not start the car. Her sons have left. Their childhood is over, her role in it done, and nothing now will be the same: this autumn, Sarah tells herself, is when the world will change.

A tractor lumbers past. A station wagon stops beside her in the gravel pull-off; then a woman with a string bag emerges from the driver's seat and limps away toward the produce stand. Her car has Connecticut plates. It is 2:53. She and the farmer greet each other; he offers her an apple and a slice of cheese. They talk together with the ease of old acquaintance; when he doffs his cap and scratches his bald head Sarah sees a resemblance between them: a brother and sister perhaps? The cider is too sweet. She turns on the ignition, then makes her slow way south.

This is, she sees, a valley full of Christmas trees; the hills on both sides of the road are lined with rows of pines. The wind is high. She tries to remember the last thing Danny said to her, not "Bye, Mom," or "I'll call tonight," or even "Wish me luck." She thinks the last words they exchanged were when he said, "Drive safely," and she offered "Love." He was standing at the curb, and Annabelle stood next to him, and both of them had waved.

Tree branches bend their outstretched arms; pines sway. Danny is her carefree child, the one who finds the world easy, the one who never seemed to mind being dropped off at kindergarten or left home with a babysitter. When he was five and sent to day-camp he went without a backward glance—unlike his older brother, who was organized and cautious and, just like his father, *concerned*. With John you had to explain every part of the day so he could understand beforehand what would happen why, and when you would come to collect him once activities were over: the swimming lessons and the tennis lessons and the music lessons and the riding lessons after school. John learned to tell time early, not because he cared about the sequence of events but because he wanted to know exactly how many minutes it took until a procedure was finished, or another would begin; he had a sense of duty from the start.

Her second son is inattentive, and it is part of his charm. He resembles uncle Peter in the casual, slipshod way he goes about his business, not pausing to consider what will happen as a result or what damage he might cause. For a boy who went to Temple and had been bah mitzvahed, he seems—so his father likes to say—surprisingly guilt-free. "Because I *felt* like it," is Danny's answer, always, when you ask him why he does the reckless things he does. "Because it's *fun*, Mom," Danny says, and dives from the high diving board or launches himself on one ski down the slope . . .

And this too, she knows to her sorrow, is the way Peter behaves. If John takes after Frederick—always calculating profit and loss, the odds of failure or success—then Daniel takes after his father's big brother, a gambler to the core. He packed a deck of cards and a chess-board in his suitcase; he had more games to play than clothes to wear, and he was good at cards. His uncle taught him to handle the deck and how to shuffle and deal. No doubt he'd played with Annabelle last night, and won their game of strip poker, if anyone plays strip poker these days, or Spin the Bottle, or Hearts. There was something in the way they stood together, waving, that made his mother certain they'd shared more than the prospect of English class, or European History, and the sweatshirt from *New Trier* is something she no doubt removed . . .

Now, following Route 7, Sarah considers her own time at Pembroke before the school joined up with and was folded into Brown. They called them "sister schools" back then; female students were protected and kept separate from their counterparts and not allowed to share a dorm or floor or shower stall. There were terms like "parietal hours"—those few hours every week the opposite sex was permitted to visit, with an open door—that have long been forgotten; today no one knows what "parietal" means. There had been a formality to courtship, and everyone was fearful—*terrified*—of getting pregnant or being called a slut. It meant "Four feet on the floor!"

During her freshman and sophomore years, she focused on

her studies and tried very hard to succeed. She had been a serious student, and there were few distractions, and the acquisition of knowledge was in its own way rewarding. Sarah was a smoker then—everybody smoked in class—and *Middlemarch* and *Bleak House* were what they called a three-pack book; the novels of Jane Austen required only one. She became a political science major, since her advisor assured her the subject of government was open-ended and could be used as a credential later on. "You don't want to foreclose on your options," the woman had suggested, and even then she'd understood this was a foolish argument, not sufficient reason to pursue a course of study. Yet now her own sons are in college she hears herself offering the same advice: *Keep your options open, don't specialize too soon.*

Frederick was learning how to drink. In the bitter Providence winter, he kept bottles on the window-ledge so they would stay cold. During parietal hours one March Saturday of junior year, after his roommates obligingly announced they were going off to Boston, he poured two glasses of gin. They both had known, that afternoon, what they would do together. She had worn black underwear, and he put a towel over the sheets, and the Beefeaters did help.

"Are you ready?" he had asked.

One Anglo-Saxon king was called—she knew nothing else about him—"Ethelred the Unready." Sarah loved the disrespectful names of rulers from the ancient stories and days. There were "Pippin the Short" and "Charles the Hammer" and "Bertha with Big Feet."

"I'm ready, yes," she said.

Silently they took off their clothes and, in his bedroom, embraced. Frederick was tentative; she helped him roll the condom down over his erection. There was a little blood, a little pain and pleasure, and then they were no longer virgins and felt like almost-adults . . .

Of a sudden clouds appear, and a spattering of rain. She does not require wipers; the sky ahead stays blue. Her romantic history was brief. There had been Frederick, and then a few others; the list of her partners while she was at Pembroke is not something she looks back on now with pride. For spring semester, senior year, once she was fitted for a diaphragm, she did allow herself—in an expression current then—to "play around." It was 1961, and Kennedy was President, and everything had changed. Sarah remembers when on graduation weekend her parents took her out to lunch and there had been two boys from RISD at the adjacent table, each of whom she'd slept with, once. She had had a secret, and the elders would have disapproved, but Frank and Bill came over and shook her parents' hands, not revealing their shared intimacy. She can remember her relief, her sense of having gotten away with something vaguely shameful, and she liked Frank and Bill much better in the restaurant than she had in bed.

Now, driving into Cornwall Bridge, she wonders if she seemed as obvious to her own parents as Annabelle had been this morning, standing next to Danny with a hickey on her neck. It all feels very long ago, and far away; it is, she thinks, astonishing that who she was is who she has become. *Fatuity*, thinks Sarah: youth wasted on the young.

The clouds disperse. She passes gas stations and diners and grocery stores and churches with steeples and white clapboard houses and barns. Her Danny-boy is starting out on what she'd promised him at dinner will be a great adventure, but her own is done. What might have been is gone. Idly, Sarah finds herself remembering—a result of her trip to the Clark, perhaps?—her Art History class. It had been her first exposure to the history of art. In a way she cannot fully understand, it connects to her experience of Frederick and Frank and Bill, the restlessness she'd reveled in that final year.

She had been exploring her options and, as her advisor suggested, taking an elective: "Early Italian Renaissance." The course focused on the art of Botticelli and Piero della Francesca and, before them, Giotto and Masaccio and Fra Angelico. There were monks who worked their whole life through in a single monastery, painting devotional scenes. Her professor liked to say that the progression from gold leaf and egg tempera to oil paint, from wood paneling to wall to canvas was the equivalent, in artistic terms, of the great voyages of exploration. "'O brave new world,'" he would proclaim, "That hath such artists in it! Shakespeare's word had been 'creatures,' not 'artists,'" the professor said, quoting from *The Tempest*, "but Shakespeare too was a Renaissance figure, an example of outreach in language. I want you all to understand how *revolutionary* these progressions were in terms of the discovery not only of technique but of this entity we call the self. The modern self. The invention of the self."

She copied down his terminology—*discovery, selfhood, technique*. "It's like," the girl sitting next to her whispered, "he's talking about sex." Her teacher wore wire-rimmed glasses and a three-piece suit and had an English accent she doubted was authentic. She had had coffee with him once, in order to discuss her essay, and he said he'd studied at Oxford and, earlier, at Duke. Before the job in Providence, he'd lived in New Orleans. Sarah felt nervous to start with, but it grew obvious from how he clapped a colleague on the back and talked about the party last night and gazed around the coffee shop that who he desired were boys. He had seemed ancient to her then—she smiles to herself, remembering—but was not yet forty, was maybe thirty-five . . .

The lectures, however, compelled her. That the rebirth of antiquity was linked to the birth of modernity seemed somehow important to Sarah: the idea of exploration felt both old and new. *Discovery, technique.* Sitting in an aisle seat because she was left-handed, and it helped with taking notes, she liked to imagine herself a painter or, more plausibly, a painter's apprentice, working long hours in candlelit space or a refectory with oil lamps and sweeping sawdust from the floor, then strewing fresh sawdust on tile. There were workers in Italy and Antwerp, she learned, who specialized in glasswork or silver work or mosaic or tiling; these were inherited skills. Or, if not inherited, at least a skill in which it helped to have a relative who was a member of the guild and could set an example of the way to work. Her sons will not, she knows, inherit an interest in warehouse construction, but sometimes she thinks it would be simpler if choice was not an issue, if you were raised to do what your parents and grandparents did . . .

In the early 1960's, in any case, careers weren't something you could take for granted; after college you took jobs in order to meet men. She had worked in advertising, at Doyle, Dayne & Bernbach, then Ogilvy, Benson & Mather, but all it was was errand-running and looking ornamental and hoping not so much for a promotion as a date. She did this for four years. She went out and sometimes went home with copywriters and art directors and, once, a married Vice President in the agency, but none of it had mattered much and nothing was important. Even then, she felt demeaned. She was part of a cadre of young women who were valued not for their brains but bodies, and it was tiresome, predictable, not what she'd dreamed of at school. She dated commodity brokers also, but did not like to think of herself as a commodity or something to be traded for on the stock-market floor.

There was the period of celibacy and the period of yoga and the time of protest against war in Vietnam. There were the years in Manhattan, and then the year in Springfield when she nursed her dying father and worked in an insurance agency. Her roommate settled in California, and Sarah thought she might move there too, but spent three months in San Diego under the unchanging sky and, feeling bored, flew home. Briefly she thought of applying to graduate school and studying Art History, but kept putting off applications. Then, at a class reunion, she met Frederick again, and he asked her, on the final day, if she wanted to go to Cape Cod. It was the beginning of June. Because there was nothing to cancel, and no one waiting for her, she agreed.

He owned a white Buick convertible—three years old. They took the top down and drove two hours to the edge of Provincetown and stayed in a beach cottage called by one of a series of flower-names: *Peony*, thinks Sarah, or maybe it was *Rose*. There had been *Iris* and *Lilac* and *Lily* also, a dozen stand-alone structures. The cabins themselves were unprepossessing but each had a view of the water. There was a sink beside the bed; the wallpaper was torn. The shabby, mildewed feel of the cottage fit her mood precisely, and her mood improved. She had been adrift, she confessed to her old boyfriend, unmoored and marking time.

They kissed. "What a coincidence," he said, "that's just how I've been feeling." They reminded each other of that afternoon so long ago when they both were virgins, and drinking glasses of Beefeaters Gin, and it seemed important, a wheel that came full circle, to become lovers again.

He first had seen her, Frederick confessed, at a Freshman Mixer. Back then he had been bashful, and by the time he did work up the nerve and make his way to where she stood she was dancing with a group of girls and he didn't dare break in. He still remembered what she wore, and when she asked him to describe it he did so with precision: the gray knee-length skirt, white turtleneck, the patent leather pumps. "I'm flattered you remember," Sarah said. "But why did it take you so long?"

"I wasn't ready."

"Ready for what?"

"To get serious. I think I didn't dare to."

"I'm ready now. Are you?"

"We used to talk about commitment, remember, and you said it was only for institutions. Jail or insane asylums, they're what a person commits to. Is committed to."

"I must have been joking," she said.

The next month, he proposed. In his courtly fashion, he got down on one knee, offering his grandmother Ilse's ring and words like "honor" and "obey." The ring was diamonds and emeralds, and when she said how well it fit he told her he had had it sized. In some ways, Sarah understood, the proposal did seem sudden, but they had known each other for nearly a decade and had a shared history. The years apart seemed part of it, as if they too were preparation for shared adult life. Again, there was nothing to cancel and no one waiting for her, and on her twenty-eighth birthday she told Frederick "Yes."

In the second year of their marriage, he bought a Steinway C. Sarah played it every day. She did not attain proficiency, or even a real competence, but was enthralled by Mendelssohn's "Songs Without Words" or Schumann's "Scenes from Childhood" and, little by little, acquired technique. Her husband played the violin, because his parents had insisted he take lessons, and sawed away dutifully at her side while they played sonatas together. He had no music in him, and she felt thick-fingered, but it mattered to her that their sons—when they grew old enough—both should learn to play. John commenced with piano lessons and then took up the clarinet; like his father he could follow notes in proper order. But it was never a pleasure; it was wheeze and tootle and cacophony every afternoon for thirty minutes until he asked for and received her permission to stop.

Danny had talent, however. Without conscious application, he seemed inside the music; he had a feel for it, his teacher said, that was very promising. She loved to hear him practice and would busy herself in the living room, cleaning, pretending to read. It was the way she'd sometimes felt with "Scenes from Childhood" or "Songs Without Words," as though melody were everywhere and harmony prevailed. From the time that he was eight he played the piano daily, and it was fine to listen to her gifted son.

Then, at thirteen, he stopped. Unlike his elder brother, he did not ask for or receive permission; he just stopped. His piano teacher protested, but Danny told his parents that the man would sit too close to him on the piano bench and hold his hand too often, demonstrating fingerings and stroking his right wrist.

Frederick said, "Enough's enough."

Now, thinking back on it, she thinks she should have noticed sooner and canceled the lessons herself. Her child had been at risk. Nothing came of it, however, as nothing came of his wild jumps from diving boards or hurtling rush down ski slopes;

Danny was impervious to harm. And an instructor's touch, she knows, is not a major threat and probably meant nothing and was only an excuse her son used in order to stop practicing. But when Frederick said, "Enough's enough"—with that conviction of his, that knee-jerk certainty—Sarah felt reproved.

"Should we get another teacher?"

"No."

"Do you want to talk to him?"

"Who?"

"Danny."

"What's there to say?" Frederick said.

There is a lane closure and announcements of construction, but she sees no workmen or evidence of labor behind the traffic cones. After some miles, a sign declares WORK ZONE ENDS, and Sarah increases her speed. When the boys were young they watched *Sesame Street*, and one of its jingles comes back to her now, with its childish lilt. "*Three of these things belong together; one of these things is not the same.*" The three men who belong together are Frederick, John, and Daniel; the "one of the things" that's not the same is Peter Hochmann, her brother-in-law.

On a Thursday afternoon she still can remember in detail, he took her by surprise. It was the only way, thinks Sarah, she could have been taken; it was 1985. Peter had been passing through, the way he used to do often, not giving them time to refuse. He had arrived three weeks before, from God knew where and God knew why, and did not say when he would leave.

It happened only once. It happened on Thursday, at two. Her husband had a meeting in New York. The children were in school. Sarah came out of her bedroom and walked down the hall and down the stairs and found Peter sitting in the library; he patted the cushion beside him and invited her to sit. The room was hot. She had given up tobacco for her second pregnancy and the year of breast-feeding her baby, so Sarah told herself she was just being polite when he offered her a cigarette he'd rolled, saying "Here," and "Have a toke."

She did. The marijuana was strong. Peter smiled. He said, "I've been wanting to ask you," and she asked him "What?"

"Should a gentleman offer a lady a joint?"

"Excuse me?"

He repeated himself. "Should a gentleman offer a lady a joint?"

She looked at him: this wanderer who carried with him everywhere a whiff of contrariety—this Lord of Misrule in her house who would not change his clothes or cut his hair. "It depends what you're asking . . ."

"That sounds like 'yes.'"

"Why not?"

They continued smoking, making small talk, not flirting precisely but not not-flirting either, and he told a joke about a one-legged sailor and a parrot in a bar. She said, "That isn't funny," and he said, "I know it's not, it's serious," and Sarah laughed. She could hear herself laugh: high-pitched and not in her usual register, as though a stranger made the sound, a whistling deep down in her throat.

"Do you know the one," asked Peter, "about the one-armed sailor and the owl?"

The sense of well-being that flooded her then, the companionable way he touched her breast and, pulling her towards him, put his arm around her and with his other hand undid the buttons of her blouse and stroked her skirt is something—even now, not on the leather loveseat but eight years later and behind the wheel of her Mercedes, entering the town of Kent—she can recall. For months she had been restless, restive, in a kind of not-so-much-depression as elation, feeling giddy and unstrung. Out of a sense of duty—fading even as she honored it—she protested, saying, "No," and he said, "Whatever you want . . ."

"Want?" Sarah asked.

He said, "Yes," and touched her knee. "There's a little hash in it."

"In what?"

"In what you're smoking, lady."

"Oh?"

"What the hell," said Peter.

"Don't swear," she said, "you're swearing."

The smell of marijuana was also the feel of his fingers and the taste of hot smoke rising to the tongued roof of her mouth. Not unpleasantly, it stung. Sarah coughed; she could *hear* herself cough. At first there was the fear of blame, of shame, of being by someone discovered, of being interrupted. She crossed her arms over her breasts.

"Whatever you want," he repeated.

She watched the clock. She listened to it ticking: tick tick *tock*. Sarah thought about her husband in his meeting in Manhattan; he had told her he'd be home by seven, maybe eight o'clock, and not to wait on dinner; he might be as late as the eight o'clock train. The gardeners had gone. The cleaning lady came on Monday and on Wednesday morning and, if she was needed, on Friday afternoon. So there was no one in the house except the two of them together, and there were hours till the end of school when she had to leave for the boys . . .

She saw the chandelier. She saw, on his left wrist, his watch. Sarah breathed; she could hear herself breathe. She heard Peter's breathing also, and her inhalations and exhalations were precisely synchronous with the rhythm of this wanderer, this almost-stranger beside her.

He dropped his hand into her lap and splayed his fingers there. "Are you all right?" he asked.

It was, she knew, her choice. It was her decision to make. She can remember kicking off her shoes, the small sound they made as they fell to the floor. Pressing herself back against the pillows of the loveseat, Sarah arched her spine and spread her legs.

"Does *this* feel good? Does *this*?"

Wordlessly, she nodded. She felt herself start to grow wet. Wordlessly she touched his crotch, feeling the stiffness there.

And then, of a sudden, he stood. Peter cinched his belt and opened the window; she felt the cold inrush of air.

"What are you doing?"

"Opening the window."

"I can see that. What are you doing?"

"We shouldn't fuck things up."

Inanely, like a schoolgirl, she heard herself echoing him: "'Fuck things up?'"

"I've been wanting to do this," he said, "since the time I saw you in that wedding dress. But you're too wasted, lady, you don't know what you want . . ."

This was such a, such an *insult* she felt herself go cold. Sarah collected her shoes. "What wedding dress?"

"The one you poured yourself into . . ."

"Were you at the wedding? I can't remember."

"I'm trying to be honest here. I've been wanting to do this forever."

"What?"

"Sleep with you. Make love to you. Hell, *fuck* you."

Her voice was high. "Except I'm married . . ."

"Oh?"

"To Frederick, remember?"

"Does it matter?"

"Doesn't it?"

He looked at her. She can picture, still, the way his expression altered in the changing light and settled, again, to the features she knew: obdurate yet malleable, her husband's older brother who was clothed in darkness. "So I should take no for an answer?"

"No."

"No?"

"Yes. Oh, let's not discuss it," she said.

When Danny was eleven, he fell and broke his arm. He had been running at the bottom of the garden where he and John would practice football; he tried to catch a pass his brother threw too far over his head, and hit the stone wall at the garden's edge and, tumbling, cracked an elbow. She was watching from the kitchen window, not focused on but nonetheless aware of her sons' game of catch, and can remember Danny standing, shrugging, trying not to cry.

She turned off the tap, dried her hands. Outside, she went to him—not running but not walking either, with an anxious urgency she attempted to conceal. "Where does it hurt?" she asked, "Does it hurt much?" and though he tried to tell her "No," he ended up nodding his head.

"I didn't mean it, Mom," said John, and she said, "Of course you didn't," and he said, "It was a accident," and she told him, "Yes."

"It *hurts*," cried Danny, his voice high.

"Don't try to move your arm," she said, "just hold it, darling, hold still." It was clear he had been injured and, when he came into the house, his white face and limp dangling hand made it clear he needed help. He lay down on the loveseat, beneath a poster by Toulouse-Lautrec of a chorus girl lifting her leg, and though she gave him aspirin and chocolate the pain did not abate. She called her doctor's office and the three of them drove to the emergency room; John did his homework while she sat with Danny and spoke with doctors and nurses and waited for Frederick to join them. He did. In the hospital they diagnosed a compound fracture and operated that afternoon; four hours later her son returned with his right arm encased in plastic, in a sling.

The cast became a kind of canvas for Danny's school-friends with their pencils and their felt-tipped pens.

"Get Better Soon," wrote Amy Gordon, and Sally Andrews drew a smiley face

and heart around her name. "Break a Leg," wrote Harry Irving, who was the class clown. Others signed their names or wrote "GO DAN" in capitals and someone with a yellow Bik wrote "Kilroy was Here."

Since Danny was right-handed he was forced to learn new motor skills with his left and less practiced hand. To begin with, she cut food for him, or helped him get his clothes on and tie his shoes and button his shirt, but soon enough he told her he could handle it, and wanted to do things himself. While the fracture healed and they reduced the size of the cast; his fingers grew shriveled and brown.

For six long weeks that autumn, Peter remained in the house. Having arrived without warning, he stayed till late December when the snow grew deep. He did not try to seduce her again, and she did not encourage him. They did not talk about what happened in the library, or had failed to happen; instead they avoided each other and, as if by unspoken agreement, remained at a remove.

It was a difficult time. Their visitor had slipped into his old insouciant madness and refused to wash. She never knew what he might say or, worse, might choose to do. She could have broken the silence, perhaps, have walked into his bedroom beneath the attic eaves and discussed the whole thing like the grown-ups they were and agreed to disagree. Or she could have shed her clothes and joined him in the attic bed those cold mornings and long afternoons they were alone together.

Sarah thought about it constantly. Each time Frederick went to work and her boys went off to school she thought about his feral presence on the couch, the marijuana he had offered and the advantage he had taken—*was* it advantage he had taken?—of her altered state. Except that she had welcomed it; except he had chosen to leave her alone, except it had been her idea at least as much as his . . .

She did talk to Judy Olesker. Sooner or later she told Judy everything, as Judy told her everything, and at some point in early December she took her friend to lunch and—over a glass of wine—confessed. Her friend was unsurprised. Ordering a second round, she said, "He's dangerous, isn't he; he doesn't play by our rules."

Sarah nodded.

"And in his own way Peter *is* sexy."

She wanted to cry.

"Thou shalt not covet thy brother's wife. Is that, isn't that one of the Ten Commandments?"

"'Thy *neighbor's* wife,' I think it is."

"Same difference," Judy said. "How long is he staying?"

"He's our only living relative. I can't just throw him out."

"Why not?"

Spitting gravel, a truck roars by. On a downhill stretch of road, she catches her own aging face in the rearview mirror. She has been Frederick's faithful wife, believing in richer and poorer, in sickness and health, for better or for worse. She had been well behaved. Then along came this prodigal brother of his, this piece of wreckage washed up at their door, and everything got undermined because he, Peter, doesn't care and didn't care and can't and won't be made to care.

In any case, she tells herself, she would not have gone with him—not even if he asked. He did not ask. He left her with his brother and their two children to raise. The children are in college now—at Dartmouth and Williams, a senior and freshman—and keeping options open although hers have been foreclosed. Peter was easy with the boys, and both of them adored him, but three of the Hochmanns belong together; one is not the same.

Sarah rolls her neck. She remembers her Art History professor's terms—*discovery, technique.* No doubt in the dark ages Ethelred the Unready and Bertha with Big Feet had sex, and perhaps they had had it together—she cannot remember their sequence or dates—but in the early Renaissance there were canopied beds to lie on and plaintive airs to listen to and sweet-smelling unguents to breathe. She knows she is drifting and making no sense but what she thinks of now are velvet robes and Annabelle and Danny looking like a princess with her prince. Her son is gone; her heart—in that archaic term—aches, *aches.*

It rains. A police car idles in a parking lot, but she has not been speeding and does not step on the brake. Sarah turns on the radio, and in this valley enclosed by high hills hears only bursts of static. There are classical-music stations in Albany and New Haven, and no doubt some stations between, but she cannot find them. Imagining herself an apprentice in Florence or—what was the center of tiling?—*Delft*, she listens to the road-sound and, beyond it, silence. The floors would be hard; her feet would be cold, and there was a solemnity to labor. She turns the radio off.

Now the volume of traffic increases, and the unattractive cities—Danbury, Norwalk—loom. She is less than an hour from home. Taking advantage of a passing lane, she passes a convoy of Jeeps. There are box-like vans and camouflaged trucks also, with billowing canvas tarpaulins: the National Guard. A soldier waves.

In every marriage, Sarah thinks, there is some sort of imbalance—a wife who loves her husband more or less than he loves her. This business of equal partners is a well-intentioned myth. She had known from the beginning that the man she married was devoted, dutiful, and loved her more than she loved him, or at any rate needed her more. From the time of their first night together in that cabin up in Provincetown, she understood he was hers for the taking, and she should not destroy what she took.

Yet more and more she feels—what were the words she used with Frederick in that cabin by the water when they met again after college?—*adrift, unmoored*. A part of Sarah lives these days in mortal fear, in mortal weariness, and what she yearns for is a strong right arm to carry her away. Her lover would reach down for her and lift her to the saddle of his prancing steed and canter—no, *gallop*—away. Laughing and holding each other, she and Prince Charming would ride through wide green fields. They would leave all this behind. Except Peter is no one's prince charming, and he did not have a horse and used a Greyhound Bus . . .

In the morning, she reminds herself, there are errands to run and appointments to keep. She will go grocery shopping; she must plan a meal for Thursday night when Frederick returns from Chicago. She will deal with the dry cleaning and a problem with the gutter and have the furnace inspected. At two o'clock tomorrow, she has a mammogram.

It is the beginning of the end. At the end of the week she has a telephone call from the doctor's office, saying there has been a small irregularity, nothing to concern her but they would like to take another set of pictures and would she come in on Monday? They take another mammogram and three days later are in contact again and this time there is indeed something the doctor would like to examine and would she make an appointment as soon as convenient, please? Sarah schedules the biopsy appointment so Frederick can rearrange his schedule and accompany her, and he does go along and offer if not comfort at least the consolation of his solid, stolid presence, his willingness to wait for hours in the waiting room until her name is called. When her name is called and she follows the nurse she turns to look at Frederick, and he smiles at her from where he sits and lifts his hand, palm out.

Time thereafter is an entity that will become wholly elastic, spiraling, curved in upon itself: the days when she is forced to wait, although she knows them already, for the telephoned results, the verdict that is not a verdict, or so Judy Olesker assures her, but only a piece of evidence in what will be her trial. She knows twenty women, Judy says, who were smokers once and have been diagnosed with cancer and have beaten it or lived with it or been declared cancer-free. You're only at Stage Two . . .

Stage Two, Stage Three, Stage Four. It will continue in this fashion until her visits to the doctors and then the hospital become the rule in Sarah's life, not the exception, the almost-routine she says she's grown used to but never grows used to in truth. There is the radical mastectomy, the radiation and chemotherapy, the years of remission and then recurrence, the shadow self within her chest that travels with her everywhere while she—who is not, has never been religious—prays or more accurately bargains with an unknown unseen ineffectual higher presence for another week, another month, another decade please. There are words like tumor and malignancy and metastasis that once upon a time meant nothing personal and now mean much, mean everything, until Sarah becomes an almost-expert on the person in the mirror who less and less resembles the one who used to stand there, applying eyeliner or rouge.

The rest of life continues. What once had been the future is the present and the past. Her sons will graduate, pursuing studies and careers and finding women to marry with whom in turn to have children, and she attends their weddings and the birth of her first grandchild and attempts to pay attention and be, for their sakes, glad. She likes Daniel's wife better than John's.

Her brother-in-law stays away. Their dog Methuselah—whom Frederick brought home because one day he saw that John was frightened of the neighbor's dog—grows old despite his name. One afternoon, he dies. She goes to concerts and museums and spends many hours at the Frick Gallery on Fifth Avenue, staring at the Piero there, and the portrait of Sir Thomas More by Holbein, and the beautiful Bellini; she no longer visits the Racquet Club except once in a while to rally with her husband if the courts are empty after rain.

From the bay window in their living room, she likes to watch the rain. For her sixty-fifth birthday they travel to Italy, planning to relive their honeymoon, but in Milano she contracts a fever and, rather than go to the hill towns of Tuscany or Umbria and take chances with the doctors in Cortona or Arezzo or Assisi, although the visiting physician in the hotel in Milano assures her that the doctors there are competent, are excellent, she and her husband fly home.

The New Millennium
1999

THE AFTERNOON IS ending, and it always moves him: how the light that comes at close of day is fleeting, evanescent, and will soon be night. Peter rocks in his chair on the porch. It is the last day of December, 1999, the string of Christmas lights sparkling, a menorah lit by way of equal opportunity, though the festivities are long gone and the worship over, the needles desiccate and dropping from the blue spruce tree. There had been a celebration—carols and a Santa Claus, the fat janitor with a white wig, the Social Director playing the piano, and eggnog without rum to drink. There had been visits and turkey and yams and "God Bless Ye, Merry Gentlemen" on a taped loop in the hall. There were also "Deck the Halls" and "Good King Wenceslas" and "Rock of Ages" and "Ave Maria" and "Hava Nagila" and "Silent Night": a cacophony of brass and strings and good insistent cheer. For the last month and week of the year.

But Christmas was six days ago and he's the single man outside, with his throw-rug on his knees and wearing his parka and earmuffs and gloves and feeling old and cold. The bell has rung, has tolled for thee; at four o'clock the shift is changing and the white-garbed orderlies and nurses intersect. Their cars (some of them with headlights on, some off) criss-cross in the drive. They dance an intricate ballet: a pause, a growl of gears: Ah, do-si-do, the square dance, the real Virginia Reel.

Except he's in Connecticut, his nursing home in Guilford,

his court of last resort. They have moved him here, his brother—upright uptight Frederick—and the lawyer his father's executor, Jarndyce v. Jarndyce, or is it Cholera v. Jaundice or simply
Little John, his nephew from the coast? What happened, he is
certain, is that someone somewhere sometime called a meeting
and an intervention and decided, nay, *decreed* that he, Peter Ernest Hochmann, being of sound mind and body, be construed
as having neither and remanded to this place. Where his lodg-
ing is and will be forever and ever pre-paid.

The light is fading, falling, and it never fails to move him:
how the dark that comes at close of day is fungible, arrested,
because of the lamp on the porch. And the lights that line
the hallway and the night-light in his bedroom and the twenty-eight electric bulbs in the crystal chandelier meant to suggest
prosperity in the reception pavilion and the rows of hanging
fixtures—sixteen, he has counted them—in the dining hall.
Dark conquers all, and always did—long before the invention
of candles and guttering oil lamps, the lanterns and the hanging
globes and chandelier—and will. And therefore this sentient
animal must wheel himself inside to eat.

What will he eat, Peter wonders—the sole soul on the flood-
lit porch—what is on offer tonight? The menu has instructed
him: broccoli tips and asparagus spears and awful cod in sauce.
Béchamel, béchamel mucho. With, at the banquet's conclusion,
maybe a nice piece pie. It is, after all, the last collation of the
month and year and century before the new Millennium; the
mistletoe is hanging by the EXIT sign, and there are conical
hats to wear and balloons to wave and pink and blue unfurling
paper horns to toot. Brief candles to blow out. There will be,
if he behaves himself—always a question and one he can't answer—the chance to sit and chat with nattering Alice McNeil.
Who was born, as she at lunch informed him, in Burlington,
Vermont, and spent her childhood on Lake Champlain, *in* Lake
Champlain, on North Hero Island, oh, Peter would have liked
it there, the sound of lake water lapping in loud concert by the
shore, the nuns who kept a convent with its marble steps and
doorway lintels and walkways at the island's edge, the way that

Sister Magdalene would offer her, when young, a piece of newly baked banana bread, my, my, but you should *taste* it. Alice sticks out the tip of her tongue. Nothing, she says, has ever equaled the delight of warm sliced fresh still moist banana bread: beats everything, that sour sweetness in the mouth, I *wish* you'd tried a piece.

"'Lo, Pete."
   "'Lo, Bill."
   "'Lo, Tom and Dick and Harriet."
   "Please pass the salt."
   "What did we do today?"
   "What day is it?"
   "Peter, do we need to go piddle?"
   "Piddle?"
   "When was the last time you went to the boys' room?"
   "Time? Time?"
   "I'm only asking."
   "No."

In the dining room, at table—although he has not reached it yet, yet in his mind's ear hears and to himself rehearses—the topic turns to politics and Y2K, the future of our great Republic and its tattered flag, the stars and stripes forever from sea to shining sea. There is space for six and maybe eight and, if they crowd together, ten at every table, an emblem of the flag and union of this our great Republic, *hah*! and he will try to tell his fellow inmates if not intimates how the Armageddon they approach this week has been of their own making, the *hubris* Aristotle called man's mortal failing: do not think yourself a God. To have aspired to such a condition is to guarantee a fall. To have construed the universe as a well-oiled and well-made piece of machinery, a kind of cosmic grandfather clock with gears interlocked and ticking, clicking, is to play the fool. The Harmony of the Spheres is what we used to call it (the Social Director playing the piano, the endless loop of "Deck the Halls," the undrinkable eggnog in honor of Jesus) and on and on and on and on until the music stops. Then they take away a chair. Soon enough it will be over, soon enough there will be one who comes alone to tell thee how the little bug will win and all our vainglorious technology (the protocols enacted by the British Standard Institute for the Year 2000 Conformity Requirements) lose:

(1) No valid date will cause any interruption in operations.

(2) Calculations of durations between, or the sequence of, pairs of dates will be correct whether any dates are in different centuries.

(3) In all interfaces and in all storage, the century must be unambiguous, either specified, or calculable by algorithm.

(4) Year 2000 must be recognized as a leap year.

Fat chance, fat fucking chance. Peter has memorized them: these stays against confusion, the criteria propounded by the British Standards Institute, their little sputtering guttering matches struck against the dark. When they built the first computers they never thought or ever dreamed or even remotely envisioned that at this nearing century's end the algorithm would change. When they first invented the digital chip they did not think or dream or even remotely imagine that a defibrillator would be implanted pit-a-pat in this my beating heart, with my blood sugar monitored and my brain-waves scanned. Or that the last two digits of the ending century would in the end fail to suffice: The number 96 stands anterior, does it not? to 97; in turn the number 97 precedes the number 98; 98 in sequence is succeeded by 99, but 99 is and in short order will be followed by the numeral OO. Oh-oh.

So inside all those calculators (your watch, your portable radio, your cash register and washing machine) th'invisible worm will turn. So those who gather on this night in the collective eating space believe themselves autonomous—*please pass the salt, the ketchup*—and behave as though the meal they eat is not a final supper and the nuns of North Hero Island do not plunge headlong screaming into th'inexorable sea. Well, lake. Th'inexorable lake.

Because the satellite will cease its signal, the transponder stop transponding and the radar end its tracking, the planes will abandon their flying or crash in midair uncontrolled, the exchange of currency go belly up and tides neither ebb nor flow. Which is why, of course, he has deferred the pleasure of their company, the nonexistent warmth of a gas fire in the vestibule, the witless exchange of witticisms with men and women gathered by the elevator shaft, beneath the mistletoe and EXIT sign—*In case of Fire, Use the Stairs and not the Elevator*—and mans his post and rocks alone in his rocking chair on the cold porch: to watch the streetlights flicker and go permanently green or red, to watch the cars veer headlong into the onrushing trains.

"Are you aware?"

"Aware of what?"

"Cognizant, I mean. Are you cognizant of what this day will bring? This night will bring?"

"Excuse me?"

"*Garbage In. Garbage Out.* That's what we used to call it."

"When?"

"At the dawn of the computer age. Which now comes to its necessary end."

For this is the third country he calls home. The third in a sequence of three. And even though there's Canada or Mexico to move to, it's unlikely there'll be four. Well, truth be told and why not tell it to those he soon will visit in the dining hall, he can't remember Germany and sees it in his mind's eye only because his parents told him way back when he was a German Jewish boy wearing no doubt *Lederhosen* and with no doubt a fondness for sauerkraut if two-year-olds eat sauerkraut. But that was long ago and in another country and water far under the bridge—the concrete bridge athwart the pond in the garden back beyond the fence—milk spilt so long ago and far away it might as well belong to fable, a country of the mind. The homeland of Otto von Bismarck and, before that, Mad King Ludwig and, before that, Charlemagne.

But *palpable* is Cuba, a place he does remember well, or thinks he can, or knows he can, and conjures up with frequency: the three-legged dog, the sea wall, and the smell of sugar cane. There was a maid called Maria who used to make him take his bath, and wash him with attention while his grandmother repeated *Swimma-Bimma* in the bathroom. He remembers the pink cloth. He remembers how she wielded it, and that Maria's hands were at one and the same time and somehow without contradiction hard yet soft. Peter puzzles at the memory: how can a person's hands be both hard and soft, strong yet tender, how do you pull that off? His grandmother's hands were only soft, and there was a wicker chair beside the bathtub where she sat and watched. *Swimma-bimma*, his grandmother said.

The Cuba he remembers now is not of course the Bay of Pigs, *oink-oink*, or Guantanamo, because he never saw the Bay of Pigs or Gitmo, which is what they call it, but a table with bananas and papayas and sweet tea. A place of palm fronds gently swaying and, rising from the patio, the sound of strummed guitars. When the bath was finished and he dried himself, Maria brushed his teeth and his grandmother Ilse would wish him good night, sleep well. *Gute Nacht. Schlaf wohl.*

So he tells his little brother, his little married brother, that one of us was born in Berlin and one in New Rochelle and it makes a *difference*, bro, except there is always recurrence. The rolling slope of Guilford, the green sward where they've put him out to pasture while the green sward turns to brown and white and storms blow in and storms blow out and he sits in his rocking chair, rocking. The Bide-a-While and Dew Drop Inn and Connecticut Elder Retreat on the Hill. Where less than seven hours hence, at the year's turning and with transmitters no longer transmitting, time will have a stop. Where Peter Ernest Hochmann waits for the end of the world.

From Australia to New Zealand and New Guinea, from Borneo to Java, from Tahiti to Hawaii and thence by slow yet certain stages to the coasts of Alaska, California, then the Rocky Mountains and the Central Plains and Mississippi Delta (for, truth be told, geography evades him, always has, and he cannot tell for certain which is previous to what in terms of Greenwich Mean Time, not to mention the International Dateline, from west to east and hour after hour, a thousand-mile span spanned while each of the time zones is crossed by the sun, or rather the revolving earth, *poi si muove*); the collapse may have happened already, he thinks, in Easter Island or Guam or the Galapagos, bells ceasing to toll and telephones ceaselessly ringing and islanders feathering paddles, adrift.

So midnight in Connecticut has been midnight elsewhere turn by turn, the millennium slouching, approaching. What Peter wonders and has been trying to assess is this: how do the best-laid plans, the best intentions gang agley, how could what's incorruptible prove so subject to corruption, we who start our dying with our first intake of breath? Our infant wailing gasp. How could it go so wrong?

He considers this. But what is your name, babycakes, he asks the nurse nearing his chair on the porch, because we are in this together and I *should* know you, yes. It is, he thinks, the human condition and wants to laugh for thinking in riddles, repeating them, *the human condition,* the *existential circumstance,* the what-the-fuck does that mean and why do you need to impress her? yet nonetheless and at the present moment in the grip of rhetoric it feels somehow *profound* that she should transfer him to and then push his wheeled conveyance down a well-worn passageway towards a set of celebrants in a place he does not recognize or in the carnal way know. Is this not, he wants to tell the nameless figure at his back, an emblem of the way we live, from darkness into darkness, from the watchman's post to supper because the bell tolls five.

"'Lo, Pete."
  "'Lo, Bill."
  "'Lo, Tom and Dick and Harriet."
"Please pass the salt."
"What did we do today?"
"What day is it?"
"Peter, do we need to go piddle?"
"Piddle?"
"When was the last time you went to the boys' room?"
"Time? Time?"
"I'm only asking."
"No."
"No?"
"*No.*"

Between the grave and cradle, astride the wintry blast and trailing clouds of glory if you turn the handle left or right, the beldam sans merci at his back has wheeled his intricate machine along the corridor that leads from porch to dining hall, that brings him to the dinner trough, the slop they ladle dish by dish and bowl by bowl that soon will be the final time and then the final hours and then the final minutes of the final century: *Shazaam!*

Once Peter Hochmann sat on a wall; once he had a brother and his brother had a wife. And he and the beautiful Sarah took a great fall, or nearly did, and all the King's horses and all the King's men went tumbling down the nonexistent hill on which the house in New Canaan was built, rolling together heels over head like laundry in the fluff-dry cycle and single rotating bin. Must I honor the commandment—the fourth, fifth, which?—against all fornication with my brother's wife? Must I know my place and wait my turn and bide my time? Of all the ladies I have loved this one is beyond compare, intact because *virga in-*

tacta, and of my regrets she is foremost and first. Am I not the very man ye seek who *knows* about the millennium bug and has been crying in the wilderness for lo these many nights? Who used to be a rambling man, who used to travel ceaselessly, who now has left the porch. But, inside, it is warm.

The long, looping syntax of things, the way they wind together then unwind, the feel of the light in your mouth, the sound you make while touching it, the slant of the sunshine precisely the angle it arrived at yesterday, only not *now*, not through the same set of trees or at the equivalent instant, not this minute of the watch he fails to wear—yet keeping watch—not needing radium strapped to a wrist, the reminder (as if anyone needed reminding how time itself is circular and deadly not least because dull, the measure of man's metronomic regularity—this man's, at any rate, who soon enough will be given a napkin they tie to his neck and patted on the shoulder and spoon-fed and wheeled back again and by babycakes prepared for sleep) of our dutiful segmenting declension, the habit of a hierarchy, compassed degrees: fifty-nine to sixty, twelve subordinate to one—and the sun where it was once and would be routinely, as if fifty-nine and sixty are and should be parallel, as if it matters, is of consequence, the sun and dial and generation rising but to fall.

"Are you aware?"

"Aware of what?"

"Cognizant, I mean. Are you cognizant of what this day will bring? This night will bring?"

"Excuse me?"

"*Garbage In. Garbage Out.* That's what we used to call it."

"When?"

"At the dawn of the computer age."

"The dawn?"

"Which now comes to its necessary end."

Six hours now; it's six o'clock and at the stroke of midnight Cinderella will discard her gown and her coach will turn to pumpkin and her matched horses transmogrify to frogs; the fairy-tale princess becomes an old crone, the prince a man who steers his walker down the hall. Once he had danced the courtship-dance, the do-si-do and by-your-leave and real, Virginia, reel. Yes, Virginia, *yes*, there *is* a Santa Claus. And once he would insert himself between the open legs of Cinderella, Sleeping Beauty, Rapunzel, Goldilocks and all who would receive him, though now they too, like the pine needles in the vestibule, are desiccate, unsupple if not dead. And, certainly, not quick. So what he has are memories—sweet Betsy, bitter Angelica—and the nameless legion promenading gaily on the Atlantic City Boardwalk or down the gritty strand of Stinson Beach. It's possible, he knows and knew, to delight in a body some twenty yards distant, some stranger who remains that way, some vision of pure beauty for which a man might lust. *Halt! Who Goes There? Stand and Deliver.* Please.

For they do keep him company: his parents and grandparents and the friends from school and college and battalion of the lost. Why, Peter asks himself, should the language he finds to describe them—*legion, battalion*—belong to the discourse of war? His memories are happy ones, his people laughter-loving, and when the world comes to an end—this world as we know it, this organized bustle—he will take his place at table with the palsied and the bent and bald and await the coming millennium with, ah, equanimity, please pass the ketchup and salt.

They eat. They talk. They smile. They nod assent or shake their heads in disagreement or avoid the topic altogether: ostriches in sand. They pass the time until seven o'clock and sing "Auld Lang Syne" and remember Guy Lombardo leading his band on the crepe-festooned bandstand every New Year's Eve in celebration and with his baton cajoling the horns and strings and winds with which to serenade the great white ball above the Great White Way. Les Brown and His Band of Renown.

Tommy Dorsey, Lawrence Welk, Glenn Miller and Paul Whiting and the rest. Benny Goodman, Artie Shaw. It's pleasant here, he tells himself, and views his newfound company, these shipwrecked survivors of North Hero Island who eat and talk and smile. They speak of band leaders, of dancing till dawn, of traveling to Harlem and the Cotton Club. He's not listening, of course, or only barely listening, and what he hears or overhears is someone else's history, some other set of memories that ravel out in time. For somehow he alone appears to be *en garde* and watchful, waiting for the shoe to drop, the ball to drop, the world to end at midnight while they dance the do-si-do. Because for reasons Peter fails to understand he has been wheeled into his room again and urged to stand and brush his teeth and take his pills and urged to sit and shit and lie down on his bed and cross his arms and close his eyes and sleep.

He does. He sleeps. He dreams. When he awakens it is two a.m., the clock on his bedstand gleaming dully as per usual, as per always, as it has done the night before and the night before that one, the night before that. And no doubt will continue to do the next night and the next. Till time must have a stop. Outside his window there's the usual halo of the usual streetlamp by the entrance gate, the hum of the furnace, the low wheeling clouds and, above them, winking stars. If indeed the world has ended, he thinks, this model of the real thing looks and feels and tastes and smells and sounds persuasive (a siren somewhere, a car driving by) where he studies it: moon, snow at the driveway's edge piled there by plows. He tries to tell, and cannot, if what he is feeling is relief or disappointment, if the failed prophecy brings comfort or discomfort where he lies. Peter reaches for the pillow and, because he has been sweating, turns the dry side up, the wet one down, and dreams Sarah his love is in his arms and he in his bed again.

Tenure
2011

HE HAS EARNED it, finally, and knows he should be pleased. This is not nothing, he knows. To have become a full professor is to have fulfilled a dream—his mother's—although she did not live to see that dream become reality. His mother would have been proud. It was only after Sarah's death Daniel took the process seriously, and these last years of working for promotion have felt like a kind of forced march: *Left* foot, *right* foot, *left*!

He made his way in lockstep through the ranks. It has been, mostly, a bore. It was not why he entered the field. But while his mother lay dying he wanted to assure her that her second son had a future; his brother was a lawyer and he himself was soon to be promoted, so she could rest in peace. From *Assistant* Professor, he became *Associate* Professor, then *Associate* with tenure, and finally *Professor* Daniel Hochmann of the Department of History at the University of California, Berkeley. *Right* foot, *left* foot, *right*!

It has not come easily and has taken time. There were dues he had to pay. The drudgery of academic labor—the articles and panels and symposia and conferences, the theses supervised and the proposals written and meetings attended and the sub-committees chaired and reference letters composed for students' dossiers and the syllabi compiled and filed, then the application process and the national and even, as he later learned, international competition for this particular job, for which he became a finalist and from which, after the round of interviews and a guest lecture given and two demonstration classes taught, he emerged with an offer in 2006—is a weight upon his shoulders he hasn't quite learned to shrug off. It's not an accident, he thinks, that his appointment at Berkeley was labeled *tenure track*. You follow the procedures like a mouse upon a treadmill, and when the treadmill stops turning you're either rewarded or dead.

Daniel gets up from his desk. The fog outside is lifting; soon, he will go for a run. He can remember, way back when, how he fell in love with history, how Castlereagh and Metternich and Talleyrand at the Congress of Vienna came alive for him and moved from hall to hall and document to document with flesh and blood and bone beneath their waistcoats and leggings and bright buckled shoes. The hands that held those quill pens once are hands he felt upon his fingers at the keyboard, guiding every formulation and shaping each line; the minds of Europeans in the Napoleonic era were minds he knew he knew.

His first book on the Congress of Vienna—an enlargement and elaboration of his dissertation at Princeton—had been a kind of game to play: when Castlereagh met Metternich and bowed, and the two men sat on their plush chairs across the four-foot width of the brightly polished table, Daniel *saw* himself as one of the attendants in the room. "More tea, Your Excellency?" he inquired, and the minister nodded assent.

"Might I suggest," said Talleyrand, "a piece of this first-rate cheese?"

"It comes from where?"

"Grenoble," Metternich said. "From a sheep and not a cow."

"A goat," grumbled Viscount Castlereagh. "I am but the butt of your jokes."

He did not write this, of course. He had known enough—even starting out, even as an undergraduate and then a graduate student—not to indulge in fantasy or put words in the diplomats' mouths. But theirs was his story to tell. The Congress of Vienna held no mystery for Daniel; he could describe the pattern of negotiations and the interplay of courtesy and what would later on be called *Realpolitik* with a near-total conviction his description was correct. That conviction took him through the thesis-draft; it took him through his PhD orals and, later on, the interview for his first job at Oberlin and the years of teaching gifted children who would rather be outside, he understood, or listening to music or smoking weed together in their dormitory rooms. When he talked about the nameless dead at Waterloo and those few who survived it—the shoeless soldiers marching, and the mud-bespattered officers on their starving mounts—it was as though the landscape beyond his classroom window became a scene of carnage where "ignorant armies clash by night . . ."

This was a line from Matthew Arnold's "Dover Beach." It provided, as well, the title of a book by Norman Mailer about a march on Washington, D.C. where, in 1968, the anti-Vietnam protest movement gathered steam. He made these points in class, and also referenced a text by the poet Anthony Hecht, "Dover Bitch"—where the figure in the Arnold poem, a man who says, "Ah, Love, let us be true to one another," becomes, in Hecht's modern variant, a man who takes a call-girl to a hotel by the beach.

The students shifted in their seats, grown suddenly alert. "I'm trying to tell you," said Daniel, "that history is relevant. It stays with us. And those who don't understand it are doomed to repeat it, correct? The war in Vietnam must seem like ancient history to you—like something that happened way back when in Greece or Rome. But I have an uncle who walked in that Pentagon protest march, who got tear-gassed and arrested by men he called 'the pigs.' What Wellington did in Waterloo has more to do than you imagine with what's going down in Iraq."

For the early years in academe he'd reveled in such speeches, the chance to make his students and, later on, his readers (however few, however inattentive) enter a time now two centuries past where cakes and cheese and port were served and nation-states created on a polished walnut table. He had embraced the theory of personality in politics: how the outcome of the Congress was at least as much a function of the behavior of diplomats as of the positions they were empowered to take.

It was a variation on the "Great Men in History" theme, except that greatness did not enter in; they had feet of clay up to their necks. Daniel *saw* it; he could *hear* it; at the podium or on the page he brought it back to life.

"Never more serious," Talleyrand said, "*Messieurs, je vous en prie . . .*"

Prince Metternich kept his eye cocked for the serving girl and pinched her well-fed rump. His footman disapproved. Talleyrand had noticed, but Castlereigh ignored them, staring out the mullioned windows at the courtyard beyond. "That *cochon*," said Talleyrand. "The little Corsican. Were it up to me I'd have him horse-whipped in the marketplace."

"It would call too much attention and perhaps arouse some sympathy. Even now, Napoleon has those who call him Emperor."

"*Ganz richtig*," said the Prince. "You are correct."

The men took snuff together and, albeit guarded and mistrustful, created modern Europe with the strokes of their shared pens. The map was four foot square. It had been folded and refolded and rolled into its carrying case; on the upper right-hand corner there was a small jagged tear. This would have to be repaired.

His time at Oberlin was hard in ways that now seem easy; the problems Daniel dealt with were those of ambition and youth. There were two he chose to focus on: the question of "commitment," the question of "career." He was twenty-five years old. In that small town in Ohio he lived alone for the first time, and most days it seemed excellent to do so. At other times he missed his family and college friends, those who had shared his graduate cohort or knew him when a child. But even as he tied his tie or adjusted the tilt of his hat-brim or put his lecture-notes and books in his scuffed leather briefcase, he was trying on identities for size. His mantra was the ancient one: *Where am I going and why am I here?* Those years, he smoked a pipe.

It was an affectation like his other affectations—the riding boots, the torn black jeans—but also a way to fit in. The faculty at Oberlin were proud of their liberal history; the college was one of the first to register women and blacks, and the Underground Railroad flourished nearby. Its liberal ethos suited him, and the concerts offered by Conservatory students were first-rate. One golden-haired harpist compelled him; from his vantage in the audience she looked little short of angelic, and when he praised her playing at the after-performance reception, she said "I do other things also, you know."

"What?"

"Guess." Just below her collarbone there was a tattooed butterfly.

"Other than pluck at the harp strings?"

She smiled.

He pursued his advantage. "The heart strings?"

"Right. It rhymes with 'pluck.'"

In his house that night, with no hesitation, she kicked off her heels and stepped out of her clothes. When she stretched across the bed, he found a matching butterfly tattooed above her knee.

"Ve make beautiful music togezzer," said Daniel, aping a German seducer. "Tonic *und* dominant, *ja?*"

All spring they slept together, and when after commencement she was offered a position in the Denver Symphony Orchestra, he promised he would stay in touch. It was not a promise he kept.

Throughout his time at Williams and then the time at Princeton there had been girls to court and date, and one of them got pregnant. The pregnancy, however, resolved itself before he'd had to deal with it, and somehow there was always slippage in the arc of an affair. Just when he told himself he'd gotten serious, or should be getting serious, he fell or jumped away. One girlfriend gave Daniel a book. It was a descriptive text about a psychological personality-type the author labeled *The Dance-Away Lover*, and that was how he saw himself: two steps forward, one step back. There were romantic partners everywhere, and none of them felt permanent the way his mother did.

Yet that very sense of permanence—his mother in the garden, his mother in the library, his mother in the car—was being undermined. The single woman in his life from whom he could not separate, and had no desire to, was living in New Canaan in a slow then steep decline. In the late spring of 2006—his final semester at Oberlin—Sarah Hochmann died.

It was John who called to tell him that the doctors had decided on no further course of treatment, and from here on out the game to play was just a waiting game.

"What are you *talking* about?"

His elder brother sounded, as always, self-contained. "The protocols are palliative, not remedial."

"Is that law-speak?" Daniel asked. "What the fuck are you telling me? Trying to tell me."

"It isn't quite time to start hanging the crepe . . ."

"What does *that* mean?"

"But, Dan, you should get yourself ready."

He hung up. His cellphone barely functioned in the empty countryside, and he had used the land-line: a yellow wall-mounted relic with a twisting spiral cord. He watched the cord coil and uncoil.

"My fucking boy-scout brother," he told the kitchen cabinet, "with his fucking 'Be prepared.'"

Outside, it rained. The downspout by the window streamed. His anger at his brother was, he told himself, irrational; he shouldn't blame the messenger for delivering bad news. Yet John's declarative calm made Daniel feel, as always, patronized; he was thirty-one years old but being condescended to, dismissed . . .

He called the house in New Canaan. "Do you want me to come home?"

Sarah told him, "No."

He asked his father the same thing, and Frederick said, "Do what your mother wants."

"I want to be useful."

"You are."

"What does she want from me? *For* me?"

"She needs to know you're settled. And not a rolling stone . . ."

"Tell her I'm settled," he said.

Yet Daniel knew from the beginning he was just passing through. In preparation for the move to Oberlin, he bought a 1967 Porsche and, after it broke down repeatedly, a ten-year-old Corvette. He liked his little rented farmhouse at the edge of town—the sense of an unchanging landscape nonetheless subject to seasonal change. The role of chicken farmer, the role of stock-car racing enthusiast, the role of gourmet—this last because, for half a year, he slept with a curator from the art museum who was serious about her food and writing a book about artists as cooks—were roles he took on turn by turn. It had been a waiting game, he told himself, while he had been deciding to decide . . .

In the early mornings, sometimes, standing by the kitchen stove or taking his dog Rufus—a tall mournful-eyed mutt he'd acquired at the Farmer's Market from a Pet Adoption Agency—out for a run, he told himself this life he was living was worth it, this happy alliance of body and mind was one he should plan to continue. The bookstore was obliging, the concert series inventive, the drive to Cleveland or Ann Arbor an easy one to make. The harpist and the curator and a waitress in the French restaurant outside of town all gave Daniel pleasure, and he told himself he pleased them too, yet it had to do with transience: *Dance Away*. He liked to sit out on his screened-in porch, nursing a gin and tonic and staring at the expansive sky or, in heavy weather, watching the lightning and rain.

But even in the flush of it, raking leaves and drinking cider with his colleagues, arguing the hermeneutics of campus behavior and a proposal for divestiture from all investments in the Oberlin Portfolio that profited from fossil fuels, he knew it was time to move on.

His second full-length effort, *Palmerston and Empire*, followed the conceptual pattern established by the first. As Geoffrey Scott had put it in *The Portrait of Zelide*—from which Daniel took his epigraph—he described a "frond of flame." Both dashing Viscount Palmerston and his wife Mary were the ancestors, or so Daniel argued, of telegenic politicians nowadays, those men whose profiles manage to convey (the jutting chin, the noble nose) strong character. So too were those eighteenth-century courtesans with powdered curls and scented arms who wound their seeming masters around their ring fingers like string. Again, as an historian, he had no trouble picturing the drawing rooms and smoky chimneys of English aristocracy, the whispered innuendos of one statesman to his rival's impoverished cousin, and how the petty quarrels of a Baron and his banker might pave the way to reform. There was a ditty of the period he used to make the point:

> A smoky house
> And scolding wife
> Are two of the worst ills of life.

Mary Palmerston abhorred the way black coal dust blew back from her chimney, soiling the armchairs and staining the silk carpets. "Oh, Benjamin," she told her suitor, "I'm sick to death of this sooty inconvenience; won't you do something, please?"

"Such as?"

She made a *moue*. "Rid me of this plague of ash."

He did. Sir Benjamin Thompson—later Count Rumford of the Holy Roman Empire—designed a chimney with an aperture that blocked soot from the downdraft and kept living quarters clean. The invention of the smoke-shelf was therefore the result of but a moment's pleading; Thompson made this new arrangement to satisfy his mistress and be, in turn, rewarded by her smile. More than her smile, of course, but Daniel left this to his students' and his readers' imagination, drawing the curtain on the scene of their hot courtship as the footman drew the drapes.

Here once again his theory was that history and human personality are interlinked: less by a one-to-one equivalence than an action-reaction formation. The yearnings and ambitions of individual players had more to do with general change than generally acknowledged. To understand air pollution in England, and the improvement of household hygiene for both the rich and poor in the mid-nineteenth century, it was useful to report upon the mating game of a London-based aristocrat and her inventive lover. The "dark, satanic mills" of Blake's great poem, "Jerusalem," were in that sense predictive of an energy-based economy as well as the industrial revolution; the "green and pleasant land" Blake mourned went up in coal dust and smoke.

This biography earned a nomination, although he did not win, for the best book on the history of modern Europe: the Ickes-Bollinger Prize. With his study of the Congress of Vienna and his biography of Palmerston—both published by Princeton University Press—Daniel staked a claim.

It was then he moved to Berkeley and there he met Eileen. She too was recently arrived in town, having come from the East Coast; they wandered through the streets and parks together and by the end of the first week were lovers. During a meal at Chez Panisse, and wondering at the rush of it, because he had known many women and had never felt this way before, Daniel asked her to move in with him and, when she demurred, proposed.

"What took you so long?" asked Eileen.

"To make an honest woman of you?"

She laughed. "I thought we were past that . . ."

"We are."

He ordered a second bottle, and she said that she was flattered and, she had to admit it, surprised. But this wasn't something she thought they could settle at dinner, or not before dessert.

Her hair was brown, her eyes blue. She was long-legged and slim-hipped and her cheekbones were pronounced; she worked

on Shattuck Avenue, as the office manager for a capital management firm. The firm had six employees and a hundred clients; it
was her job to manage schedules and to maintain the files. After
their first night together, Eileen read his book on Palmerston, in
particular the chapter on the dalliance of Lady Mary with Benjamin Thompson. Speaking carefully she said that—contrary to
available evidence and, no doubt, his own experience and, she
may as well confess it, hers—she believed in marital fidelity, not
infidelity, so if you make a vow it's one to keep.

"I plan to," Daniel said.

Then, as if a "To-Do" list were written on her napkin, with
agenda items to attend to, and she was crossing them off, she
looked up and touched his hand. "It sounds like a change of
subject," she said, "but it isn't, really." He should know she
wanted children, and if they were going to marry she wanted
children soon. Eileen hoped to meet his father and she planned
to meet his brother—who was living, after all, in San Francisco,
a short ride across the Bay.

He demurred. He told her that he didn't have much use for
John; his older brother was too straight-laced for his liking, full
of disapproval and a pattern of behavior that made him a perfect example of—did she remember the phrase?—"the man in
the gray flannel suit."

"I thought that went out with the fifties."

"It did. Or should have anyhow. But he's a throw-back . . ."

She shook her head. He told her, then, about his uncle Peter who had been a—no better word for it—hippie, and how
Peter and his father were almost total strangers who didn't like
each other much, and maybe that was passed along unto the
next generation, two ways of being in the world that seemed,
if not irreconcilable, at odds. He himself had loved his uncle,
had tried to *be* like Peter, who made each visit seem a celebration. Everything would lighten up and be unpredictable, and
the windows of their closed-in colonial house in New Canaan
were thrown wide.

Now, Daniel understands, that rush of air had been intended to mask the pot his uncle smoked, the constant smell of

marijuana on his clothing and hands. But when he was still a boy and Peter came to stay with them—practicing his card tricks and delivering long speeches about the nature of democracy—those open windows were an emblem of the life to come.

"Your brother wasn't buying it?"

"It's like that nursery rhyme, the one about Jack and Mrs. Spratt and how the two together lick the platter clean. If I played baseball he played chess, if I wanted chocolate cake he chose vanilla instead. When I grew my hair long he sported a buzz cut—you know. We staked out ways of being that edged up against each other but didn't cross the line."

"Makes me glad I was an only child . . ."

"That has its limitations too, I imagine."

Again Eileen considered him, her blue eyes unblinking. She wiped her lips.

"What you have to understand," he said, "is I come from family that's both family-proud and ashamed of itself, both glad to have survived the Holocaust and guilty for having done so. Not unusual, I'd guess; I only learned a little while ago of great-uncles dead in Auschwitz and aunts sent to Dachau. As if we should be embarrassed that they hadn't quite escaped . . ."

There was a space between her two front teeth he found endearing, exciting. "Are you serious?"

"About."

"Wanting to get married? About what you just asked me? Or is it the wine talking?"

"I'm serious," he said.

The waiter came to ask if they were finished and he could clear the plates. Daniel shook his head. "No worries," the waiter declared. His accent was Australian, and the skin of his cheek was abraded and red.

Eileen spoke about the men she worked for down the way on Shattuck, their private clients and corporate accounts, the *bonhomie* in the office and how it pleased her to have found this job because her duties were specific and work-tasks defined. Office management was easy; what was hard was the rest of her life. When he asked her what she meant, she said other people's

problems were problems she knew how to solve. But she wasn't
so efficient with her own . . .

She herself had been married once, briefly, and it was a mistake. Mr. Wrong had been the very picture of dependability—a
lacrosse-playing Brooks Brothers type out of Groton and Yale
who worked long days on Wall Street and was renting a pent-
house with a view of the Statue of Liberty. He had just the right
"cut to his jib."

"Can you imagine,"—mirthlessly, she laughed—"those were
the words he used: 'Cut to his jib.' I should have known from
the get-go it was all for show, a matter of playacting. But he had
me fooled."

Their first few months were happy ones—late-night dinners
and Broadway shows and a timeshare in the Hamptons. The
mood swings and the violence were matters she could deal with,
and she told herself, when he came home at three a.m., it was
the pressure of Wall Street and he needed time to unwind. So
for a year she let him and, for a year, he tried. Staring out the
window, or on their little balcony, he would raise his glass of
Grey Goose to the illumined statue, quoting Emma Lazarus,
"'Give me your poor, your huddled masses yearning to be free.'"

And then he turned to her to say, "They got it wrong, of
course. The last word should be 'fleeced.' '. . . yearning to be
fleeced.'"

When it snowed, the statue's arm acquired a white sleeve.
When it froze, the torch nonetheless gleamed. It took her longer
than it should have to discover Harry had the habit of cocaine
and a Puerto Rican boyfriend who was dealing on the side . . .

Eileen shook her head; again, she touched his hand. Impulse
buying, she continued, isn't such a good idea, and this time
through she planned to be more careful, so he would have to
wait. Financial planning is a long-term proposition, or ought to
be; and if that's the case for stocks and bonds how much more
true it is, or should be, for romance.

"Agreed?" she asked.

"Agreed."

Her manner and matter-of-factness intrigued him. When

the time came to take away the leavings of their bouillabaisse, and the waiter proffered a fresh set of menus, she said she couldn't manage a dessert.

"I'll ask again tomorrow," Daniel said.

His third book proved both more ambitious and less easily accomplished. It took a full five years. Daniel wrote about the crucial half century from 1820 to 1870, when Europe rearranged itself into a kind of precursor of the contemporary continent—when a sufficiently discerning witness could predict and track in retrospect the contours of incipient nationalism and therefore the political and cultural and economic alliances to come. The modern idea of empire and that a nation-state could consolidate shared borders—the very notion of hegemony and of "spheres of influence" (as opposed, say, to the model of invasion and military subjugation)—was conceived of in that period and place. The revolts of 1830, 1848, 1870, as well as the spasmodic upheavals and small protests in between were also, he argued in *France Sneezes*, a function of the attitudes and personal antagonisms of the Heads of State.

"Hegel remarks somewhere that all great world-historic facts and personages appear, so to speak, twice. He forgot to add: the first time as tragedy, the second time as farce."

So wrote Karl Marx in *The Eighteenth Brumaire of Louis Napoleon*, and this framed Daniel's project: a pairing and comparison of its antecedents with the present day. By "present day," he meant mid-twentieth-century Europe, but the figures of Churchill and Hitler and Daladier and Mussolini were presaged by their predecessors in the birth of the contemporary nation-state. He did not suggest, of course, a full-scale replication, but the types of rule and ruler had been established early on. From Napoleon I to Napoleon III and, by extension, Charles de Gaulle, it was possible to trace the slow relinquishing of the dream of empire, and *France Sneezes* focused on (though radiating outward from) the years 1830 to 1848.

Therefore the self-described "citizen king," Louis Philippe, with his umbrella and his waddling gait became a kind of caricature of the present-day politico seeking to ratify power; his time spent in America and England was both a form of exile and a source of education. The portly scion of the Bourbon line called himself not "King of France" but "King of the French," and much was entailed by that change. Now the few remaining hereditary monarchs—witness Queen Elizabeth II—must expect to be the subject of cartoons. In her great predecessor's time an indecorous phrase could cause an earl to lose his head, not to mention his castle and lands; in Rupert Murdoch's info-empire, the royal family's behavior was fair game for headlines and unflattering front-page photographs. In this regard, both François Mitterrand's illegitimate daughter and Camilla Parker-Bowles were part of an ancient declension; from the Sun King's momentary favorite to an elected official's thrice-married consort is less a tragedy played out as farce than a line of indirect or collateral descent. *Tout commence en mystique et finit en politique.* So wrote Charles Péguy. "All that begins in mystery ends up as politics."

This text earned him his promotion. It was—one of the reviewers wrote—"a compelling display of erudition, but not for erudition's sake. Rather, Professor Hochmann's inquiry does what good history should do: bring the past to present life." Daniel spent a semester in Paris doing primary research, and the book did wear its learning lightly; he was aiming for an audience not only academic, and his language was clear and concise. *France Sneezes* was published by the University of California Press as their featured title for the fall of 2010. The publication party resulted also in an evening's celebration with Eileen, though he could not shake the sense, even as she moved above him, her breasts swaying and her neck arched back in seeming ecstasy, that she was going through the motions of delight. "Was it good for you?" she asked him later, joking, stroking his still-erect penis, and he told her, "Yes."

"Are you finished?"

"No."

"I didn't think so," said his wife and straddled him again.

Theirs is a good marriage. He respects her, and she him; they share the household's tasks. When he returns from a speaking engagement, or she comes back from the office, it is always a comfort to see her: the cheekbones and the pale blue eyes, the managerial competence with which she unpacks groceries or whips up a stir fry of soft-shell crabs. As had been the case with his mother, Eileen is an excellent cook. She meditates each morning, and although he knows not to intrude he likes to watch her sitting cross-legged, eyes closed, palms raised, half humming. This Friday will be her thirty-fifth birthday, and he has planned a family outing to the Post Ranch Inn. It is expensive—frivolous, even, to take the children to a place exalting silence—but he knows she will be happy in Big Sur. It gives him pleasure to please her, and the weather is predicted to be fine.

With the arrival of their son and daughter, Daniel has shifted allegiance; he wants to spend his time at home and not in his office at school. William and Sue are four and two years old respectively, and already they have staked their claims on who does what. Little Susie is a charmer, an attention-getter, her big brother likes to build things, or play Candyland for hours. She smiles; he scowls; she burbles, disrupting his silence. Between the two of them, he thinks—and can remember saying something of the same to Eileen at Chez Panisse—they lick the platter clean.

By pooling their joint assets (his wife's salary is smaller, but with her annual bonus there's a rough equivalence), they have bought a gray shingled house on Lewiston. It is worth two million dollars, and Frederick provided the bulk of the down payment and counter-signed the loan. The monthly charges stretch them, but the house is sizeable, and they have room to expand. There's a triangular garden patch, a porch that needs repairing, and a portico with wisteria curled tautly to the crossbars; each year, it must be pruned. There are three bedrooms on the second floor and a studio with bookshelves. On both sides of the entrance hall, bay windows give onto the street. Rufus likes to lie on the living-room bench and, jumping up from it, his every muscle straining, bark at the neighborhood dogs.

So here he is at thirty-six, the father of two children and a tenured full professor in a steeply mortgaged house. That he has settled down to domesticity surprises him a little, but his unmarried colleagues are not an occasion for envy, and he wishes Sarah had lived long enough to meet his wife. He would like to be friends with his brother, and from time to time does try.

The desire is reciprocal, and once in a while John calls to say there's an afternoon free. Two weeks ago he did so, saying Saturday could work, and was Daniel busy?

"We could watch the Preakness," Daniel had suggested. "Post time is 6:18 in Baltimore; why don't you come on by at two, two-thirty?"

"Great. Or you could come to us?"

"My turn to play the host, I think. Last time we went to you . . ."

"OK."

"I'll have mint juleps ready. Do they serve juleps for the Preakness?"

"They don't grow mint in Maryland. Or if they do, it's not for that drink." With his habitual precision, John declared, "Juleps are for the Kentucky Derby."

Despite their good intentions, these meetings are not a success. Daniel feels uneasy with his sister-in-law: her hair-trigger temper and ready disapproval, her sense that she goes slumming when she drives across the Bay. Harriet makes her preference for San Francisco clear. Her own house on the slope of Nob Hill has been designed to a fare-thee-well: half French chateau, half English country cottage; what he thinks of as his own companionable clutter is, to her way of thinking, a mess. Nothing the Berkeley clan can do seems right to her; nothing he says strikes a chord. He tries to pretend the dynamic is easy, and that they share more than the family name, but it doesn't work.

Eileen is sensitive to this, and shares his dislike of the woman, yet they do what they can to pretend all is well, and hope to make the cousins get along. Harriet and John also have a son and daughter, Colin and Carrie: teenagers who have little use for Will and Sue except to call them cute and stare into the middle distance; when they arrive on Saturday, they eat more than their share of the cake.

"Free radicals," says Harriet. "Isn't that a term from mathematics?"

"Yes."

"So why are they called radicals here? The ones, I mean, on Telegraph Avenue?"

"You mean the homeless?" asks Eileen.

Daniel tries to intervene, but the two of them start arguing, and the argument is not of course about its ostensible subject—the *laissez faire* treatment of the homeless by the Berkeley City Council, the price of curbside collection when it means that cans and bottles are picked over by street people so there's no revenue available for Recycle Berkeley itself—but about a way of life.

The horses and their riders exit the paddock, prancing, and approach the starting gate. He wishes he could say to them, "Oh, let it go, let's watch the race," but one thing he has learned about his wife in the five years of their marriage is her tenacity in argument, her refusal to be bullied, and he and John stare at the flickering screen.

The song "Maryland, My Maryland" has the same tune as "O Tannenbaum," a German Christmas carol their parents used to sing. He does not know the words to "Maryland, my Maryland," but starts to hum along.

John interrupts. "Do you think it was immigrants missing *Der Vaterland*?"

"Not likely," Daniel says.

"I thought it was Lord Baltimore who settled Maryland. Why would he choose a German song about a Christmas tree?"

"He wouldn't have," Harriet says.

Across the room the children have begun to play Monopoly. The two elder cousins are humoring the younger ones; Susie is only two years old and unable to follow the rules.

"It's *this* way," Carrie explains, "you roll the dice and do what it tells you to, see? You move as many spaces as you count black dots."

Susie tries. She rolls the dice and throws them at the board. They bounce and knock over the racecar and a house on Marvin Avenue, and her brother swats her and she starts to cry. Someone kicks the board. For a moment there is bedlam; Susie wails, Will shouts, and Colin and Carrie start laughing. Then, as if on a prearranged signal, they turn away from Monopoly and consult their phones.

The brothers each have picked a horse, although they do not bet. Daniel's choice, a tall black beauty, breaks free at the starting gate, then falters in the stretch. He loses by twelve lengths. John's horse does win, but had been the favorite, with odds of five to four.

"If this were a real bet," he says—demonstrating what Daniel thinks of as needless pedantry—"you'd owe me eighty dollars. Assuming, that is, we followed the odds and bet twenty each."

When Harriet announces they have a dinner engagement that evening and must get back across the bridge, he does not try to dissuade them. He thanks his brother for coming, and walks them to their car.

In the department meeting on Tuesday afternoon, there had been a discussion of next year's "Theme Semester." His colleagues planned to focus on the plight of indigenous peoples, how California had been built by and was still dependent on the labor of Mexicans and Chinese workers, not to mention the original settlers, who are today almost extinct. They would offer a collective course on the Spanish–American War, and Daniel volunteered to lecture on the brief quixotic rule of Maximilian and Carlotta, two Hapsburg adventurers installed on the "throne" of Mexico in a bid for annexation that was doomed from the start.

Napoleon III, the Emperor who sponsored them—his uncle's large pale shadow—was a case study not so much in delusions of grandeur as of overreaching; had he not emptied the national coffers for a set of pointless wars (Maximilian and Carlotta's importantly among them), he might have died in peace. The parallels to Bush and Iraq and Afghanistan were too obvious to belabor, but "tragedy" and "farce" have played out here again.

The head of the sub-concentration in Women's Studies called the situation in the Middle East merely the most recent of America's "macho wars." "It's a sequel to the prize fight our government picked after September 11. There was Teddy Roosevelt with his 'Big stick!' and Ronald Reagan with his cowboy hat and the Iraq war with that parachuting idiot from Texas; now there's Obama with 'selective intervention.' You guys wave your little popguns and assassinate a cleric and persuade yourselves it's God's great work."

"Marla, be civil," growled the Graduate Office Director.

"Do you call assassination 'civil'? A SWAT team or the mess in Kabul—not to mention Nicaragua, Granada, and the rest. Define the difference, please."

"There's all the difference in the world! I resent the implication that the masculine hegemony—*if* there's any such thing any longer—is implicated here."

"It isn't personal," said the Department Chair. "Let's not get personal."

"*All* politics are personal," insisted the outgoing head of the Curriculum Committee. "Remember Tip O'Neill? Most of you are much too young, but he was the House Speaker with a genius for compromise, and if he went out for a drink with his counterparts in the Republican party they'd end the evening in agreement, not—the way it happens now—stalemate."

"Why is this relevant, Fred?"

"Because each time we make a decision we're changing the face of the theme semester. And, as I scarcely need to remind you, we voted on it last year. *Two* years ago, in fact, when we commenced this debate. And, let me remind you, our subject here is *history*."

Daniel looked around the room. Half of those present were male, half female, but their gender made less difference than their age. There were the old and the bespectacled and garrulous, the young and the severe ones with metal studs in their ears. The department's language theorist disagreed with the specialist in Gramsci—his "Prison Notebooks"—and their disagreement grew loud. Iraq and Lebanon and Libya were referred to turn by turn, although the true equivalence—so stated the Director of Women's Studies—is Palestine. Lacan, Derrida, and Walter Benjamin were each invoked as central to the indigenous imprisoned population; so were Foucault and Fanon. What the Native Americans of the Northwest and the displaced Arabs have in common is deracination-*cum*-a-despairing-rootedness; it's not too much, said the specialist in Gramsci, to claim elective affinity here.

He drew in a deep breath. The terms of their discussion were not ones he wished to credit, the discourse not something he shared. Daniel reminded his colleagues that their expertise lay elsewhere, but the drum-beat for engagement was beating in the room. These people were impassioned, yet he found himself unable to follow the drift of the argument, unwilling to take seriously the serious issues they raised. What, he wondered, had happened to his love of scholarship and the work of history; would he, starting out again, have made it his chosen career?

He doubted it. Castlereagh and Palmerston and Metternich and Talleyrand and Louis Philippe and the Napoleons had been his familiars, once; now they are ghosts gone mute.

Eileen drives off to work at eight each weekday morning, and Isabella—a thirty-year-old from Costa Rica—arrives. She cleans up the kitchen, and does a daily laundry, but most of the time she occupies herself with Will and Susie, watching TV and using her cellphone and speaking rapid Spanish to other people's nannies. She takes the children to the playground and, when he learns to use a tricycle, pushes Susie in a stroller while Will peddles ahead.

Daniel wishes his mother were alive to enjoy his son and daughter, but Frederick appears to, when he comes to visit or they travel east. They have managed to make the trip twice. It's no simple thing to organize: the drive to the airport, the interminable plane ride, the drive from Kennedy or Bradley, if they choose to change planes in Chicago, the children sick or restless and their tempers frayed . . .

He feels concern for his father. But when Eileen says, "We should ask him to move in with us," he disagrees.

"Why not? In other countries and other cultures it would happen in a heartbeat."

"Right. But Dad is far too private . . ."

"And?"

"And John would think he's playing favorites. If he came to Berkeley and not San Francisco."

"Well, what about some somewhere between the two cities? Some retirement community up in Marin County, maybe, or Richmond?"

"Can you see him there?" asked Daniel. "He's happy where he's living. Or at least as happy nowadays as he knows how to be."

"I suppose that's true. But still . . ."

Her own parents are in Florida, living near a golf course in a gated condo complex at the edge of Longboat Key. They are younger than Frederick, healthier, and they extol the virtues of the climate in their newfound home—except, of course, for summertime, when they return to New Hampshire.

Daniel laces up his running shoes and pulls on a sweatshirt and lets himself out of the door. Having stretched, he jogs through the low streets and starts up Tunnel Avenue. In the hills of Berkeley it's not easy to maintain a pace, but once he reaches the top of Vincennes he has a level run.

At eleven o'clock, the fog has lifted, and the day has gone

from crisp to warm; the route he has planned is three miles. It comes to Daniel, finally, that what he wants to write about is his own family—their succeeding generations and what was gained, what lost. The views of the Bay and the high scudding clouds still have the power to move him; he feels his spirits rise. *This is not nothing*, he repeats to himself, and, on a steep cobbled downhill slope, windmills his arms as he strides.

Finale
2018

HE LIES ON his bed with two pillows beside him. He lies on his left side. They keep the bedroom windows closed, but the blinds have been raised and the curtains stay open—bringing warmth as well as light. Frederick enjoys the view, or claims to, although he can no longer see it with precision. It doesn't matter, he says; a loss of hearing would have been more difficult to bear. He knows the landscape well enough; diminished detail and the blurring do not alter what he sees. Beyond the window lies the garden, and past the garden stands the hedge, and down past the hedge runs the street.

His bedroom gives out on the easterly view, and also the view to the south. He has owned the house in New Canaan, now, for more than forty years. At first it was too large a place, but he and Sarah "colonized" the property. This had been Sarah's joke, since the structure was built in colonial style, with porticos and wings. The previous owners had whitewashed the brick, and there are dark green shutters, and the roof is patterned slate. "We'll grow into it," she told him, although he felt uncertain and thought a "starter" house would make more sense. She said, "It feels just right."

His wife had been correct, of course; her judgment was better than his. What had seemed excessive to Frederick came to fit their growing family, and as his business prospered the place even came to seem modest. There were beds and television sets and paintings and etchings and rugs and quilts and lithographs and rocking chairs and desks in every room; they could sleep twelve people easily and, with some crowding, fifteen. For years their children and their children's children filled the halls with music and shouting and traffic and laughter. But, as Sarah used to say, "This too shall pass." It passed.

The nurses plan a party. They don't want to surprise him, they say, so he shouldn't be surprised if old friends come to visit, and the children and grandchildren. He will turn seventy-nine. "It's not every day we celebrate a birthday, now do we?" asks Maureen, with that mix of compassion and condescension that marks the professional nurse. She has the nightshift, Jenelle the morning, and Miriam the afternoon; between the three of them, says Miriam, they lick the platter clean. Then there are the people from Hospice, and if you add the social worker and the supervisor and substitute nurses it's quite a chorus line.

He knows he should be grateful; he tries not to be ungrateful, but it irritates him nonetheless to be so *handled* by a bunch of women he would otherwise have had no occasion to meet. They are intimate with him in ways he finds *surprising*: not erotic, certainly, and not any longer embarrassing, but surprising he should find himself on a first-name basis with so many strangers, plump women wearing cardigans and sneakers, thin ones with glasses on ribbons and their hair in nets . . .

Still, he does want this party; he looks forward to it avidly, imagining who will and won't attend. He tries to remember who promised to travel, and who proved unable to come. Balloons and paper hats and ice-cream cones are not perhaps appropriate—the kind of celebration a young child would hope for—nor are middle-aged festivities: a dinner party possibly, a night at a concert or play. For years he and Sarah had honored each other by going to Carnegie Hall or the theater; her birthday came on July 23, his on December 18.

This meant, she used to tease him, she was an older woman and he'd better mind his manners or she'd send him back to school. His wife had not reached seventy, and for reasons he can't understand it seems important to Frederick that he will outlive her by twelve years. He does intend to make remarks and blow the candles out; he has planned his thank-you speech.

Judy Olesker comes to visit; her husband, Sam, is dead. They are, she says, a pair of survivors, the last man and woman standing though he's mostly lying down. She drives over for the afternoon in Sam's vintage Cadillac, and complains about the cost of gasoline and, when she dented the fender, how much it cost to repair. They drink tea or sherry together, although lately Frederick has not been drinking sherry. He would like to start again. Before the summer came, when he was feeling, as she put it, perky, *up to it*, Judy drove him into the center of New Canaan and a restaurant they used to frequent, or the Farmer's Market if the weather was propitious and the peaches or sweet corn were fine. Over the Early Bird Special or the Seniors' Discount Dinner they would have what she called an "organ recital," discussing their various ailments, and then by mutual agreement put the topic of their health aside and reminisce instead about the days when Sam was alive, and Sarah alive, and the parties they had thrown and the mixed-doubles tennis they played as couples together.

His wife and Judy were intimate friends; there was nothing they did not discuss. Sarah called it "girl talk" and said it was par for the course. It's what we mean by friendship, she said, it's the way women behave. Then, when she lost her long battle with cancer, on her death-bed—so says Judy—she made Judy promise to keep an eye on Frederick and keep him in the world.

This the Oleskers had done, taking him along with them on a trip through Eastern Europe. His visitor reminds him of a concert in Vienna the three of them attended—Yefim Bronfman playing Brahms—and a hotel they stayed in on the Ringstrasse near the Opera House. Did he remember how the elevators stopped functioning one evening, and by way of apology the concierge had offered champagne? Hotel guests gathered in the lobby by the piano player, and a group of South Africans started to dance, and by the time the elevators were working everyone was drunk. Judy talks about the trip through Austria and Hungary, then the Czech Republic, and how in Germany they visited his mother's—no, it had been his father's—house.

"Charlottenburg. Do you remember?" she asks.

"Of course I remember," he says. The trip was a success. On the last day Sam suggested, "Next year, let's do wine country. Let's take a trip to Burgundy and maybe the Loire Valley; let's do some serious tasting in France."

They planned the trip for May, because Sarah died in May, and it was good to leave Connecticut that month. But before they had a chance to finalize their itinerary, on April Fool's Day Sam Olesker had a heart attack he'd had no warning of, and no way to prepare for. The two of them were sitting in the library reading the newspaper, says Judy, and Sam got up to answer the phone and stumbled and fell as he reached for it, and by the time the telephone stopped ringing he was dead.

She purses her lips, shakes her head. The one good thing about a lengthy sickness—though she wouldn't of course wish lengthy sickness on an enemy much less on her dearest friend— is you get the chance to *think* about it, to prepare for what's going to happen. But she had had no time to do so and had made no plans.

"It isn't something you prepare for," Frederick says. "And anyhow it takes you by surprise."

"Not *you*," says Judy, "I don't believe it, nothing takes you by surprise."

She means this as a compliment, he knows, but today it does not feel that way, and he explains: "I knew Sarah was dying, of course, I'd been prepared for it. The doctors made it clear. So it wasn't in that sense surprising—but I was unprepared. You go through life together and do everything in lockstep and attain a perfect unison if not a perfect harmony, until one fine day there's no one walking at your side."

She sips her tea. "That lockstep you're talking about," Judy says, "you make it sound as if we're majorettes, drum major-ettes. In some college marching band."

Then she makes a gesture with her free left hand as though she were twirling a baton, and throwing it, and catching it, then drops her hand to her hip.

He laughs. She has, he assures her, not lost a step—a half-step at most—and Judy says that isn't true. "I'm an old bag. A hag."

"Oh no," he tells her, courtly, "you look just the same to me."

"But you're legally blind," she reminds him. "And anyway"—this is an expression she and Sarah used to use—"you're one cucumber sandwich short of a picnic, my friend."

He laughs again. He can hear himself laughing: wheezily, high-pitched. No one had ever suggested that Frederick Hochmann was "short of a picnic" or anything other than up to the job; all his life he had been praised for managerial skill. All his life he had made plans. He still can manage, for instance, to maneuver himself on the pillows; he shifts them perceptibly and takes a new position in the bed beneath the coverlet so he and Judy are no longer in Miriam's sight-line, and winks at Sam's widow, his wife's closest friend—the one whom, thirty years ago, he might have made his mistress, except that thirty years ago he was happy in his marriage and did not want a mistress—and says, "'Have some Madeira, m'dear.'"

His brother too has died. That had been less of a loss. Peter had memory lapses and—depending on his medication—fits of depression or wild flights of fancy and, for the last five years, congestive heart failure and diabetes and glaucoma and a list of problems he would recite in a loud voice when Frederick arrived in the establishment in Guilford. Before relinquishing his driver's license, he'd visited his brother in the nursing home—more out of duty than desire—twice yearly. The last time, when Peter was dying, he hired a car and driver, taking a day to go from New Canaan round-trip.

They were not, had never been, close. Their attitudes and memories diverged. Peter, for instance, had few happy recollections of childhood and at every chance complained about their parents—the severity, the what-he-called hypocrisy of their standard of behavior, the way they bought into a system of which he (who had been a charter member of the "Flower Power" movement, who hitched a ride one brief shining afternoon on Ken Kesey's bus in Oregon, who had dropped out by dropping acid, as he liked to say, with "the best minds of my generation," and who never held a job for more than a year or stayed with the same woman for two) disapproved.

It has taken Frederick much of his adult life to understand his brother did not like him, was full of old suspicions and a sense of past injustice. *You were the one,* he thinks Peter thought, *our mother doted on, the one she sat up all night long with when you had a fever; you walked the straight and narrow line and all your life you've had a poker up your ass.*

In his bed now, he shifts.

"Are we feeling sleepy?" asks the nurse.

He shakes his head.

"Do we have to go potty? Tinkle?"

Again, he shakes his head.

"Are we hungry at all?"

"Are you hungry?" Frederick asks Judy, and she tells him no, she has to go. She will return for the party, she promises, and be here to help on Saturday, first thing. Meantime, he should save his strength.

"Don't you want to stay?"

And sweetly, kindly, sadly, Sam's widow tells him "No."

His sons arrive. John, the elder, flies from San Francisco; last year, he filed for divorce. John's son is a sophomore in college, his daughter still in high school, and since her mother has returned to Cleveland she goes to high school there. But they are all, he tells his father, planning to join the celebration and coming up on Saturday to say hello to the cousins. Dan and Eileen and the gang are getting here tomorrow, says John, but I had to take a deposition in New York. And so I took advantage of the trip to visit Colin yesterday; he loves it at Columbia, he's majoring, or planning to, in economics and then he wants business school.

John shakes his head. "What I mostly think he loves is the Upper West Side and all those bars and coffee shops and Barnard girls. You're only young once, is what I tell him, take advantage of it while you can. Right, Dad?"

Frederick nods. But this is a subject they need not pursue: the subject of college and youth. Its pleasures are self-evident, as are its disappointments and distractions and finally its evanescence: we all have once been young. We all have been to school and frequented a coffee shop or bar. What he wants to tell his visitor, but does not, is that the last occasion the whole family assembled here was at Sarah's funeral, and this is a rehearsal for the next such time they'll meet.

He holds his tongue. He does not say, for instance, how it troubles him that everybody in the Hochmann clan has settled in the West—or Midwest, if you add John's daughter Carrie—as far away as possible from Connecticut. Why should we have a continent between us, he wants to ask his children; what does it mean that there are now three thousand miles of distance between members of the family? It is, of course, the American dream—one son a lawyer, the other a tenured professor—but to Frederick in his empty house it feels like failure not success. Why should I lie here by myself with these nurses in attendance who know nothing of my history, *our* history; why do you come to see me *now* and not when I need you each day?

They would offer no adequate answer. It is—Sarah's expression again—Fortune's wheel. Or, as his mother used to declare, "Such is life."

His head hurts. The dull pain has stayed with him, and he cannot feel his feet, and he needs to pee. An ache nags at his shoulders and across his upper arms. It is, he tells Maureen—when, checking his oxygen level, she asks—not severe but a discomfort, and it's not unusual; he's used to it, lord knows, and just answering her question: "How're we doing, hon?"

You live, he wants to tell his visitor, with the sense that you can *manage* things and will be unsurprised. I knew, of course, your mother was dying; the doctors made it clear. So it wasn't in that sense surprising—but I was unprepared. You go through life together and do everything in lockstep and attain a perfect unison if not a perfect harmony, until one fine day there's no one walking at your side.

But this is something he has said before, or thinks he has, or knows he has, but cannot remember when he said it, and to whom, and why. His son looms above the bed—those beetle brows, that dimpled chin—and says "I'm glad to be here, Dad, I hope you're in no pain."

"Tell me what you're up to," Frederick manages. "Any interesting cases?"

John is a real estate lawyer who, visibly relieved, begins to talk about a case of adverse possession, a neighborhood in San Francisco where neighbors had walked through an outlot for years, on a shared path which is now being fenced, and the developer who bought the land has a whole raft of Title Insurance attorneys, and is claiming ownership, so those who walked the path for fifteen years and more have lost their access to it, and—pulling up a chair—his son discourses on the intricacies of precedent and how, although he has no doubt his clients have been wronged, and have justice on their side, they might well lose.

At times like these, John confesses, he loses faith in the process; it's not, lord knows, a question of manifest injustice or false imprisonment or some life-threatening issue at stake, but there's a way in which this little case has gotten to him, is causing him to question the whole procedure of evidentiary hearings and depositions and settlement discussions, the apparatus of law courts. He proceeds to talk about the matter of adverse possession and the evidence he gathered from the owner of the outlot, whom he had deposed the day before at his office in Manhattan—one of those places with so much glass and polished wood you have to ask yourself who *works* here, who gets anything done in such a building except the custodial staff? And listening, half following and half not-following the details of the legal case, the nature of John's argument, Frederick finds himself adrift and marveling that this large man beside the bed had once been a small creature clamoring for his parents' attention and wanting nothing so much as to climb in beside them for comfort; how does this happen, he wants to be told, how can the litigator standing there impeccably above him now be someone who came crying when he hurt his thumb?

Maureen appears. "Your father maybe needs to sleep."

"Oh?"

"It's maybe a surprise to you. But he does love his catnap."

No, he wants to say to her, that isn't it, not it at all, we're talking here about adverse possession, we're having an adult conversation and you interfere. My son and I don't visit much; he hasn't had the chance to tell me what went wrong with Harriet, and how Carrie fares in Cleveland, and if he has a new, what would you call it? *companion*; just look at him wearing his striped shirt and flannels, his black suspenders and cufflinks: my son the fashion plate. I have had weeks and months to sleep, I will have an eternity, and if it's all the same to you I'll take a glass of sherry with this expert on outlots, this man who intends to file next week for summary disposition—and I require him but not a catnap if you please.

Here too he holds his tongue. It is, Frederick thinks, surprising—or perhaps more accurately not unsurprising—that the spool of language in his head unreels in silence and need not be voiced. It is, he tells himself, a function also possibly of his loss of vision, how he sees only nowadays what he wills himself to see. On the screen of his shut eyelids he and Sarah raise a glass. The children in their yarmulkes, the children in their tennis whites, the children drinking root beer with a scoop of ice cream and a straw to stir it with, the children eating oysters the first time they tasted oysters, the children drinking beer . . .

"If he wants to sleep he'll sleep," says John. "I only just arrived."

How long has it been, he inquires, since you last came to visit; how many days and weeks and months has your father been lying alone? Well, not alone, not really, there are all these substitutes, these paid attendants at my side who wash and wipe and help me pee, these nurses who control the oxygen supply. And, lucid again, he struggles upward in the sheets while Mau-

reen plumps up the pillows, and asks: "Tell me, how long can
you stay?"

"I've got three days," says John.

"Is it the weekend?"

"Yes."

"A person can lose track of time. You don't believe me, but
it happens. It can happen."

"Oh, Dad, you need a smart phone. Or a scheduling app on
your iPad."

This is, he understands, a joke. John has a calendar to keep
as once he, Frederick, kept an appointment book, and not a
schedule on the bedside table with the morning pills, the afternoon pills, the evening pills to take. They number—he has
always had a memory for numbers—twelve, though some he
takes twice daily and the total is therefore sixteen. There are
some you buy over the counter (the aspirin, the multi-vitamins)
and some the doctor must prescribe (the Lipitor, lisinopril, the
metoprolol) and some to help him urinate and some to help
him sleep and some to regulate blood sugar whose names he
cannot name.

Maureen, Jenelle, and Miriam are very good with pills. They
pay close attention.

They fill a row of little yellow plastic boxes with the pills he
needs to take each week, the daily allocation, and this is how
he knows—it's his own form of calendar knowledge—if the day
is Monday or Wednesday or Thursday and how many days remain before the tray is empty and needs to be refilled.

"What went wrong with Harriet?"

"Excuse me?"

"Your wife. What happened between you?"

John makes a dismissive gesture. "The usual."

"The *usual?*"

"Dad, you don't really want to know."

This does not require an answer. He waits. He lies in his
bed like King Solomon, resting, ready to dispense a judgment,
and listens while his son explains that he and Harriet had disagreed about approximately everything, the way to raise their

children, the place to take vacations, the neighborhood of Nob
Hill, where they had a carriage house, the fact he had married
an atheist, or anyhow an agnostic, and it hadn't therefore mattered that she was a Catholic, but these last years she went to
church at first with seeming nonchalance, then regularity, then
with more and more devotion, and it bothered him who even
if unobservant was nonetheless a Jew; there were waitresses in
restaurants and secretaries in the office who gave him more of
a sexual thrill—not, he hastens to assure his father, that he'd
been unfaithful or taken advantage of what was on offer, but
when your wife won't put her hand on your arm, or touch your
shoulder in passing it's hard not to notice the women who do.
Vivacity is what he means, and what he found himself missing;
it had been painful to notice how often Harriet enjoyed herself
in the company of strangers, and how rarely she did so at home.
She'd been exuberant in public and in private cold. So little by
little they drifted apart, he spending time at work and she with
her book club and girlfriends. In San Francisco, John explains,
it's not unusual that women spend free time together, as do
men, and he'd been easy about it, he'd been—to use Mom's
word—*copacetic*, but over time their marriage was a marriage in
what you'd call name only. Last year, when Colin got accepted
at Columbia, and was packing up and leaving, his wife turned
to him and said, "I'll take him east. After that, I'm staying there
with Carrie," and he was unsurprised.

John continues in this fashion, saying what kept him married all this time was the example of his parents, *you*, who
seemed so entirely happy, so absolutely bonded that divorce
had been unthinkable, not a thing real grown-ups do. "You're
a hard act to follow, Dad, and certainly our mother was, but
one fine morning I decided that I didn't want to settle for what
felt like second best"—he spreads his hands—"and the kids are
handling it. We'll see."

He needs to sleep. He thinks of a phrase out of Shakespeare—"shuffle off this mortal coil"—and wonders what
Prince Hamlet means, and if the mortal coil is rope, and how
you shuffle it off. "Shuffle off to Buffalo" is also somehow a

phrase in his head, and he remembers one winter business trip to that city, the lake and the amazing snow, the wind rattling his hotel room's window, and how he telephoned Sarah to say, "I'm selling storage units to a bunch of would-be Eskimos, how does *anybody* live here?" and she said, "It isn't worth it, Freddy, come on home."

"I am not dying yet," he tells his son. "But I am more ready for death than for life."

Maureen says, "He's asleep."

Daniel and Eileen arrive from Berkeley, with their two children, William and Sue. He cannot remember their ages, but Eileen reminds him sweetly: eleven and nine. She is his confidante, the one Frederick can talk to, or would if he wanted to talk. Instead he contents himself looking at her, pleased with the color of her hair, the tight taut line of her stomach and legs, the confident assertion of her breasts. It pleases him that Daniel has married so lovely a woman, and that *this* marriage—so far as he can tell—is strong; they have all been camping near Vancouver, on an island you get to by ferry, she tells him, and William insisted on building and tending the fire, and was good at it; his sister was learning to steer a canoe. Always before Susie sat in the prow, but now she can handle the stern.

"They're growing up," says his daughter-in-law, "our little hellions; we're proud of them."

"Yes."

"We wish you'd moved to California . . ."

And he believes her; she means what she says. It is not possible, of course, not something he can do these days—you'd *moved* to California is not the same formulation as *move*, the tense is past, the chance is past—but after Sarah died he might have gone. He could have sold their house and settled near his family and become, as it were, a dependent. His father, Johann, died here in this very house, he might have gone to his son's home and done the same.

Daniel's expertise is Europe, the beginnings of the nation-state, and at Berkeley he teaches a course called "*1830: Europe has a cold.*" This is, he says, a reference to the saying by Prince Metternich, "When France sneezes, all Europe catches cold." He used the first part of the sentence for a title for his book. In 1830, and again in 1848 and 1870—not to mention the Napoleonic Era, or the Revolution before it—what was happening in France had ripple effects far beyond its borders, which were in any case more mutable than fixed.

Frederick coughs. He could have been an Eskimo and walked out on the ice. The story of old Inuits who in the bitter winter when supplies of food are running low walk out on ice for the good of the tribe, and freeze, and die, is one he likes to consider. It's how elders should behave. Sam Olesker said it isn't true, just a fantasy concocted by the advocates of Assisted Suicide; it's a story used to make us look unreasonable; all this money spent on prolongation of what's mostly misery, but I'll bet you those old Eskimos are huddling near the TV set and saying pass me some more of that seal butter, please, this tusk's too hard to gnaw. Another helping, *yum.*

Sam—who'd made a killing in commercial real estate—was always debunking the value of things, saying it's only money and why bother saving it, why bother if there's any wine in the bottle when you're not there to drink? New wine in old bottles or old wine in new; it makes no difference really; let's *do* the Loire next year. Over brandy or a game of bridge, Frederick kept himself from pointing out the obvious: if you have no children and more money than you can manage to spend, there isn't any virtue in an act of generosity. To go wine-tasting in the Loire is to acknowledge privilege; to live in the house of your daughter-in-law is a good deal easier if you yourself foot the bill . . .

Still, it would be seemly to sleep on the ice, to let the cold wind chill you and the snow drift down. The ice floes and the leaden sky and hibernating bears and seals—he'd seen a television documentary about an arctic winter—would be the kind of landscape where a man might expire unnoticed, and all this attention distracts him: Eileen's soft hand on his arm. She smiles down at him carefully, and something in her downward glance convinces him (in ways he has not understood, and with a certainty he'd otherwise have gainsaid or objected to) that he is going to die.

"I'm dying, aren't I?" Frederick asks.

Eileen is speechless. She nods.

There are children in the house. Colin and Carrie and William and Susie arrive. There is commotion everywhere, a perturbation in the air. He welcomes it. He is a being of sound mind and body who attests in this last testament to laughter and traffic and music and shouting, and from his bed discerns the scraps of utterance, "How goes it, man?" and "Mine!" and "Trump!" and "Lookin' *good!*" and "*Nur einen Augenblick*" that echo down the halls.

Colin talks about Columbia and Will and Susie talk about their camping trip and Carrie tells him Cleveland is not like San Francisco except she's getting used to it, and he can tell which one is which by the decibel level and pitch of their voices, but if entire truth be told (and why should it not, why should he deal any longer with lies?) he does not deeply care about a course in macroeconomics or the neighborhood of Shaker Heights and a best friend called Alison or the way to feather your paddle and light a fire with sticks.

Frederick lies on his right side. He distributes his blessings to the clan. He would like them all to know how much he has been gratified by their arrival, their willing suspension of whatever it is they have had to suspend to attend.

Disbelief, that was the word, a willing suspension of disbelief, yes, for it grows hard to understand and if not understand accept the flat inescapable fact of transience, the loss of Sarah by his side, this journey he has undertaken that so soon must end. He will leave behind the property to sell. He has bequeathed them a good deal of stock. He will depart a world more populous

than the one he entered, if just as torn and bellicose and subject
to disaster, though the disaster does not seem as imminent to
him now lying in New Canaan as would have been the case perhaps for his ancestors in Theresienstadt and Bergen-Belsen or
arrested at the borders or pulled from trains and ocean-travers-
ing steamers while attempting to escape. There will be drought;
there will be fires and plague. Among the beneficiaries of the
Frederick Hochmann Trust there will no doubt be discord and
distrust. Susie will, he understands, be lovely as her mother, and
she in time and times to come will also have her suitors, and no
doubt marry one of them, and have children and grandchildren
he will never know, nor will they know (when leafing through
old albums and seeing the family photographs Eileen has pasted
to the page, the colors yellowing, the black-and-white images
faded to sepia, although it has been written down) his name.
The apple tree, the singing and the gold. The Biedermeier desk
his father sat at, keeping the ledgers and doing accounts, the
Schubert Impromptu No. 3 they played at Sarah's funeral, and
at her request . . .

On Saturday morning the caterers appear. He knows this
because he can hear them, doors slamming and the sounds of
commerce, the clatter and bustle of men bearing trays, the fuss
of rearrangement. He has been showered and shaved. He has
been clad in his good dressing gown, the one Sarah gave him
for his birthday with the warm lining and the purple silk with
moons and stars emblazoned down the sleeves and the black
tasseled sash. He holds the tasseled sash. He is wheeled along
the hall from the master bedroom that once had been a library
but two years ago was reconfigured for usage since it means that
he avoids the stairs, with east- and south-facing windows and
an adequate bathroom adjacent, with railings in the shower stall
and a wide entry for his chair. There are books and family photographs and a CD player and the portrait by Rouault. After his
triumphal entry in the living room he will be positioned by the
window with the oxygen canister at his feet and offered a glass
of champagne. He will see his children and grandchildren and
his business associates—those several who remain alive, whose

names he will try to remember—and the nursing staff and Hospice staff and the woman from the clinic who had helped his dog Methuselah depart this earth with a biscuit in his mouth and painless final injection.

That had been years ago. He can remember driving his dog to the animal clinic—Methuselah so weak by then he had to be lifted to the seat, who earlier had jumped up to it lightly, his tail nonetheless wagging and tongue hanging down—and wanting to cry and needing to do so but not in front of the Golden Retriever, the one who grew up with his sons.

Lacrimae rerum: the tears of things. He can remember walking with Methuselah down bridle paths, or by a stream, and how the dog would run to fetch the stick he'd throw, splashing and drinking and then, emerging, shake himself dry with a fine spray of water and pride in retrieval and dropping the stick at his feet. Then Frederick threw it again. They would do this often, repeating the throw and catch and throw and catch until the dog grew weary or he himself had wearied and would be lifted to the wheelchair and guided down the hall.

The caterers wear aprons. One woman in a white toque is the one who gives the orders and to whom others turn for instruction—positioning cutlery, setting out glasses and ice and trays of flutes; why should the word be *flutes*, Frederick wonders, what in the shape of the glass suggests music, a wind instrument, or is it the way a person's lips approach the rim, the soft *embouchure*, diminished song, the bubble and froth there contained? What he recollects, he understands, feels less and less clear, a kind of echo and an aftertaste like the residue, swallowing, of champagne—the way the photograph he passed just now of his wife standing on a hill is something he sees in his mind's eye only, because it seems a yellow blur, the third in a series of photos he hung, that was her dress and hair.

Within the burnished silver frame there is a blue and green arrangement also of the noontime sky and beneath it a flowering tree. He knows it was noontime because of the shadows, or rather the absence of shadows; she stands before him quick, not dead, with a solidity he could embrace as once he held her on that hill. There had been a picnic hamper and a blanket spread beneath the tree, there had been bread and deviled eggs and cold fried chicken and olives and cheese, the Pentax he preferred to use, so accurate of focus he could focus on the sweat-beads at her neck. There had been a cold bottle of *Liebfraumilch* or possibly prosecco, sweet drinks she used to like. He uncorks the bottle and pours. At the end of the hall past the powder room there hangs a series of prints framed in black metal frames, six studies by Francisco Goya of the technique of bullfighting, the *Tauromachia*, with bulls and horses and toreros in the ring en-acting their murderous dance. One picador leaps above a bull, implanting steel; another has been gored.

In the living room they wait for him, expectant. He fingers the dressing gown's sash.

"Our birthday boy!" proclaims Maureen.

"*Felicidades*," says Jenelle. Her family has come from Cuba, and he wants to tell her how his family also sojourned in Cuba, but he hadn't yet been born, and wonders and cannot be sure if Jenelle is a name from that island or something her parents made up.

"The man of the hour!" Miriam says.

"Here's *Johnny!*" Daniel does his imitation of Ed McMahon on the *Tonight Show*, exhorting the audience, raising his hands.

The birthday boy and man of the hour can see them—hands outstretched, a cluster of relatives waiting and just above his head a floating assemblage of purple balloons, a garland of crepe paper twined and gently moving in the created breeze. Someone has cut out his name in large letters and affixed it to the crepe, so FREDERICK bobs and twirls as though he stood on a receiving line or there beside Prince Metternich reviewing troops and trying to stifle a sneeze.

He can read the purple letters; they spell, after all, his name.

"Welcome, welcome," Frederick says.

"We're glad to be here," someone says.

"You can say that again," says another.

"To a long and happy life," says John.

"A long and happy life," they chorus, raising their glasses

in unison, singing "For he's a jolly good fellow" and repeating "Happy Birthday" till the din subsides.

"To absent friends," says Judy Olesker.

To her he turns. She is a blur of yellow and orange—wearing a dress, he thinks, not unlike the one which Sarah wore in the framed portrait in the hall, displaying too the double strand of amethysts and opals Sarah had bequeathed her, the white hair stiffly coiffed. This he can see. He does not need to touch her head to feel again the stiff resistant springiness of hairspray or trail his hand along her cheek to feel the wrinkles there. Judy is—he hunts the word—*game* to join his raucous family, to stand beneath the cluster of balloons and raise a glass and toast their absent friends. They make a sad processional, the long line of the disappeared who once were near to hand. His mother had died rapidly, his wife had done so lingeringly, and though they both had died of cancer it had been separate forms of the disease. His vision now is blurred not by the glaucoma but tears.

The family and then the guests make toasts. They raise glasses and click flutes in honor of their host. They tell him Happy Birthday and how excellent it is to celebrate a long and happy life, to follow his example of—no other word for it, Dad—dignity. Why *toast*, he wonders, what does such a celebration have to do with heated bread? They say how good it feels to be in this house again together, how much the place has meant and means, how grateful they are to be home. They do not dare to wish him many happy returns of the day. Jenelle adjusts his oxygen, then slips it from his nose.

There is also, Frederick remembers, a *roast*, a way of making fun that suggests both an oven and method of cooking; he is not being *roasted* but *toasted* by the guests. But what does being *roasted* mean, he asks himself; what sort of group assembles to cook an honoree? That thing called dignity is something he relinquished when the first nurse wiped his drool and shit, when the first visitor from Hospice said, "We're here to help you, dear."

He puts his left hand in the pocket of his robe. He rubs his index finger and his thumb together, and the friction soothes him; it is as though he makes a fire using two fingers as sticks. *Triangulate*, he tells his boys, *make sure the kindling and logs form a tent.* On this afternoon his breath comes charily, and his desire for continued life—so truncate in the scheme of things, a bird of passage in a barn, a tidal rising—ebbs. *Orion the Mighty Hunter. Cassiopeia, the Crab.*

"Can I refresh your glass?" asks a dark figure, approaching, and Frederick shakes his head. From darkness into darkness, silence to silence he flutters, and it all seems very distant, a brief encounter only, for he feels neither pleasure nor pain.

Now it grows clear to everyone—in the orchestrated hush and pause—it is his turn to talk. He has prepared his speech. He knows the men and women in the room he must remember to thank; he knows what ground to cover and which topics to avoid. Although the state of politics is everybody's subject now, he will not talk of politics or how the better instincts of this nation have collapsed. He will not talk of corruption and the stupidity that triumphed in the last election, the rage and the ravening greed. Because he does not wish to spoil the mood by naming our President's name, he will not discuss Donald Trump. At this party he has planned instead to be worthy of the confidence of those arrayed before him and, if not their confidence, respect. He will honor the distinction between duty and desire: the way to behave when your grandparents and parents and your wife and brother are lying adjacent in Ferncliff, dust to dust and hip to hip.

After some time, he speaks. Civility is something Frederick can manage still, and he starts out well. "I'm very glad you're here. I'm glad to be with you, my children. Friends. And my children's children who come from far away. This is a joyous occasion, a chance to remember our dearly beloved, the ones I will be joining soon if there be any justice—a prospect we have some reason to doubt—in the world above, providing of course there *be* such a world, which we have reason to doubt."

As Frederick continues, however, he hears himself spewing nonsense and careening off the track of things he planned to say. He *meant* to say, he means to say, how happy he is they're all here together, how sad that some are gone and necessarily absent, except they remain in our hearts. My heart. Instead he launches, possibly out loud, on a speech about the afterlife in which he, an unbeliever, has no actual belief, but as the Talmud tells us—what *does* it tell us exactly?—the idea of immortality consists of remembrance, of being remembered, and therefore he hopes to stay green in memory, to sprout there like the weed he was, to spread like the thistle and burdock and the expanse of clover and crabgrass he'd been in the habit every Saturday morning of mowing on that lawn beyond the living-room window until it became a green glade.

There behind them at the edge of vision they hover: the stout pianist playing Brahms's Second Piano Concerto, the one in B flat major, *was* it B flat major?, the rock that wrecked his mower's blade, the gardener—Larry? Harry?—his wife hired when he grew too old to mow, the dog beside his bed.

"Are you all right?" asks Elaine.

Although he is fond of his daughter-in-law, her honeyed breath, her lissome frame, he thinks this such absolute nonsense he cannot forebear to frown at her, *Of course not, what a stupid question, no, I'm not not not all right.*

Frederick steadies himself. He needs to start again. "This is a joyous occasion, a solemn occasion, a chance to remember our dearly beloved," he says. "And I'm very grateful you're here." You live, he wants to tell his guests, with the sense that you can *manage* things and will be unsurprised. We all are born to die. The doctors made it clear. But what exactly makes us think this life we live is other than a storage unit, a receptacle of bric-a-brac and cherished memory, those objects we hold dear? The handkerchief he fingers in the pocket of his robe. The apple tree, the singing and the gold. This country called America his parents found a refuge in, where he himself was born. Therefore to shuffle off the mortal coil is to do a dance step, and there's nothing wrong with counting, a-*one*, a-*two*, a-*four*. There's nothing wrong with practicing: *the ice beyond the door*. What else he says is lost to him, to them, because the roaring in his ears is tantamount to silence, and the shapes that flit about the room are permeable entities through which the past now leaks.

By the fireplace stands Penny Dean, his first school crush, the girl across the aisle he never did dance with in dance class—and there is Alan Silverwhistle, with whom he roomed sophomore year. By his own side, indeterminate—first young, then middle-aged, then old—Sarah hovers, smiling in that way of hers that means, *You fool, you can't fool me*. By the window gather men with whom he used to work in Warehousing and Real Estate, the CEO and CFO and junior partners of the company, the CPAs and others with initials on the pockets of their shirts.

The ABC and XYZ, the quiddity of things. There is Methuselah's leash entangled now about his feet except as an oxygen chord. Deftly, a nurse straightens it and coils it back again. Deftly he completes his toast: "It is enough. My thanks."